The Hospital Murders

THE HOSPITAL MURDERS

Means Davis

WILDSIDE PRESS

www.wildsidepress.com

To
Donald, Gerald
and Jimmy

Contents

》《

»I«
An Unconscious Intruder

Docterr Ste-earling, Junyior, Doct-terr Eth-err-ridge Ste-earling, Junyior. Calling Doct-terr. . . ."

The loud speaker whined through laboratories, permeated kitchens, rasped in corridors. In the service corridor of Medicine Clinic the orderly rolling the laundry bin halted to listen and expectorate. Four floors above, Cub Sterling pulled in his long stride and reached for a nurse's desk 'phone. His voice pushed through the mouthpiece and almost immediately severed the monotonous breathing of the loud speaker. He said:

"Doctor Ethridge Sterling, Junior, is answering from Ward D, Medicine Clinic."

The dead voice of the operator responded:

"Doc-terr Ste-earling, Jun . . .?"

Cub's patience and his ear were closely allied. He cocked his head and barked:

"Well, what is it?"

Her voice dropped several octaves. She cooed:

"Justa minnit, Docterr Sterrling. Docterr Barton's calling. . . ."

Barton's voice intervened:

"Cub? Harold Barton. Will you go over to Weber's and telephone me at my home, please? Right away."

Five minutes later, Doctor Ethridge Sterling, Junior, turned from an elevator on the first floor of the Medicine Clinic of the Elijah Wilson Hospital, gave a vacant nod to two internes and shambled through the door, into the accident corridor and out into Beeker Street.

In Weber's restaurant he folded himself into a telephone booth and said:

"Riverside 7863."

While waiting for the connection his long fingers manipulated a cigarette. He was more excited than he dared to admit.

What the hell could Dr. Barton, a life-long friend of his father and Pediatrician-in-Chief of the Elijah Wilson even before he was born, have to say which was too confidential to transmit over a hospital telephone?

The operator invaded his curiosity.

"Deposit a nickel. Five cents, please."

Cub Sterling's rangy legs began untwisting. He begged:

"Hey! Wait a minute!"

Folding back the door of the booth he bellowed:

"Gimme some nickels, quick, Otto!"

Otto Weber had been bartender, confidant, and advisor to the staff of the Elijah Wilson when Cub Sterling was in short pants. He waddled from his bar:

"Sure, Cub!"

The temporary Physician-in-Chief gave the bartender a boyish grin and arrayed the nickels in front of the telephone box. Then he said:

"Here are two nickels, lady. If I talk up a dollar don't you interrupt me. This is Wilson 7390. I'll pay you after I'm through."

"It is against the rules. . . ."

"Lots of things are! Thank you, mam!"

A slight giggle was her response and Dr. Barton's voice drowned that.

"Cub?"

"Yessir."

"Ethridge Sterling, Junior?"

"Yessir!"

"Harold Barton. I had to make sure. I'm in a terrible mess, son. I need your help! If I take time to come over to the hospital . . . it'll be too late!"

With his left little finger Cub gave the interior of his ear a violent shake and transferred the receiver. He moistened his lips, but Dr. Barton forestalled his words:

"Don't interrupt me, Cub! Time is valuable! My brother, the Attorney-General, is slated to be elected senator next fall. The cards are stacked. Today the Governor gave a political barbecue at his camp. Half an hour ago, while returning, Herb had an automobile accident . . . out on Lincoln Highway. No, he wasn't hurt. Much too drunk for that! But the girl was. A newspaper reporter. What? Couldn't tell you. Never saw her.

"Another car of newspaper people came by. They had an A. P. man along. Of course Herb could 'hush' it locally, but the A. P. man refused to kill the story nationally unless Herb promised to get the lady into the Elijah Wilson and foot all bills.

"She's in an ambulance now. On the way. Internal injuries. No, you miss the point! The man insists her reputation as well as her . . . organs . . . must be intact. Will you take her under an assumed name . . . in case she dies? Say her father is a friend of yours, and you recognized her. Anything! If that won't do, think up another one. Awfully unethical, I know! But I can't stand behind any more relatives . . . right now . . .!"

The last sentence contained a note Cub had never heard in Barton's speech. A helplessness. . . .

Outside in Beeker Street an ambulance screamed up the long hill. Cub's cigarette was adding another hole to the already scarred floor of the booth.

He said, and his voice had its steel under which he buried real emotion:

"Certainly, Doctor Barton, I'll take her in. But everything is occupied except a dying patient room off Ward B. Will the Attorney-General pay for frills? Private nurses . . . so on?"

"For anything, son! And Cub . . . please . . . you know MacArthur and Herb admire each other. If you don't mind . . . ?"

The clanging bell vibrated down Cub's free ear. He snapped:

"Between ourselves, Doctor. Suppose we leave it that way? Hear an ambulance now! Report to you later, sir. Not at all! 'By!"

Otto Weber flicked his towel and shouted when Dr. Ethridge Sterling, Junior, flung open the door of the telephone booth:

"Stoop, Cub! Stoop!"

As the tall, angular body shot across Beeker Street, Otto plodded into the booth, picked up three nickels, stomped out the cigarette and replaced the receiver upon the hook.

Across Beeker Street two firemen were lifting the padded stretcher from a municipal ambulance. One of them ceased pulling for a second and changed his tobacco wad to the other side.

A big man bent over him and snapped:

"Did you get this accident out the Lincoln Highway?"

"Yeah . . . looks like them dolls in the waxworks down to Holiday Park."

Cub Sterling's left shoulder rose abruptly. His voice ascended, too:

"Be careful. Take it easy . . . easy . . . these steps are high!"

While the stretcher was rolling into the Accident corridor, Cub lurched into both accident rooms, saw that the tables were occupied, and turned to the internes:

"I'll take her up to Medicine Clinic, myself. Internal injuries. Just got a telephone message. Father's a friend of mine in the East. 'Phone Miss Kerr to prepare Room Two off Ward B."

Halfway up the corridor to the Medicine Clinic a student nurse and an orderly stepped briskly. The orderly gripped the handle bar of a swishing stretcher. Upon the stretcher, completely covered, lay an inert figure.

Five feet behind, his shoulders stooped, his body tense, slouched Dr. Ethridge Sterling, Junior. Upon either side of him, like stubby pencils, a fireman tiptoed. Cub bit his lips and said:

"Who called you?"

"Where? When? For what?" the one with the cud growled.

Cub threw his hand forward, motioning.

The younger fireman answered:

"Fellow used to do fire chasing for *The Call.* And say, Doc, he promised us a new stretcher, but he didn't say when . . . if it's the same to you . . . ?"

The student nurse and orderly pranced out of sight. Cub Sterling moved toward the fireman and said:

"It's still yours! I'm scared to move her more than necessary. Send it down in the elevator as soon as she's transferred. You wait at this door."

Inside the door of Medicine Clinic, Miss Roenna Kerr, head nurse, accosted Dr. Sterling. The pompadour which overhung her long face was a blueing-water white.

Beside her with the quiet diffidence of a poodle, a fat interne was anchored. Miss Kerr said:

"Dr. Mattus, and Dr. Sarah James, the floor interne on B are off this afternoon, Dr. Sterling, so I brought the interne from A. . . . And am I correct in understanding that you ordered this patient into a dying patient room off Ward B?"

Dr. Sterling's voice was crisp and ominous:

"Room Two. You are."

"But Dr. Ethridge. . . ."

Her bust began to inflate. His reply corroded her vanity:

"I'll see you later, Miss Kerr."

The student nurse, the orderly, the stretcher swished aboard the elevator, Dr. Sterling and the interne followed. Dr. Sterling, the professor, made the interne forget the friction. He snapped:

"Give you instructions after examination, Doctor. One of the most interesting things in Internal anced. Hair as fine as a baby's and filled with sunshine. Skin so transparent you could almost poke your finger through it. The eyes should be . . . blue . . . brown . . . ? No! Something else . . ."

He lifted a lid gently.

"Ah, violet . . . of course! Only violet eyes could go with lips that curved that way. . . . She was too swell to be true. . . ! Something must ruin her . . . the teeth, probably. . . ."

His fingers actually hesitated as he pulled back the lips; then, as they relaxed again, he drew his right forefinger down the cheek, as though examining the jawbone. The motion was soft and utterly gentle. It carried a sense of private approval. . . . The teeth were perfect. . . .

To cover up this sudden finding of a live flesh and blood perfect person, his dictation clipped and became intricately anatomical.

During the chest examination he noted the nasty bruises against the cup-like breasts, and decided it was time to pull himself together. She probably murdered the English language and slept with all comers. The Attorney-General, for instance. . . .

His irritation vibrated into her leg, when he felt for torn tendons. The girl roused herself momentarily and screamed:

"I don't give a damn what kind of general you are! I'll slap your face again! Take y' dirty hands off me!"

The interne had been called away over the loud speaker; the floor nurse was busy at the ward telephone. Cub Sterling tiptoed to the door and closed it swiftly.

The tired wrinkles around his eyes began to crinkle, a fine humor relaxed his brittle body. He came back to the bed and squeezed the curly head of the unconscious figure against his long leg.

Then he leaned over and whispered in the little ear:

"You are all right, kiddo! But for God's sake, wake up!"

Then he went back to methodically examining her legs and laughed shortly at the downy patches where the calves curved behind the small ankles; at the lopsided little V's in the big-toe nails. . . .

Never before in all of his medical experience had he had a devastating, unconscious, perfectly private patient. . . . He lifted a foot and laid it from the nape of his palm to the ends of his fingers. It was half an inch short of his nail tips and the little finger of his left hand could extend entirely under the instep without touching flesh. . . .

The girl groaned deeply and Dr. Ethridge Sterling, Junior, intervened. . . .

He took her pulse again. Noted the excellent heart action. Began carefully going over the abdomen. Once or twice she cried distantly, and he decided the best thing to do was to put her out of her pain. The heart action was so splendid that the wisest way to keep her from babbling to the nurses would be to narcoticize her.

So he took her head in his hands and went, painstakingly, over the skull. There were no masses, no abrasions, no visible signs of anything extraordinary. She was in shock, of course. But an accident coupled with an endeavor to make old Herb Barton keep his distance. . . . That recollection killed his critical faculty for an instant. He lifted the head slightly forward and massaged the curls which nestled in the hollow at the base of the skull.

The fat interne and Miss Kexter, the floor nurse, returned simultaneously. Dr. Sterling resolutely replaced the head among the pillows and said, shortly:

"No signs of concussions, or injuries; with the exception of that abdominal sensitivity. Case of extreme shock. Acute pain is from strained ligaments and bruises. Nurse, give her an eighth of morphia injection. Doctor, keep your eye on her respiration and notify me at ten. I'll be in my rooms, probably. Main thing is to keep her quiet."

The nurse's flat voice replied:

"Yes, Doctor. Do you wish a night nurse, Doctor Sterling?"

"Depends. Let you know later."

She blocked his exit. Her voice was embarrassed:

"They called from the Admitting Office, Doctor, to complete her history. They said Miss Kerr told them you knew her name. Miss Jaunts asked me . . . ?"

Cub Sterling swirled and glanced swiftly over the face of the patient.

"Thank you. I'll call by the Admitting Office, myself." Then he shot at the mouse-haired woman a barrage of questions about the ward patients.

The interne gave the Sleeping Beauty a pouty stare. There would be no decompression. By now the blood sugars would have increased to six. They must be done before supper, too!

The nurse followed Dr. Sterling onto the wards and he began his rounds and gave his instructions. At the patient in Bed 11 he stared carefully and turning, snapped:

"How was that thyroid's basal?"

After her response he walked over to the bed, took the woman's pulse and said very absently:

"You are doing splendidly. Keep it up!"

The nurse followed him to the elevator and begged:

"You *are going* by the Admitting Office, Doctor? Will you return the blanks, or shall I keep them until tomorrow?"

He scowled and his black eyebrows met. Then he pushed the elevator button with precision.

"Fill out the details, hair, eyes, that bunk, and give them to me tomorrow. The Admitting Office can wait . . . for once. . . . I'll telephone over the important particulars. 'Night!"

His " 'Night!" was another way of saying, "That's all! And no more questions, madam!"

The elevator began ascending and the girl operator asked timidly:

"What floor, Doctor?"

Cub Sterling appraised her vacantly:

"Huh?"

The girl's voice quavered:

"Where to, Doctor?"

"Top floor!"

"Yes, sir."

When the elevator halted, he quickly raised his head:

"By the way, how's your cold?"

"What cold, Doctor?"

"Haven't you a cold?" he growled.

"No, Dr. Sterling. Thank you. I haven't."

"You're welcome. Other operator, I guess."

He stepped from the elevator and began his rounds. A whole avalanche of nurses galloped down the hall and he realized it must be time for the shift. He squinted at his watch and saw that it was almost seven.

"Damn it to hell!" he muttered.

Hot hash was bad enough. By now it would be slime. Better finish the rounds and eat at Otto's. Herbie's hands had messed things up! Damned old spider! His memory was focusing upon the girl when the floor interne hurried forward and began to report.

One hour and a half later Dr. Ethridge Sterling, Junior, tilted back in the swivel chair in his private office. His left heel held the edge of the seat, the telephone was balanced upon his left knee, the receiver wedged between his left shoulder and ear. His eyebrows were parted; he had just given his pants a comforting jerk. His mouth twitched occasionally; in his free hands he held a copy of "The Love Books of Ovid" and his eyes measured a familiar illustration. He decided that the legs weren't up to hers. His father's voice centered his attention, again.

"Yes, son?"

"Your thyroid, sir. Did a remarkable basal. Pulse is down to 110. Lowest . . . so far. . . ."

"Fine! I'll operate tomorrow if you advise. Drop around later and give her a final once-over. Be there in half an hour."

"But Father, I'm hungry . . . I missed . . ."

"All right. All right! You always were! Go get your supper. I don't need you dancing attendance on me! Still know an operative patient when I see one. Don't interrupt me! You talk too much! Always did! Goodnight, son!"

His gruff affection blacked out the illustration. Cub placed his right foot against the center drawer of his desk and began wondering what he wanted to eat. Shad roe? Lamb chops? Roast beef?

His telephone bell jangled sharply:

He propped open a recent copy of the *New Yorker* and read four passable cartoons, turned the page, then lifted the receiver.

Dr. Barton's voice begged:

"Cub?"

"Yes, sir. Yes, Dr. Barton. Been trying to get you all evening, sir. Think she's all right. Pull through. Can't tell for a certainty yet. Mostly shock. What's that? Aw, she's average. Kinda tinselly. By the way, better say none of those paper people can see her for a week. No beaus and no flowers. Righto! Not at all! See you tomorrow, sir."

Cub replaced the receiver, rose, straightened his tie, changed to a blue serge coat, tore three wedding invitations on his desk to shreds, slung the shreds into the waste basket, slammed the door and slouched up the stairs, whistling.

The jingling of a telephone bell followed him. That's why he whistled.

Five minutes later, the woman in the Admitting Office wrote Thursday, May 12th for the fourth time, and Sophie Merriweather, Newark, N. J., for the tenth time, and Cub Sterling barged into Weber's deserted restaurant and said, pathetically:

"Otto, fill me up."

Otto said:

"Sit down, Cubbie!"

Then he lifted the hose of a talking tube and ordered:

"Three-minut-steak-two-vrench-vrys-asparag-gus-on-toas-celler-y- an'- ollivs- VRIGH-TER-VAY!"

He slid the tube onto its hook, filled two steins with Schlitz, blew the foam, carefully refilled them, and with a "from the heart" motion, pushed them across the counter and soothed:

"Y'tired, son?"

"Yeah."

Cub raised a stein and drained it.

Otto eased it away, refilled it and stood it beside the full one. Then he lifted his belly onto a stool, leaned his arms against the bar and said, earnestly:

"Fut you need, son . . . iss to get marriet. . . . Tonight you see you haf vent viddout your supper. No vivfe allows dat. . . . No! Fut you need iss . . ."

Cub put down the empty stein and lifted the third one.

"Oh hush, Otto. . . . I'll get married when I want to!"

A bell tinkled in the kitchen, below. Otto disengaged his stomach, threw back his head to balance it, and before he turned, announced:

"Dat's it! You *don't vant to!*"

Cub set down the stein and laughed.

"What are you going to do about it, Otto?"

The little German drew himself slowly erect. His words were carefully chosen:

"Cub Steerlink, I *von't* stand-hit!"

Cub laughed again and begged:

"Aw, Otto!"

Otto turned his back and began lifting the food off the dumb waiter. His dignity surrounded him.

He placed the platters in front of the doctor, re-filled the empty stein and announced placidly:

"You are as fin as dried-herrink!"

Cub cocked his head seriously and replied:

"So you advise marriage, Doctor. Is that how you got prolapsus of the stomach?"

With three quick "Ach! Ach! Ach!" Otto blew himself to the far end of the bar and turned his back. But he was careful to turn it so that he could still see Cub's thick curly black hair and the way he jerked his head. So the internes said he was crazy! Otto rolled his own head, proudly. . . . You had to know Cub Sterling to understand him. . . . . All the really famous doctors . . . like Semmelweiss . . . were queer. Dr. MacArthur, himself, said that Cub Sterling had the flare . . . !

Cub slid off the stool and started for the door, and Otto relented:

"Vus it satissfact'ry, Docturr?"

Cub jerked his head and grinned:

"Yeah. Always is. Send me a bill soon, Otto."

"Sure, Cubbie. Sure!"

Outside, the sky was a pincushion of diamonds. So reachable, and yet so distant. An unexplained joy, that was ribbed with restlessness, pulled Cub's feet away from the hospital. He began strolling down Beeker Street. A silent, tuneless whistle tickled his lips. The recesses of his brain squirmed over the flat vacant center which was usually crowded with sick people. The way he used to coast this hill on a bicycle when he was in medical school! Whew! Lucky there were so few automobiles, then, or he'd have busted up a sight more test tubes.

Lord, that was long ago! Ought to begin going to debutante parties again, just to keep his foot in. He turned the corner and made his way back into Wilson Boulevard, and started the long climb to the hospital.

A glittery night, no dying patients, a full stomach! An interior champagne began to flow, and then his eye caught, in front of him, the august figure of his head nurse, Miss Kerr, sailing toward the hospital. Walking carefully and firmly in the glare of the street lamps; her tightly rolled umbrella protecting her virginity.

His left shoulder began to rise. He stooped quickly, picked a brick-bat out of a trash can and slung it at the light just behind. The action was involuntary and unpremeditated. It was an active example of his inner abandon, and followed by all the reflexes natural to a little boy.

He ducked into a shadow. He peered. His knees trembled slightly.

Miss Kerr turned and scrutinized the street. The search showed enraged dignity but bore no traces of fear. After a fruitless survey, she carefully raised the umbrella and proceeded toward the hospital.

Ten minutes later Dr. Ethridge Sterling, Junior, strode through Ward B, Medicine Clinic. Beside him the fat interne sweated profusely. He was gasping:

"The morphia didn't hold. She's awake and raising . . . raising . . ."

"Hell?"

The interne gave a relieved nod. The night nurse rocked her heels in tune with theirs. Cub turned to her and said:

"I understand. I understand. Nurse, you go back to your ward. Doctor, you may return to Ward A. I'll tend to her myself. . . ."

The interne hesitated and a fine hope glistened:

"Doctor Sterling . . . are you . . . is there to be a decompression?"

"Not unless absolutely necessary." Cub's voice was very grave, "I'll call you if I need assistance, Doctor."

The interne plodded helplessly off the ward. He

thought the student nurse's haughtiness was aimed at him.

Cub Sterling entered Room Two, pulled down the window shade of the glass inset opening onto the ward, and snapped on the wall light over the bed.

Then he gripped the bedside table and stared. Among the pillows, eyes wide with amusement, a wispy smile tracing the pale lips, was the head he had held in his hands three hours ago, alive, alert, intelligently vivid.

It was as though Cleopatra's understanding had flowed into an Egyptian mask.

The lips moved slowly and she asked, in a monotone:

"Who are you? And where am I?"

"I'm the man who knows your father, and you are in my hospital."

The composure ran out of her face. She muttered:

"Don't be funny, please. My father died in the War."

Cub Sterling straightened a pillow, slowly.

"Of course he did. Now you go to sleep again."

A bitter wry smile began searing her lips:

"So you think I'm 'nuts', too. He did! He and she both did! They were reporters on *The World*."

Cub caught the pride of the inflection, turned his back and adjusted the shade again.

The girl's voice was husky and amused.

"Will you give me a cigarette, please?"

He swung around:

"Of course not! You are too sick to smoke! You've just been in a horrible automobile accident. You had a narrow squeak. Be quiet and behave yourself!"

Her pupils turned black with amusement. She drawled:

"Used to having your way, aren't you?"

Cub blushed slowly, then announced:

"Speaking of having your own way, the night nurse and interne say . . ."

"I'm a hell-raisin'-huzzy, Doctor?"

He bit his lip:

"What *have* you been doing?"

Her eyes and voice dilated softly:

"Just asking questions. I'm a newspaper reporter, you know."

Cub nodded grimly:

"Yes. I know."

The girl overlooked the sarcasm. She asked levelly and with deference:

"Was it much of an accident? Did I lose my reputation or just a couple of teeth?"

Cub moved toward the foot of the bed and fenced:

"Publicly speaking, neither."

She shot back, "Privately speaking, the teeth are permanent."

He stood at the end of the bed and looked at her critically. She met the look and returned it. A short laugh finished her estimate. She said:

"Don't you think it might be wise if we told each other the truth? You snap like a police dog, but your eyes are honest."

Cub's legs collapsed under him. He sat upon the bed. The girl continued:

"How bunged up am I? I've got to get out of here quickly, or I'll be fired. . . ."

Cub's hands deprecated the statement. She sneered:

"What does a medical man know about life? Ever been poor and discriminating?" Then she threw the gesture back at him and ordered, "What's the story?"

He swallowed twice and said:

"You are in this hospital because your father is supposed to be a medical man in a distant city, Newark, New Jersey, to be exact, and a friend of mine. You are recorded as the victim of a bus accident. The bus went ahead with your luggage and pocketbook. Your name is Sophie Merriweather. As for your injuries, I'm not certain myself . . . yet." His words were beginning to clip. "Does that satisfy you?"

The girl shut her eyes and lay silent. A minute later she opened them, cocked her head upon one side and gazed critically down her chin, at her body. Then she looked reprovingly at Cub Sterling:

"So-ph-ie. How could you? Sophie Merri-weather, Newark, New Jersey! I haven't got the breastworks for a Sophie!"

The belligerence flew from Cub's face and his eyes began to dance:

"Breastworks, or no breastworks, madam, Sophie you are and Sophie you remain until you are well . . . or else a famous elderly medical man and I get kicked in the pants. . . ."

Without looking at him, she replied:

"You appeal to my finer feelings! I'll be Sophie forever, Doctor, if you'll promise me that the At-torney-General gets the kick and I get a cigarette, immediately!"

Cub's mouth and feet twitched. He rose and became professional:

"I'm sorry, Miss Merriweather. The cigarette is forbidden. Hospitals are pure places."

"Rats! Ever look in the trash cans in a Nurses' Home?"

"No, of course not, Sophie!"

She lay silent a minute and wiggled her toes. Then her voice grew small, and she said:

"Sounds like you've been very nice to me. Darned nice! But you have to know sometime and I guess you'd better know now that I haven't any money to pay you. I'm really a waif."

Her eyes blacked. She finished, "Respectable though . . . very!"

"But you're too loquacious! And you are pretty sick. Shut up and go to sleep!"

"How sick?"

"I told you I'd tell you tomorrow! As for your bills, they are being taken care of, so don't worry."

The mouth drew to a line, she demanded:

"Who's paying them? The Attorney-General?"

Cub evaded:

"You were riding in his car when you were hurt, weren't you?"

Sally Ferguson sat erect and put one hand quickly over her mouth. Sterling caught her by the shoulders and forced her back among the pillows.

"Where was it? Where did it hurt you?"

"Here," she put her hand on her abdomen and groaned.

Cub began examining her carefully and thoroughly. When he stood up again he said:

"I'm sorry, Sophie! We'll stop it if you want us to. The bills and the pain, too. Talk about them tomorrow. You must get some rest. Lie quiet. Be still. . . ."

Her mouth fell into a fighting straightness. All of the childish freshness which had charmed him when he had first seen her was gone. She lay tense and hard under his hands. Suddenly he knew she was trying not to cry. Calmly he began talking again:

"Accidents knock a darned lot more out of you than you ever suspect at the time, you know. You see, Sophie, if you don't help me, then . . . if you get terribly sick and I have a consultation over you . . . it'll mean sending for your father . . . and it'll be a hell of a mess all around. . . ."

Her body relaxed under his grip. She smiled again and gasped:

"May-I-please-have-a-drink-of-water?"

When the glass was empty Cub eased her into the pillows and she laughed:

"I didn't mean to hiss in your ear, Doctor, but if I hadn't completed the sentence in one breath, you'd have yelped: 'NO!' "

Dr. Sterling ignored the remark and asked:

"Is that comfortable?"

Then Cub barked:

"You ought to have better sense than to antagonize your doctor!"

The patient responded:

"Extremely comfortable, thank you."

The girl answered:

"The hair of the dog is good for his bite," and before Cub could reply, she relaxed her eyes into his and almost whispered:

"Thank you . . . for . . . taking me . . . in."

With a brusqueness he switched off the light and bowed:

"Pleasure's all mine! 'Night Sophie. When I look in later, please be unconscious again!"

After he was gone, she lay for five minutes convinced that she had been dreaming, and then she began to really dream. . . .

»II«
Murder

"THE HOSPITAL IS FACING A FUTURE which cannot be prophesied. So far, we are running no more than the usual deficit and our problem will not be how to continue on our course, but rather how to meet the increasing demands which, in such a year, automatically become our lot. That, from the administrative side, is the situation, gentlemen.

"It is, of course, a condition of which you are too painfully aware; but I conclude the conference with the mention of it, because it has been upon the ability to cope with the desperate that the reputation of the Elijah Wilson has been founded. . . ." Dr. Henry MacArthur hesitated, his eyeglasses carefully poised between his right thumb and forefinger. "Have any of you some special problem you wish the staff to consider?. . . If not. . . ." His penetrating blue eyes and pointer nose questioned. Men said he could sense a situation in the hospital with the certainty of a dog.

The doctors around the long mahogany table shifted in their chairs and prepared to rise, but

Cub Sterling's voice checked them:

"I have, Dr. MacArthur. A problem which I should like very much. . . ." Cub began unwinding his body and adjusting his bushy head, unconsciously balancing that list in his left shoulder, Dr. Hoffbein, Psychiatrist-in-Chief of the Elijah Wilson, noted.

"The matter you told me about yesterday?" There was a note of patience in Dr. MacArthur's question. "Why not wait until you are certain, Ethridge?"

"No, sir. With your permission, I would rather. . . ."

Words came out of his mouth as though shot by mental force. They were chosen with a clarity, spoken with a certainty and uttered with a velocity which tired the ears of these men whose minds had learned the defense of slow speech.

Dr. James Harrison raised his shaggy brown eyebrows which had not turned gray with his fringe of hair and his beard and reached for his watch. Twenty years ago a smart-alec student had said he looked like Christ in a Derby hat. But even that didn't stick. A man whose hazel-brown eyes had spent sixty-eight years laughing at life received no permanent nicknames. After thirty years of urology and literature, he still believed that the wages of sin were occasionally a damn good living.

Cub moistened his lips and hunched forward.

Dr. Harrison stroked his Vandyke beard and measured the intensity of young Sterling's excitement. Since Monday staff meetings usually lasted from four to five and that was an hour when nobody ever died, he could give the boy fifteen minutes. After five, the really sick patients didn't wait for an audience. . . .

"Perhaps the best way to state the situation we suspect is through the facts." The eyes of the other seven members of the General Staff of the Elijah Wilson Hospital turned to Dr. Ethridge Sterling, Junior, temporarily Physician-in-Chief, aged thirty-eight, whose present importance came about through the premature death of Dr. Merritt at fifty-two, and the natural advantage of being his father's son.

Cub continued, "Two patients in Medicine Clinic, B Ward, have died of causes which seem to our staff not natural in origin and which cannot be traced."

Dr. Harrison snapped his watch shut and interrupted:

"Ethridge, isn't it possible you are taking your Hippocratic oath too seriously, son. . . .?"

"Please, Dr. Harrison!" There was a note of almost childish pleading in the man's voice. "Dr. MacArthur has gone over all of this too, and he thinks it is. . . ."

MacArthur took his hands from his graying

temples and stated: "The deaths have occurred in the same bed."

With that phrase the waters parted, and Cub's father, Dr. Ethridge Sterling, Senior, Dr. Harrison and Dr. Barton braced themselves for the nervous antagonism which was rising in Doctors Peters, Paton and Hoffbein.

"The same bed?" Doctors Peters and Hoffbein inhaled the phrase as a patient does the ether.

Cub gave one of his quick, emphatic nods and continued:

"The first was a goitre I was preparing for Father. Normal case with a good prognosis. Basal average, and nerves in excellent shape, considering the nature of the ailment. The patient died suddenly and unexpectedly."

"Who attended her?" cut in Flannel-feet Hoffbein, as he was known to medical students, and Dr. Otto Hoffbein, Psychiatrist, to the world.

Cub Sterling's internal barometer began to rise. The antagonism between these two men was like that between a mule and a shetland pony.

"Dr. Mattus, resident, saw her Thursday morning, Father and I saw her between seven and nine Thursday night and Dr. Sarah James saw her about ten-thirty. She was dead by dawn."

A grunt escaped the set lips of Dr. Harold Barton, Pediatrician-in-Chief.

"Dr. James came to us from the Johns Hopkins

Medical School and is one of our best," Cub defended.

The men held their peace.

"And the other death?" Dr. Virginus Peters, Ophthalmologist-in-Chief, asked, fingering his Sons of Cincinnati rosette which in the private opinion of the majority of the staff should have been a dollar mark. His face was as open as a peach blossom.

With a careful politeness Cub Sterling answered:

"The second was a heart case of a certain type. Also a very good prognosis. Nothing to interfere with an ultimate and complete recovery. She was put in the bed the night after the goitre died. A whole day was given to a complete and thorough examination and the findings were as stated. Upon the second night, Saturday, the nurse saw her at twelve and at one. She died, suddenly, between then and daylight."

"Any autopsies?" Dr. Peters' face photographed emotions as a stage does lighting effects. It now held interest.

Cub stalled for self-control by lighting a cigarette. MacArthur and Bear Sterling watched carefully. When the cigarette was smoking Cub replied:

"No, Dr. Peters. Not on the first one. We

thought that was a 'fade-out.' Upon the second there was a thorough autopsy. Father did it."

Princeton Peters turned his lavender eyes upon Dr. Ethridge Sterling, Senior.

The only man in the room who appeared to have no interest in the question was Dr. Harrison. He was scrutinizing the shadows of the afternoon sun upon the tops of the trees outside.

Doctors Peters, Hoffbein, Barton, and Paton sat, as much as their respective builds allowed, upon the edges of their chairs, and looked at Bear Sterling.

Bear Sterling resembled his famous nickname. But as the years wore on, it should have been changed to Polar-Bear. He riveted his decisive steel-gray eyes into Peters and growled:

"There were no findings."

The sentence fell upon the table.

MacArthur, who had sat by judicially, started to close the conference.

Prissy Paton, who had been an obstetrician and gynecologist so long that the staff had grown to consider him partly feminine, blocked MacArthur's move with his high, soothing purr:

"What do you think is back of it, Ethridge?"

"Can't seem to find anything, physically, sir."

Dr. Harrison continued contemplating the leaves. Dr. MacArthur realized the thing must be seen through and settled back in his chair.

Dr. Hoffbein, Psychiatrist, who was perfectly aware that the staff didn't think so much of "black magic", therefore enunciated his words with an incisive clarity and leaned forward:

"What is your personal impression, Sterling?"

He inserted his sentences the way other men did hypodermics.

Cub Sterling gave himself an angular brace and replied:

"Must be something other than natural causes, Doctor. Everything has been checked. Everything! Dr. MacArthur and I have combed the department. The superintendent of nurses has checked the supervisor, the head nurse, the graduate floor nurse, and I've gone over my internes thoroughly . . . man by man . . . and woman by woman. . . . The reason I'm bringing it before the staff is I'm stumped. Your experience . . . then, too, medical patients are often in the hospital six weeks to two months. We can't have the thing repeated. . . ."

"Fear psychosis," Hoffbein grunted.

Bear Sterling heaved his thick shoulders and began fingering his key ring. Hoffbein and his foolishness!

This small oddly shaped brass key, and people dying when you least expected, made him think of the door to the cupola of the Administration Building: the door nobody had ever entered since that night so many years ago when he had fixed Flossie

Matthews for Ted Longstreet . . . before he was old enough to see why a reputable surgeon never had any business. . . .

Ted had held the chloroform rag, and after giving her a transfusion of his own blood, had fainted and fallen against his operating hand so that the scalpel punctured her femoral artery . . . and Flossie hemorrhaged; and Ted lay in the pool of blood. When he came to, she was dead . . . of chloroform. In the meantime he had tied the artery, somehow. . . .

"Gone" . . . he could still hear Ted's voice and see that hoggish splotch of blood his coat made upon the white plaster wall as he leaned against it and stretched his slim hands out toward the lids of Flossie's staring blue eyes.

Murder! Murder! He'd slipped in operations since, but Ted Longstreet was the first man he ever heard cry. That night, even now . . . they were all so young! She was a Tribly, Ted an interne, and he. . . .

Not all the honors in the world would ever make him forget how they got the cadaver down the obscure winding stairway behind the Director's office, the Nursing office, the pharmacy, into the elevator and down to the old cadaver vat. . . . Whew!

It was before they began ticketing stiffs and just after they changed from the hook system and the vat was a slimy mass of bodies, under which they were pushing, sliding, hiding. . . .

Then that vile job of cleaning up the cupola. That blotch of blood Ted's back had left and which wouldn't come off and Ted's saying:

"Sterling, every sunset the sky will reflect that I've broken my Oath and murdered. . . ."

And the next day Longstreet had committed suicide.

He had never been back to that cupola! Nobody had been there. The only key remained upon his ring day and night. Since he was famous, he had tried to believe that the blotch was faded, but there came spells still where he'd lose the key in his dreams and hunt and hunt; when he couldn't make himself enter the hospital by the main entrance; when he would be unable to look at the cupola.

It took ten years of dissecting medical students to finish Flossie; even then her legs were perfect enough to carry over to the new pathology building. They had a curve, even to the last . . . an irresistible curve. . . .

Why couldn't he ever learn that he must not look backward? If he had looked backward *then*, he could never have married old Dr. Jemison's daughter and been the proud father of Cub and honorary this and that.

The only people who had ever known were dead. Long dead. . . .

Dr. Sterling was cut back into the tense antagonism which was rising between his son and Hoffbein, when Hoffbein remarked:

"Have you no private conclusions, Ethridge?"

"This is no psychiatric examination, Hoffbein," said Bear. Bear's eyes also knew the hypodermic trick.

"My son has told you the facts, and asked the staff's aid. He suspects an unnatural situation in his department, and asks, in relation to the hospital, how our experience would lead us to handle it. That's simple, and like all simple things, complex enough, isn't it?"

Dr. Harrison took his eyes from the leaves, looked at his watch and rose. He had said nothing for minutes. His action had the effect of a seine upon minnows.

They were caught in his force. He said:

"What is being done with the bed now, Ethridge?"

"It is in use, sir. A patient of Father's."

"Excellent."

Then with the steady stroke of a masseur, he went on:

"I see nothing the staff collectively can contribute which Ethridge and Dr. MacArthur have not already covered. Mysteries in medicine are more frequent than recoveries and Ethridge has my profound respect for acknowledging himself up against one. When one has toyed with homo sapiens as long as Bear and I have, one realizes that they are so damn full of mystery . . . after all, people will die!"

"After the most beautiful operations!" Bear exploded.

"And the ugliest babies," Prissy Paton's lifelong impulse to fawn had tricked him again.

With his remark, the opposition collapsed.

The most respected and the weakest member of the staff had declared themselves. There was nothing more to be said.

With several passing pats upon Ethridge's shoulders the meeting broke up.

Bear Sterling lowered his iceberg brows at the utterly self-righteous bows with which Hoffbein and Princeton Peters retired and growled:

"Come on out to dinner, Mac, and I'll tell you about the golf I shot yesterday."

Flannel-feet Hoffbein drew his half-expended smile back into his facial muscles and slithered out of the Administration Building and to the right down the long corridor.

Princeton Peters pulled on his gray gloves and sailed into the main lobby, past the statue of Elijah Wilson, founder, through the front door of the Administration Building and into his waiting Packard. As the car slid down Wilson Boulevard he turned his stately head and gave the Administration Building a regretful stare. The architects had been at variance about the period and the structure screamed their different tastes. The four corner turrets were the desire of Elijah Wilson's engineering-brother. The cupola was the addition of a New York consultant; and Princeton's educated-man's knowledge of the arts was always upset by the bastard byzantine building. If he had been on hand forty years ago. . . .

The car slid down hill and he folded his hands sorrowfully.

Dr. Harold Barton squared his stocky body which had never outgrown the reach of any child's hand, and forged to the right down the corridor behind, well behind, Hoffbein.

Prissy Paton stuck his smooth, pudgy and wonderfully capable hands into his vest pockets, turned down the long corridor to the left and in what his students called his "delivery walk," caught up with the lengthy stretch of Cub Sterling's legs.

"Remember, Ethridge, my boy, we are behind you. We have every confidence in. . . ."

A group of internes passed and Prissy's green eyes noted that Ethridge barely acknowledged their greeting. Then that report about his never speaking to anybody except with a nod was true. Too bad! Too bad! He had been against his elevation from the first. Too young! Told Peters and

Hoffbein so; tried to tell MacArthur, but the meeting came the day, the very hour the Governor's wife. . . .

"Great confidence, Lad," he purred paternally and pattered away.

Cub gave the door of Medicine Clinic a shove and strode into the elevator.

Two minutes later he walked into Room Two, off Ward B, and closed that door. The inclination to be comforted, when harassed, was new to him. He thought he was being medical and "carrying on."

Sally Ferguson turned over languidly and slit her eyes slightly.

She was damned tired of being poked at by that Jew resident and that hen medic; of figuring out a career and a medical school for her famous father; of taking cascara and mineral oil; of being a sport and trying to like it.

Her long lashes raised. The slits widened.

Cub forgot his irritation and gazed helplessly.

Her lips began to part scornfully and she said:

"Well . . . at last! Unchaperoned and alone! Can I believe my own eyes? Give me a cigarette while I regain my composure."

"No, Miss Merriweather. You are much better, but you mustn't smoke!"

She turned her back and lay utterly silent. Then in a husky pleading voice she began:

"Of course you are too famous to be human!
I didn't know you were famous. I ought to though!
Famous, dictatorial, and snappish. So overbearing
flies won't even bite you! One of these pure-women-
men. No smoking allowed in His Presence!"

Cub laughed spontaneously, and the girl flopped
over furiously.

The eyes blacked and the lashes began to wilt:

"Shut up!"

Her voice had tears in it. Cub's amusement fell
through his lips:

"Sophie!"

She sat bolt up and every curl on her head
shook:

"You devil! You. . . ." Her face changed desperately and she fell backward.

"Where? Where was it?" Cub leaned over and
demanded.

"In my leg. My left leg. . . ." She sighed.

He threw back the sheet and began examining.
His brows had knit heavily. His mouth was inex-
pressive and controlled.

The girl bit her lips, but when her eyes caught
his, she said, flatly:

"Come on. The truth. What is it?"

Cub's medical cloak lowered. He replied cheer-
fully:

"Just a strain. These things crop up like burst-
ing blisters after accidents, Sophie."

Her voice was frighteningly quiet and shocked him out of his shell. She said:

"It doesn't do any good to lie to a person without relatives. I report murder trials, you know . . . and I have a hellish imagination. No truth is as bad as imagination!"

Cub's hand covered hers quickly. Their eyes locked and his voice was calm and certain:

"It may be nothing. It may be a touch of phlebitis. In either event, I'll take no chances. That leg is to be bound and remain bound for twenty-four hours. And you are to lie absolutely still and leave all of the worrying to me."

He gave the hand a squeeze and began sliding too deeply into her eyes. He said banteringly:

"What brand do you smoke, Soph?"

Twinkles pleated around her nose, but her lips were sober:

"What's phlebitis?"

Cub shook his head threateningly:

"My dear little question mark, won't you ever relax?"

The twinkles burst through and she threw back:

"If I did, I'd be an exclamation point!"

Their laughter interlaced, and he switched the conversation and asked:

"How's Dr. Merriweather?"

"Living with his second wife, still operating every morning, writing textbooks in the afternoon.

. . . No! he couldn't do that. . . . Those bitches
would have to know the titles. . . ."

Cub laughed uproariously:

The girl asked:

"How's your father?" A fine radiance wakened
her features, and she continued, "I like your
father. I heard him talk at the Medical Convention
Dinner last winter and I like him, tremendously."

Cub bowed quickly. Then, to cover his embarrassment, asked:

"What were you doing there?"

She twisted her head in the pillows and replied,
demurely:

"Oh, I was sitting among the medical wives and
daughters."

Cub laughed again, and the timbre of it made
her blush. She said quickly:

"Truth is, if you remember, Doctor, that dinner
took place the day after New Years. I was in the
Press box pinch-hitting for . . . believe it or not
. . . the star reporter!"

"Queer I didn't see you." The tone carried admiration.

"You couldn't very well. I was behind a curtain
trying to keep up with your father's mental ball-
bearings."

"They roll," Cub said admiringly, then he asked,
slowly:

"What's your name . . . really . . .?"

Her mouth twitched slightly:

"According to medical records, Doctor, Sophie Merriweather. But according to the church register, Sally Ferguson. To the reporters on *The Call*, 'Ferg' . . . to my father I . . . was . . .'Salscie' . . . I like that best of all. . . ."

Her body began to stiffen and Cub straightened the cover over her legs. His voice was casual:

"She *sounds* like a cigarette smoker. What's the brand . . . Miss Salscie?"

She looked at him slowly. Then she smiled.

And Cub said, "Camels, Chesterfields, Old Golds . . .?"

She nodded and he repeated:

"Old Golds?"

She nodded again, and he said:

"Try to get you a pack at Otto's. Bring them over later."

Her voice returned:

"Who's Otto?"

He walked to the door before he spoke and then he said:

"A bartender who gave me my first belt, first suspenders, first razor . . . and my first drink! May be late tonight before I get over there. After eleven, probably. My house staff meets in ten minutes. Then supper and after that . . . rounds. Be a good child, Salscie. . . ."

Her eyes and mouth broke into a natural smile, which followed him out of the door.

When his footsteps echoed out of hearing, Sally Ferguson remembered that she hadn't asked him any of the things she had intended to find out.

When Dr. Ethridge Sterling, Junior, again appeared in the main corridor he had changed to white hospital coat. The sun had left the trees in the back garden of the great hospital and the nurses were switching past in lines of five or six on their way to supper in the new Nurses' Home.

Had he put it to his staff in the proper way? It was troublesome having women in a meeting. No matter how hideous they were. They always listened to what you said and divined what you didn't say, and whatever else came of this thing he had to stick by his staff. If for one half second they suspected. . . .

And in a time like this why in the hell. . . . If love was as easy to diagnose as disease . . . if he could be perfectly sure! He had been married to medicine for thirty-eight years and they had got along pretty well. . . . Why not leave well enough alone! He glanced up at the corridor clock and swung 'round and returned to Medicine Clinic again. This was no time to walk along reflecting upon what a smile could mean. Better tell Miss

Kerr how things stood. If your head nurse got down on you. . . .

He lit a cigarette and considered. The proper thing was to go to his own office and send for Miss Kerr. But if he handled her with a touch of gallantry, she was always easier.

As the corridor light threw his shadow across the doorsill, Miss Kerr laid down her pen and carefully smiled. Before she did either of these things one was always aware that she knew whom her eyes would appraise.

"Dr. Ethridge!"

She always called him that. When he was "a darling little boy," she had come from Massachusetts General to "help make the Elijah Wilson."

Cub folded his frame into a chair and adjusted it into angles of dignity.

"Miss Kerr, at the General Staff Meeting this afternoon I reported the two unexplained deaths on B Ward."

"Why, Dr. Ethridge! You . . . you . . . wasn't it a little odd . . . to . . . er. . . ."

"I don't believe so. Dr. MacArthur and I. . . ."

"But you," she interrupted him and Cub felt instinctively that the fire had reached the ridgepole, "you put the nursing service in a *very compromising* position. A matter which reflects so unfavorably upon the *whole* medical unit should, I most emphatically feel, have been discussed with

the head of every department before being presented to the General." A sanctimonious note entered her heaves of indignation.

"It was."

He scratched his nose with such care that unless
Miss Kerr had been painfully aware he was contemplating her large flat feet she would have noticed it. He knew that the nurses since time im-
memorial had called her "Foots," and she knew he
knew it.

"Discussed. Yes. Grilled, perhaps better suits
what the nursing staff has been subjected to. But
before we were disgraced I do think. . . ."

"You speak as though you alone were bearing
the whole thing."

"Really . . . er . . . er," her pompadour and
bosom ascended, "Dr. Merritt always. . . ." then
her china blue eyes protruded and she snapped:

"*You* speak as though you suspect my service,
Doctor. In all the years Dr. Merritt's staff. . . ."

"We suspect nobody, Miss Kerr. We do *expect*
the nursing service to coöperate and do as it is
ordered to by the medical. This is not a time for
disagreements. Wherever the blame, until that
blame is placed we are all culpable.

"Dr. MacArthur asked me before the meeting
if there were any special nurses on B Ward. Are
there?"

"None."

"In what classes are the five student nurses?"

"Two in the class graduating in January, two in the next year's class and one entered training last fall. Really, Dr. Ethridge, hasn't my service been probed far enough? For you, Dr. MacArthur, the superintendent of nurses, and the head of the training school, to suspect my staff. . . ."

Cub cut her short.

"We suspect nobody . . . and everybody, Miss Kerr."

But woman roused without consent of will is always woman who will not keep still.

"But to humiliate me before Dr. Paton . . . he's always been against me . . . and dear Dr. Hoffbein and even in front of Dr. Peters . . . without allowing me to utter one single word in my defense. . . ."

"My dear Miss Kerr, will you never realize that you haven't been, as you call it, 'humiliated'? As your line of duty in a crisis, your service . . . like ours . . . is suspected of a failure . . . somewhere."

He rose and turned.

She towered from her chair with the determination of a mule.

"The idea! After all of these years! I can answer now . . . and later, Doctor, for *my* staff . . . and *myself*."

The last word came in two ascending notes of inquiry.

"I trust you are correct, Miss Kerr. Good evening."

The water-off-a-duck's-back nonchalance with which he quitted her office left Miss Roenna Kerr, Class of '90 M. G. and head nurse in Medicine Clinic Elijah Wilson Hospital since 1900, with a sensation of standing with her feet in a puddle.

As the elevator girl respectfully bore him to the top floor where his early rounds began, Dr. Ethridge Sterling, Junior, slouched with his tongue in the corner of his mouth. He was thinking:

"Could break her damn neck! Sex-repressed old maid."

Miss Patricia Withers had been night superintendent of nurses so many years that she had developed an hourly routine.

From two to four-thirty, after all of the clinics had checked-in their midnight patient rounds, she read mystery stories.

After thirteen false clues and flukes, she had just reached the place where the real murderer was to be revealed when her telephone bell intervened.

With an intensity, every motion of which was profane, she snatched up the receiver:

"Well," upon a rising note.

The voice at the other end quaked:

"General Superintendent's office?"

Miss Withers checked her: "Yes. What do you want."

"This is Medicine Clinic, Ward B, Miss Evelina Kerr, Student Nurse, speaking. The telephone of the night supervisor Medicine Clinic does not answer, so I am reporting to your office the death of Alice Tuck, patient in Bed 11."

"What?" Miss Withers' breath pushed each letter through the receiver.

"Reporting the death . . ." the student nurse's voice began to quaver it out again.

"I heard you before, child! Are you sure? No pulse? No respiration? Draw the curtains and leave everything exactly . . . exactly, you understand until your superiors come. . . ."

There seemed to be no response and Miss Withers feared the nurse had fainted.

"Can you hear me?" the authority in her voice would have revived the dead woman, if she had been nearer.

"Yes'm," the girl breathed.

"Then do as I order."

The night operator of the hospital was interrupted in her regular reverie as to whether she could get into the movies, by Miss Withers:

"Get Dr. Mattus. Get the morgue. Get Dr.

Ethridge Sterling, Junior. Get Dr. Sarah James
. . . and get Miss Kerr."

The telephone girl decided that was enough for
the present and rang off.

"Hell-let-loose," she muttered and began ringing Mattus' 'phone.

Miss Withers sat drumming her desk. Again.
That's the third one! Superstitious! Like three on
a match!

Dr. Sidney Mattus turned over in his white iron
bed in his "Germicidal Cell," and reached for the
ringing telephone.

"Huzzies!"

He spat the word with sleepy vehemence born of
unconscious fatigue. The contact between his ear
and the receiver took several motions.

"Nayaa." The inflection bore no interest, it was
simply a sign that contact had been established.

"Dr. Mattus?" Miss Withers' voice was like a
splash of cold water.

"What is it?" he was bluntly and resentfully
awakening.

"Miss Withers, speaking. The woman in Medicine, Ward B, Bed 11, is dead."

"Humh? Dead? Couldn't be!"

"Alice Tuck, Bed 11, Ward B. . . ."

Mattus now wide awake thundered, "Who says
so?"

"The floor night student nurse has just reported to me. That's the bed. . . ."

Mattus, too, had realized that it was. He was busily pulling on his pants. The receiver lay upon the pillow and he was calling into the mouthpiece.

"Get Cub Sterling. Notify Dr. MacArthur. Keep the day staff off the floor until notified. Call the morgue. Call. . . . My God, Miss Withers, call everybody but the police! No you don't. Don't call anybody but Sterling until I verify the nurse's statement."

He ran from the room, the telephone receiver still upon the bed and the lights burning. He started around the octagonal hall toward the stairway. Three flights below . . . in the center of the lobby . . . he could see the statue of Elijah Wilson.

As he reached the second floor he finished buttoning his pants and started toward the door of Dr. Sarah James, then remembered:

"Spending the night with her mother in Cincinnati. She would be!"

With an indignant grunt he had passed the statue and was letting out his stride down the long corridor.

As neither Dr. Cub Sterling nor Dr. Henry MacArthur answered immediately, the operator rang Miss Roenna Kerr.

Miss Kerr and Miss Withers were classmates at Mass. General and it seemed only fair to tip her. . . .

The bedroom of Miss Roenna Kerr was bare as an operating room. It was also a front line trench, but the enemy in this case was age. Upon one chair reposed a specially built corset to hide the collapsing stomach. Under the bed stood, like a pair of dachshunds, two large white shoes with built-in bunion-rests. Under her chin nestled a wrinkle strap and her hair was in "papers." Kid papers, too. She snored with heavy precision.

For the first time since the fire in Ward M she was awakened by the insistent clamor of her telephone. She arose, put on her wool wrapper, loosened the chin strap, and walked over to the 'phone.

"Eeenie, the patient in Bed 11, Ward B, Medicine Clinic, is dead!"

As quickly as the voice had come it had gone and for the first time in all the years she had been a nurse Miss Kerr stood inefficiently looking into a silent telephone!

Then, in her highnecked nightgown, she assumed her military bearing and muttered:

"I don't care whose son he is!"

As assistant to Dr. Merritt, Cub Sterling had occupied a series of rooms on the second floor of the Administration Building. Graduated to "golden oak," the internes called it. The furniture had belonged to Elijah Wilson.

Sterling still used the rooms.

When his telephone began ringing, he lay caticornered in his golden oak double bed with a pillow nestled into his neck. He had reached that second sleep where even an insistent telephone cannot cut the purple mist.

But the night operator of the Elijah Wilson had awakened Cub before. She began ringing in short hysterical jerks like the throbs of a bad heart.

Cub awoke.

The pillow—when he became aware it was a pillow—flew through a door and landed in the bath tub.

He took his fury out upon the 'phone.

" 'Lo!"

The result was the same as if he had said "Boo!"

Miss Withers actually lost her speech.

Cub repeated the process and then in exasperation rung off.

In the interim Dr. Mattus had cut in upon Miss Withers' line.

"Miss Withers? Dr. Mattus. She's dead!"

"Dead?"

"Stone! Get Dr. Sterling . . . wherever he is . . . get him . . . quick!"

Cub had decided, now he was awake, to smoke a cigarette. The pillow was no go . . . but that lovely little laugh when he handed her the cigarettes. . . .

The 'phone interrupted him.

He repeated his " 'Lo !"

"Dr. Sterling, Miss Withers," the words were tumbling. "Pupil nurse Medicine reported patient in Bed 11, Ward B, dead four minutes ago. Dr. Mattus has confirmed the. . . ."

The cigarette followed the pillow . . . but was aimed at a different receptacle.

"Dead! You're wrong. I saw her at rounds. About seven. Dead!" His incredulity almost stopped his speech. "Gimme Mattus!"

"Dr. Mattus is on Ward B. . . ."

"All right. All right. Tell him to wait till I get over there before . . . and Miss Withers, call Dr. MacArthur right away. It's. . . ."

He had started to say murder . . . but he hung up instead. . . .

The night operator snapped to the exchange:

"Now keep on ringing and let me know when you get Riverside 7892, Dr. Henry MacArthur."

"Say, what's the trouble. Can't you wait. . . ."

"Listen, Pal," the night operator responded. "You know as much as I do. A woman 'went out' and the whole place is raisin' hell. . . ."

"Aw girlie, quit y'kiddin'. What did they expect her to do? That's a hospital, ain't it?"

In what the architects refer to as "The Master's chamber" of a white colonial house replete with early American antiques—mostly genuine pieces inherited from his wife's mother—Dr. Henry MacArthur snored peacefully. His wife was in Paris and he had spent from ten to midnight propped up in bed, smoking cigarettes and sipping whiskey highballs. The enjoyment of sprees is based upon comparison.

He lay with one arm against his head, the other thrown out, from habit, toward his wife's side. He snored with vehemence; he had had a grand time. . . .

Upon a bedside table lay a volume of Osler's essays and several medical journals. They were dusty. Only the telephone appeared to have been used within the last week.

The telephone was as necessary to Dr. MacArthur's existence as his eye-glasses. To be so excellent a director of so tremendous a hospital demanded that at any moment of any hour he must be immediately available and ready with a wise, sane, judicial decision upon any subject under the sun. Therefore wherever he went, whenever he went, whyever he went could be known by any head nurse who cared to inquire. That was why he had enjoyed his spree.

It had been the servants' night off.

It had been utterly private.

He was topping it off with uninterrupted snores.

But the night telephone operator at the hospital worked upon the principle that all men past thirty snore. Therefore she took several surreptitious puffs of a cigarette, cut in upon the exchange and settled herself to the task of drowning out a snore . . . long, continuous, vibrating, insistent, monotonous. . . .

She was successful.

The monotony of the bell dripped through to Dr. MacArthur's consciousness. He turned over and put the pillow over his head.

The operator took several more puffs and began again . . . this time in the angry insistence of a crying baby.

MacArthur succumbed and reached feebly for the receiver. It was no use. She rang like a wrong number. But it was no use.

He was fully awake but kept his eyes shut, in an endeavor to keep them from aching, which they did anyhow . . . terribly.

He fumbled the receiver off the hook.

His "yes," was like a cow's "moo."

The voice which responded hit his brain with an impact. He opened his eyes and listened:

"This is Cub Sterling. The patient in Bed 11, Ward B, is dead. Found by the night nurse fifteen minutes ago."

"Dead?"

"Yes, sir. Mattus and I have both examined her. There are no signs of . . . of anything. It. . . . What shall we do, Dr. MacArthur?"

"Remove the body to the autopsy room. Order immediate autopsy. Keep entire staff intact. Notify your father. Keep everything and everybody composed and wait for me."

The clearness in his head seemed to recede and he crawled out of bed with a horrible weariness.

He had fought death, deceit, politics, criticism, financial panics, women . . . but this was his first experience with . . . murder!

»III«
Autopsy Findings

Bear Sterling was tilted back
in the desk chair. The half-egg-shell ceiling light
blazed in his face. He wore the surgeons' apron
in which he had performed the autopsy. His lower
jaw lay relaxed against the cushions of his chins.
His eyes were peacefully closed. He was asleep.
When the Elijah Wilson had been founded he had
been the youngest surgeon, and had learned to
sleep between crises. He did it automatically, naturally and silently.

Cub Sterling had twined himself around an un-
comfortable office chair and was smoking cigarettes.
His left shoulder was hysterically high.

He watched his father's innocent repose with a
visible irritation. He had struck no matches for
over an hour. The smoking was incessant and the
old butt served to light the new cigarettes.

Dr. Sidney Mattus sat stiffly in a straight chair.
His head rested upon one corner of the back and
his feet tucked into one of the chair rungs. He
watched all of the men and held his eyes past them,

apparently upon the coming dawn which could just be discerned through the high window.

Dr. Henry MacArthur sat across the double desk from Bear Sterling. He had shielded his brow from the glaring light and was soothing it like a man in constant pain. Occasionally he lifted his free hand and twisted his left ear thoughtfully.

No man had spoken for many minutes.

The air of the room was heavy with smoke, tension, the odor of formaldehyde and the chilliness of dawn.

It housed all the suppressed horror of a death chamber, and its occupants had the appearance of men awaiting execution.

Dr. MacArthur's shoulders were hunched as though prepared for a blow; even in Bear Sterling's slumber there was a sense of watchful waiting.

Cub was thinking. Shall I keep my mouth shut and watch that night student nurse. . . ? She is a niece of Miss Kerr . . . remember that . . . old fellow!

Dr. MacArthur raised his head as though to answer and said:

"What did your father say about the heart?"

Cub's eyes met his and he responded:

"In normal condition, considering the history, sir."

"Strange. Was that your understanding, Mattus?"

"Yes, Dr. MacArthur."

Silence lay over the air again. MacArthur put his head back into his hands and began checking it all over: Cub, Mattus, Bear, the student nurse, the orderly, the Head Nurse in Medicine Clinic . . . the . . . was there anybody else? Was it possible. . . .

He stopped his mind and decided not to think until he had some facts. There would be no sense in clouding his faculties with hysterical superstitions. A clear head was what must be maintained.

The morning light was beginning to fill the room; it began to suffuse the faces of the four men.

MacArthur straightened and turned to Cub Sterling and Mattus, and smiled.

"I'm sorry boys if I've been taciturn . . . but the Elijah Wilson is my only child . . . and as a parent I guess I'm hopeless."

"Good God, sir, we understand."

Cub Sterling was upon his feet and towering over MacArthur. Mattus' manner dropped from him and he became almost a schoolboy in his shyness.

"Of course we do," he affirmed.

Bear Sterling stirred in his sleep and awoke. His steel-gray eyes were softened by the coming dawn. All three men turned to him. His eyes became pin points.

"Any news?"

"Not yet."

"Wish Heddis hadn't gone to that damn convention."

"I've telegraphed for him. Could that sleeping potion have been administered hypodermically?" MacArthur's voice was thin and old.

"Improbable. The order was for capsule," Cub Sterling snapped.

"Then that puncture was from. . . ." Mattus' voice slid into the opening each man's brain had already made.

"Durn these pharmacologists!" Bear announced and closed his eyes.

MacArthur took his watch from his pocket and said:

"Boys, since all tests are being done upon those organs, it may be hours yet. Go get some sleep and prepare for today. You'll have a twenty-four hour job ahead of you to sit on the suppressed hysteria in Medicine Clinic . . . and you have *got* to sit on it!"

Mattus and Cub Sterling rose. Patients, another day, . . . Tuesday! . . . rounds, diagnoses . . . they had forgotten it all! And within three hours it must be faced again.

They turned toward the door and it was opened in their faces by the second assistant chemist.

He was a small damp man whose limp black hair sweated into his muddy forehead. He said:

"Dr. MacArthur, Dr. Heddis and Dr. Maids are at the convention in Cincinnati, so I did the tests upon the organs you sent over. . . ."

His voice was matter-of-fact. Its uninterested monotony awakened Bear Sterling.

He rivetted his eyes into the fellow and growled:

"Who in the hell are you?"

"A gentleman," Dr. MacArthur said, "who is reporting upon some organs I sent over to the chemical laboratory, Dr. Sterling. Dr. Heddis' second assistant."

The chemist wiped his perspiring lip and continued in the voice of a bell-hop.

"None of the organs show traces of any foreign substance except the ingredients of a sleeping potion, which I believe was administered in powdered form, capsule probably. I have not proceeded with any obscure tests. Dr. Heddis will be back this afternoon. I regret I can make no further report until after a consultation with Dr. Heddis."

Bear Sterling's regular breathing was the only noise.

"Dr. Heddis is flying back. He should be here within two hours. Sorry to have called you at such an hour. Please keep on searching and consult Dr.

Heddis immediately he returns. In the meantime, will you be so kind as to have a typed report of your findings in my hands by nine this morning? So kind of you!" Dr. MacArthur stated.

He ushered the chemist through the door and shut it after him. He turned to face the three men. He stood so erect that his wife would have known he had lost a battle and a tremendous one.

"Bear Sterling, did that body show a hypodermic puncture?"

"It did."

"Then that syringe contained something . . . I can't seem to make my brain . . . understand."

At nine-fifteen, Dr. Henry MacArthur sat in his own office chair and peered intently at the innocuous findings of the second assistant chemist and the addenda which Dr. Heddis had written an hour before.

His long brow was pleated with straight thin wrinkles.

He was reading Dr. Heddis' supplement with fascinated horror. It indicated, what he had feared, that the patient in Bed 11, Ward B, Medicine Clinic had not died of a sleeping potion. That somewhere in the Elijah Wilson. . . .

His door into the corridor of the Administration Building was open. Except during meetings it was always open.

His secretary appeared in it and said, "Here is your mail, Dr. MacArthur."

The tone of her voice braced him.

He smiled as she advanced and laid the letters upon the desk.

"I won't dictate this morning, Miss Sadler. There is an important staff meeting. Please call off my appointment with the Woman's Board, and that luncheon engagement with the man from the Duke Foundation . . . and . . . take all telephone messages unless they come from the staff, or Dr. Heddis."

He was interrupted by the tall shadow of Cub Sterling.

The secretary turned and passed out.

Cub took the proffered chair and said, "Can they all come, sir?"

"I'm afraid not. Your father is doing a brain tumor on the Bishop's aunt, Paton is scheduled for a historectomy on the president of the Woman's College, Peters is demonstrating his new retina operation before some visiting medical students; but Hoffbein, Harrison, and Barton will be here, and we have the others' approval to go ahead. I'm sorry they can't come, but I do not feel I can assume the responsibility of delaying the meeting. Is Mattus coming?"

"No, sir. He's doing my teaching rounds with the students."

"Heddis believes. . . ."

Dr. MacArthur slid the typewritten findings toward Cub. The young man lit a cigarette, looked away from them and frowned.

"Dr. MacArthur," his voice had assumed its steely quality under which he always hid his emotions. He held out an envelope.

MacArthur took it automatically and asked, "What is it, son?"

"My resignation, sir."

MacArthur straightened as though he had been struck by an electric eel. His blue eyes shot into Cub Sterling's and he muttered:

"Are you afraid to face the music, Ethridge?"

"No, sir!"

"Then do it without hysterics," MacArthur ordered, tearing the envelope into shreds as Prissy Paton's purring voice interrupted:

"What, am I the first one here, MacArthur? Good morning, Ethridge. Pleasant morning. Cancerous through and through. No use removing anything. Fine woman, and great influence in her generation. Sewed her up again. No use. Will probably live several months. Are the rumors I hear true? Has there been another? I thought it was that yesterday. I said to myself, 'it certainly has all the symptoms. . . .' "

"Blow your bubbles out of the window, Boy Blue," Dr. Harrison chuckled easing Dr. Paton into a chair. Then he walked over and shook hands with Ethridge Sterling, Junior, and with Dr. Mac-Arthur.

He seated himself, took out his pipe and began talking of the tremendous discoveries of the ruins of Roman towns which had recently been ascertained in England by means of the airplane.

He filled the room with sanity. Dr. Paton went to his usual morning manicure, and Dr. Barton came in quietly, nodded, sat down and joined the listening group. Nobody noticed Flannel-feet Hoffbein's entrance.

Dr. Harrison stopped and turned politely to Dr. MacArthur; like obedient schoolboys the other four men turned to MacArthur also.

"Gentlemen, I know it is most unusual and inconvenient to be called to a staff meeting without notice and at this hour. Still I believe the occasion justifies the summons. The thing of which Ethridge told you yesterday afternoon, is this morning. . . . At three A.M. the patient in Bed 11, Ward B, Medicine Clinic was found . . . dead. There was an unexplained puncture from a hypodermic syringe in the left arm."

"MacArthur," Dr. Harrison's voice had become an august bass, "are you s-u-r-e?"

MacArthur stood up and walked toward Dr. Harrison. In his extended hand was the typewritten sheet. He was even straighter than he had been

in the autopsy room. For thirty-odd years his and
Dr. Harrison's great passion had been the Elijah
Wilson Hospital. Harrison rose. They met in a
patch of morning sunshine, which threw the sheen
from Dr. Harrison's head into a mirror over the
mantel and back into Prissy Paton's eyes.

Prissy gave a hysterical gasp and prepared to
scream. Dr. Barton, in the voice he used with children, remarked, "Easy, sister. Easy!"

Nobody laughed.

Nobody registered it.

Hoffbein breathed like a returning pearl diver
and enunciated carefully, "Read it, Harrison."

As Dr. MacArthur returned to his chair and
Dr. Harrison cleared his throat, the door into the
corridor opened slightly and Princeton Peters'
peach-blossom face vied with the morning sun. Cub
Sterling saw it and winced. Before any other man
had taken it in, Princeton tiptoed into the room
and his lavender eyes had assumed their death-
mask purple.

With a precision which carried the force of bass
waves against a rock ledge, Harrison began en-
graving into his brain and into theirs, the report of
the second assistant chemist. As he turned the page
to Dr. Heddis' supplement, the men stirred nervously and Hoffbein's eyes took on a mountain-out-
of-molehill scorn.

Dr. Heddis' addition stated: "The routine tests,

afore referred to, are being checked by my first assistant, Dr. Maids, who returned with me; so far they reveal nothing other than the ingredients of a sleeping potion. These ingredients tally with those prescribed in the order filed upon the patient's chart. Toxicology, like other branches of the Profession, is partly guess work. Since the cadaver bears evidence of a hypodermic puncture, and indications are that the potion was not administered that way, my belief is that this patient died of a syringe of some obscure drug.

"Therefore I am immediately beginning upon the obscure tests. It may take days to prove or disprove my conclusions. In the meantime, I repeat, a sleeping potion prescribed in capsule form, which the pharmacy compounded and the student nurse states she administered, explains neither the syringe puncture nor the death.

"Indications, it seems to me, point to an obscure and deadly drug. Possibly a drug which may be administered *per os*, and may have been so administered in the two previous cases. Any findings will be immediately reported to the General Staff or Dr. MacArthur."

As the last words scraped into the consciousness of the men, a solemnity comparable to that which shadows the faces of pallbearers as they watch the coffin of a beloved comrade lowered, blanketed the staff. Whatever their petty hates and puerile quarrels, so far as the reputation of the Elijah Wilson was concerned, they agreed. It must not be damaged.

"He might be wrong," Prissy quavered.

Nobody heard him.

"An obscure and deadly drug. Poison. And it may take days to discover it. Something we never heard of, probably." Dr. Harrison's voice seemed to be directed toward his own mind.

Dr. MacArthur replied:

"Let's wait for Heddis on the chemistry, gentlemen. Ethridge and Mattus have spent the last two hours searching texts. They could find nothing. We would only waste time surmising." Then, as though Prissy's statement had just reached his brain he turned to him and said, "Yes, he might be wrong. But we can't have this thing continue, and until he is proved wrong. . . ." He shook his head slowly, "The effect was obvious. The woman is dead."

For a full minute after Dr. MacArthur ceased speaking, no man spoke, and it was Prissy's high treble which cut into their consciences.

"Ethridge . . . er . . . how was she last night?"

"I saw her around seven," his voice took on its protective clip. "Her pulse was around a hundred. Considering her condition that was not odd. Her spirits were excellent. Eager for Father to go ahead

with the operation. He saw her between eight and
nine. Found condition quite in line with the way
she was when I saw her. Is that your understanding, Dr. MacArthur?"

"And . . . er . . . by the way, where is your
father?"

"He is doing a brain tumor, Dr. Paton," Dr.
MacArthur cut in.

"And how did your resident . . . Doctor . . .
er?"

"Mattus."

"Yes . . . thank you . . . Dr. Mattus, consider her?" Hoffbein slid his question into Cub.

"He saw her before she went to sleep around
nine. He reports her pulse had dropped to around
ninety; otherwise her condition remained un-
changed. Anything else, sir?"

Hoffbein never answered verbally questions
which did not flatter him. He shook his head
thoughtfully.

By that time the staff had regained some measure
of its equilibrium and Dr. MacArthur continued.

"Between the time Mattus saw her and three
A.M. she was . . . was. . . ."

"I'm in favor of turning the whole thing over to
the police," Princeton Peters said most righteously.

"I'm not!" Dr. Harrison was vehement. "Outside of this room . . . with the exception of Bear
Sterling and Heddis . . . no living person is

aware of the situation," he pointed the paper at Peters' face. "Some linen is too foul to wash in public. Want to ruin the hospital, d'ye? We think we are pretty good at death and birth . . . and we shall not be downed by. . . ."

He waved the paper at them.

"Precisely. . . ."

Then Dr. MacArthur realized he had expressed an opinion himself. . . .

"What is your conclusion, gentlemen?" he hurried to say.

"Mistake to form one without an examination of the witnesses, I think . . . if you can call them that . . . suh," Dr. Barton interposed.

"Quite. Ethridge and I decided upon that during the autopsy. And I have arranged with my secretary to call them quietly . . . and separately . . . in order to avoid. . . . We would have questioned them minutely this morning; but the seriousness of our decision . . . whatever it is . . . must be a responsibility we *all* bear. D'y'see?"

"The night student nurse on Ward B is waiting. Shall I have her brought in, gentlemen?"

Hoffbein sensed a suppressed motion of Cub Sterling's, a slight movement in the chair, an intangible gathering of forces.

"Isn't this rather cruel?" Dr. Harrison suggested.

"Terribly. But how else will we ever. . . ?"

Princeton Peters interrupted Dr. MacArthur.

"Murder is cruel, too."

It was the first time the word had been mentioned. It rushed into the faces of the seven men like an angry wind.

During the ensuing vacuum, Dr. MacArthur lifted his telephone:

"Miss Sadler, will you please bring that pupil nurse to my office."

The girl entered tensely.

Dr. Barton noticed her eyes were blue and too closely set; Prissy thought the face was sweet; Princeton Peters felt she had been nicely brought up; Dr. Harrison's brain flashed "kitten lined with ox-hide"; Cub noticed her feet were flat, and Dr. MacArthur was too benevolent for a personal estimate.

"Won't you sit down, Miss . . . er. . . ."

"My name is Evelina Kerr."

Her voice held a note of defiance as she took the proffered chair beside Dr. MacArthur's.

"My child," he said soothingly, "this is probably the most trying duty you have had in your whole training . . . and we regret that it is unavoidable. Will you please tell us plainly . . . and as minutely as you can remember, exactly what happened after you went on duty in B Ward last night?"

She sat with her feet together, her hands folded in her lap, and a sullen calm in her voice.

"At nine o'clock, Dr. MacArthur, I went on night duty on B Ward of Medicine Clinic. Aunt Roenna . . . I mean Miss Kerr . . . was on the floor and Miss Kexter, the white nurse, who had waited to give me my instructions."

"White nurse?" Princeton Peters' voice was polite, but demanding.

"Slang for graduate floor nurse in charge," Cub Sterling supplied.

The student nurse was silent in her resentment. Finally she continued:

"They left together. Then I took my temperatures, counted pulses, prepared the patients for the night."

"The patient in Bed 11, Miss Kerr," Hoffbein began in his mesmerizing voice. "How was she?"

The girl started and turned toward him with the underlying resentment of a schoolboy stopped midway through the multiplication tables.

"She was all right, Dr. Hoffbein. She had no temperature and. . . ."

"Her pulse?" he interrupted again.

Cub Sterling stirred restlessly and lit a cigarette.

"It was between ninety and a hundred. By nine-thirty I had given all of my medicines. . . ."

"Did she have any medicine?"

"Yes, Dr. Hoffbein, she did. She had a prescription of Dr. Sterling, Senior's. A . . . a sleeping potion."

"Do you know what it was?"

"No, sir. It came up from the pharmacy filled."

"Wasn't the duplicate on her chart?"

"It was pheno-barbital," Cub Sterling cut in raspingly.

The girl hesitated. She seemed to have lost the thread of her thoughts.

"Go ahead with the story, child," Dr. Mac-Arthur soothed.

She sat silent a moment and then continued:

"By ten o'clock I had finished my medicines, temperatures and pulses. The ward was quiet and I started to work upon the fever charts.

"The orderly was in the kitchen straightening up and fixing the breakfast trays. Two patients called for bed-pans. The orderly came to tell me that we were short two milk bottles. I telephoned the kitchens about them.

"Otherwise the ward was perfectly quiet, except for an occasional cough.

"At ten-fifteen, Miss Willis, the night supervisor in Medicine, made her rounds, and told me to watch the patient in Bed 11 very carefully.

"At eleven-forty I went to the medicine closet to prepare the hypodermic Dr. Mattus had ordered for another patient."

"What kind of hypodermic?" Dr. MacArthur inserted.

"A strophanthin mixture. She's a cardiac case."

"A dispensary case of cardiac insufficiency," Cub Sterling cut in.

Miss Kerr's resentment was again expressed by silence. She seemed to be debating with herself.

"What happened?" Hoffbein demanded curtly.

For the first time since she had come into the room her speech came spontaneously.

"I . . . I . . . was boiling the syringe and had my back to the corridor door, and suddenly I felt someone passing in the corridor and turned around, and ran to the medicine closet door. There was no one in sight. And then I remembered the boiling syringe and went back to turn it off. I couldn't leave until I had. It would have been ruined, and if the patient didn't get her dose in time she might die.

"So I made myself finish filling the syringe and then went into the ward. There was nobody there, and all of the patients were sleeping, except Mrs. Witherspoon, who is queer in the head.

"I asked her if she had seen anybody and she said, 'Yes.' "

The girl's speech died in her throat and the seven men held their breath.

MacArthur regained his first.

"Whom did she say she saw, Miss Kerr?"

"She said she saw Dr. . . . Dr. . . . Sterling
. . . Junior. . . ."

The girl turned her close-set eyes, acid with hate,
upon Cub Sterling. Princeton's lavender eyes,
death-purple, Prissy's green ones glinting, Hoffbein's black ones deep as wells and the brown eyes
of Doctors Barton and Harrison, gravely inquir-
ing, turned upon Cub Sterling.

Only Dr. MacArthur's eyes remained the same.

Cub Sterling answered the inquiry sharply.

"The patient is deranged, gentlemen. I was in
my rooms."

The door opened and Bear Sterling, his brows
beetling, entered. Cub rose and gave him his seat.
Dr. Harrison pulled up a vacant chair and motioned Cub into it. The chair was between his and
Dr. Barton's.

Prissy Paton looked at Princeton Peters and
both of them decided they had better not speak
. . . now.

"And what happened next, Miss Kerr?" Hoffbein insisted.

"I went and asked the orderly if he had seen
anybody and he said 'No.' So I went and looked at
the patient in Bed 11 again. She was sleeping
peacefully."

Dr. Harrison leaned suddenly forward. His voice
was acid:

"Did that deranged patient see anybody else?"

"No, sir."

Then his voice stabbed:

"Did you?"

The close eyes shifted quickly. Her response came instantly:

"No, Doctor Harrison."

A silence began stretching. The girl continued abruptly:

"Then I went back to my desk and finished my fever charts."

"You did not call your supervisor?"

"No, Dr. MacArthur. I finished the fever charts and then made the midnight rounds. The patient in Bed 11 was still sleeping peacefully. I called in the rounds to my night supervisor and began studying my nursing manual. Three patients rang their bells between then and two. One wanted a glass of water and two, bed-pans. At two I gave the special medicines and then went back to my studying."

"You did not look at the patient in Bed 11?"

"No, Dr. Harrison, she had no special medicine. At three I again made rounds and found the patient in Bed 11 was dead. I called my supervisor and failed to get her. I then called the general superintendent. She told me to draw the curtains around Bed 11 and wait further orders until Dr. Mattus came.

"He and Dr. Sterling, Junior, came within the

next fifteen minutes. Dr. Sterling and Dr. Mattus rolled the bed off of the ward and into the elevator.

"I did not see the patient again. I finished my ward duties by seven, woke the remaining patients and told them that the patient in Bed 11 had been operated on in the night and removed to the Surgical Clinic, like Aunt Roenna told me to. . . ."

"When did she tell you that?" Cub Sterling inquired.

The girl hesitated and flushed. For the moment she seemed to have lost her control.

"She didn't. I had forgotten. Miss Willis, the night supervisor told me."

"Thank you very much, Miss Kerr. Are there any questions any of you gentlemen wish to ask Miss Kerr, before she is relieved?"

"How long have you been in training?"

"Two years and five months, Dr. Harrison. I finish in December."

"Thank you again," Dr. MacArthur said as she rose, and then finished:

"Of all the people concerned in this, Miss Kerr, you are the youngest. Please do not forget that two years ago you took an oath concerning silence."

Princeton Peters, who was sitting by the door, rose and opened it for her.

"Thank you, my dear!" he beamed.

No man felt she had told the entire truth.

After her departure, they sat silently awaiting the next witness. The horror of the thing seemed to have enveloped them.

The night orderly on B Ward entered. A thin, tubercular looking man with frightened eyes. Everything about him seemed collapsed, and yet still able to move.

Dr. MacArthur looked up:

"Good morning, William. How are you?"

The man's appreciation spread over him.

"Well as can be expected, thank you, Doctor. How's yourself?"

He turned to Prissy, Bear, Cub, and Harrison with a respectful "Good morning, Doctor."

"William," Dr. MacArthur began addressing him before he could enter into a personal conversation with each man, "were you on duty last night?"

"Yes, sir, I was. As usual. And a frightful night, too, sir."

"How?"

"Well, Dr. MacArthur, to begin my rheumatism was bothering. And then everything seemed to have hid itself. And then that girl just in here was like a kitten on a brick, sir. Got my hair prickled, so to speak, by running back and asking me if I'd seen anybody on the ward about eleven-fifty and then saying she had *felt* somebody."

"Was there any basis for it?"

"None, sir, as I knows. It's true I was in the

kitchen during her feeling spell, so to speak. But, if you will pardon my remarking, sir, I been on that ward ten years coming August and it's as hard to get past me as a watchdog, sir."

"Yes, William. I know it is."

"Thank you, Dr. MacArthur. Thank you."

"How many times did the nurse come back?" Hoffbein smiled encouragingly.

"Only wunst. And then when she found the woman dead, sir! I was resting with my eyes shet, sir, and she well nigh scared me out of my wits!"

"Was she frightened?" Hoffbein insisted.

"It ain't fur me to say, Doctor. I was too mad at having my rest ruined and too scared myself to see, sir. It wasn't till Dr. Mattus came that I could stand away from the wall, sir. When Dr. Cub . . . begging your pardon, son . . . Sterling got there I was all right again.

"I been in the hospital long as most of you and I seen death every day, but. . . ."

"And we know how proud you are of the hospital, William," Dr. MacArthur cut in, "and what a help you have always been to it. So you must promise me, upon your oath, before these gentlemen, that you will not repeat to any living soul a single word of what you know or suspect about the trouble."

Dr. MacArthur drew the old man's eyes to his and William replied:

"I promise, sir."

"Thank you, William."

Dr. Peters held the door open.

The old man started toward it and turned midway.

"Dr. MacArthur, do I . . . do I . . . ?"

"You do. Tonight and every night."

It was apparent that every man felt from the minute William began speaking that he was innocent. During his interrogation they had relaxed.

In the interim between his exit and the entrance of Peter Rathbone, Chief Pharmacist, the tension had fallen considerably.

"Baldy" Rathbone shook them out of a reverie.

He had a body like a triangle upside down. His wide shoulders showed strength and assurance. He was a youngish middle-aged man. A spreading part ran up the center of his scalp and connected his wide forehead with the bald spot on top.

He had been raised an orphan and worked his way through college at night, and then worked his way up at the Elijah Wilson. There was a sense of definite knowledge about the face and figure. His eyes bore the marks of childhood suffering, but his smile heartened the men.

"Good morning, gentlemen."

His voice was a deep resonant baritone.

"Sit down, Baldy," Dr. MacArthur motioned to the "witness chair"; then a deep blush steeped his face, and he smiled. Rathbone returned the smile, took the chair, and ran his eyes over the staff. He had never seen any of them so perturbed.

Dr. MacArthur said carefully:

"Er . . . er . . . Rathbone, did you check the prescriptions?"

"As far as possible, sir. A compounded prescription, as you know, cannot be checked as to relative quantities and so . . . but the ingredients from the remainder (I understood from the order that I was to have two capsules compounded, in case the first failed to take effect) were checked. They tallied as to substance, perfectly."

"Who compounded the prescription?" Dr. Hoffbein queried.

"McInnis, my first assistant, sir. He can be trusted."

He was interrupted by the telephone bell. It jarred the men like a steam siren. MacArthur's, "Yes, Heddis. Are you sure? Soon as possible. Thank you," held the eight men to a dead silence. A silence which screamed for knowledge.

Dr. MacArthur placed the hook too carefully upon the receiver, Hoffbein thought, and then he spoke:

"Coniine, gentlemen. One of the deadliest poisons. Heddis will be over in fifteen minutes."

"Whew!" Dr. Harrison ejaculated.

"Hypodermic syringe, then," Bear Sterling growled.

Cub Sterling jumped as though he had been shot.

They all turned toward him.

"What's the matter, Ethridge?" Dr. Harrison put his hand on his knee. . . .

"Nothing. Except she was giving hypodermics all night. She. . . ."

Dr. MacArthur's pointer nose had a dreadful struggle with his judicial brain.

"We must make no decisions . . . nor allow ourselves any prejudices, until we are in possession of all evidence."

His voice was stern.

"You were saying, Baldy . . . ?"

"That Dr. Heddis believes it was done . . . hypodermically. He suspected coniine and called me twenty minutes ago, and as a result all of the medicine closets in Medicine Clinic have just been checked. Nothing was found."

"Ever have any obscure poisons in the pharmacy?" Cub Sterling was leaning arrogantly forward.

"Rarely. None, at present."

"How can you account for the entry of this . . . coniine?" Cub Sterling lowered his brows and scowled.

"*I* can't, Dr. Sterling," Rathbone turned his

body around and looked through Cub searchingly.
His doming forehead added weight to his eyes.

Cub shifted his position, and Bear Sterling who
had missed the by-play growled:

"Is it hard to obtain?"

"Sir?"

"I said is coniine difficult to get?"

"Since we never have any use for it, I don't
know, Dr. Sterling," he hesitated as if endeavoring
to hide his irritation and then continued "Shall
I find out, sir?"

Dr. MacArthur interposed:

"Good idea. See where and in what quantities the
big pharmaceutical houses have sold coniine within
the last year."

"Perhaps we can trace the person quickly that
way," Dr. Barton affirmed.

Rathbone rose and turned, "Is there anything
else, gentlemen?. I'll let you know directly I find
out. Do you wish all syringes in the hospital
checked, Dr. MacArthur?"

"Do you, gentlemen?" Dr. MacArthur turned
toward Harrison and Bear Sterling.

"Plenty of time for that," Hoffbein inserted.
"Check the supply sources first."

When Rathbone was gone they felt as though a
strong support had been removed. His incisive up-
rightness rested them; but he had shot them so full

of information they were still dazed when Miss Roenna Kerr entered.

She came, her hair waved, her face firmly set, the bust and rear defiantly inflated, her enraged vitals midway between. She had been there as long as any of them. Her work had always been perfect. She wore her new pair of bunion-rest shoes.

Princeton Peters took her arm in his, patted her hand and murmured:

"Dear Miss Kerr, brace up!"

He eased her into the "witness chair" and tip-toed back to his own.

He was worth a million dollars to the Elijah Wilson . . . in his way. To every other man in the room she had appeared *too* braced!

In response to their "good morning," she smiled, generally, cocked her head on one side and said to MacArthur:

"You sent for me, Doctor?"

"Yes, Miss Kerr," his slow methodical fairness was beating against his natural inclinations. "We want you to tell us exactly what you know about the death of the patient in Bed 11, Ward B, Medicine Clinic, please."

"The last one?"

"Yes. Thank you."

"Well, before I begin I should like to say that the Elijah Wilson is as dear to my heart as to any of yours, and my humiliation is. . . ."

Again Princeton came to the rescue.

"We know it!"

She flopped her bosom, took a snort of air and continued.

"The patient in Bed 11, Ward B, was admitted Sunday as a patient of Dr. Ethridge Sterling, Senior, under the observation of Dr. Ethridge Sterling, Junior. . . ."

"Yes, Miss Kerr. But the thing I wish you to report upon is the nursing-staff angle. . . ."

She flopped her bosom again and said:

"Miss Kexter, my white nurse on Ward B is one of the finest women I have ever met in the nursing profession. And she had been most surpassingly brave through this entire . . . investigation. . . . I think it has come to that, now. . . ."

"Trained with us?" Dr. Harrison asked.

"Yes. Stood second in her class. She has under her five student nurses into whose records I have gone most thoroughly . . . and who have been cruelly grilled. . . ."

"Miss Kerr," Dr. MacArthur interrupted, "we have all been cruelly grilled as you call it. Please try to realize that it is not because we suspect your department . . . any more than any other . . . that we are questioning you."

"Dr. MacArthur," she bit her lips, "my department has been my life; when it is criticized. . . ."

"We know you do! And so does everybody else

concerned," Dr. Harrison interposed. "Really Miss Kerr, please stick to what has happened. Your niece has night duty on Ward B, I believe?"

"She has."

"She says you gave her orders about what to say to the patients about the death. Did you?" Cub Sterling had forgotten his manners and become bitterly stern.

"I wasn't on duty, Dr. Ethridge."

"Did you talk to her over the telephone?"

"Of course not. How should I know of the death?"

"Did you talk to her on the ward?"

She inflated entirely and said with a defiant calm:

"Doctor Ethridge, I just answered that question."

"Then how do you explain her statement, Miss Kerr?"

A sudden terror flicked her china blue eyes. She dropped the lids instantly and replied with studied slowness:

"The child has been through such an ordeal, she was rattled."

"Thank you."

Bear Sterling shifted, Dr. Harrison stroked his beard, Dr. MacArthur frowned and took up the questioning before Cub Sterling had regained his composure.

"Who has charge of the hypodermic syringes on your floors, Miss Kerr?"

"The white nurse in charge."

"Who has access to them?"

"She and the student nurses on duty."

"At all hours?" Bear Sterling rumbled.

"At *all* hours, Dr. Sterling. *Night* as well as day," she defied.

"I see."

His two words nicked her composure. She questioned shortly:

"Why aren't you questioning my night supervisor?"

"She was not available when your niece discovered the murder, and therefore her testimony would have no value."

"Where was she?" Dr. Harrison drawled.

Miss Kerr began to turn purple.

"In the lavatory, Doctor."

"What time did you get into the Clinic this morning, Miss Kerr?"

She turned her defiant eyes upon Cub Sterling and struck:

"At four sharp. The night superintendent had called me at three-thirty and told me. I came over immediately. You were still with Dr. MacArthur, I believe."

Again his "Thank you" cut her down.

Dr. MacArthur realized she was useless, so he said:

"Thank you, Miss Kerr. You have been a great help. Of course I do not have to ask a person of your integrity to realize the necessity of silence."

Princeton took his cue and opened the door.

Miss Kerr rose majestically and smiled inclusively.

She left every man in the room irritated.

"Gentlemen," Dr. MacArthur soothed, "that is all of the testimony, except Mattus' story, and Dr. Sterling, Ethridge and I went over it with him while we were awaiting the autopsy findings. Any questions or decisions before Heddis comes?"

"What was Mattus' statement?" Dr. Harrison asked.

"That he found the patient in the condition Father and I did when he made his rounds, and the next time he saw her, at three-five, she was dead," Cub Sterling responded.

"Could the murderer have any animus against the patients?" Barton asked leaning forward.

"Not likely," Cub said. "One from out of town and genteel poor, second dispensary admission, and the last old patient. Been in the hospital before."

He was interrupted by a knock upon the door and Dr. Heddis' stout, round body, with its piano-post legs and lion head protruded through the opening. His wide-set yellow-brown eyes, even in

repose, dominated his highly intelligent face. Dr.
MacArthur motioned him into the "witness chair"
and he began speaking in a high, tired voice which,
because of his increasing deafness, had a sing-song
quality.

In ordinary conversation his impediment required a "raising" of his questioner's voice, so upon
a subject of which men spoke in whispers any information he had to give automatically became a
soliloquy:

" 'Morning, gentlemen. Luck, pure luck! Organs
appeared perfectly normal. Began the obscure
tests alphabetically. It would have taken two days
to reach coniine, if my nose hadn't been haunted
by an almost imperceptible odor; after about a
half hour my brain finally diagnosed it.

"The tests are conclusive. She died of an infusion
of coniine, $C_8 H_{16} NH$, *per os* or hypodermically.
Puncture makes syringe theory conclusive as coniine administered *per os* would be remarked by the
patient. Smells like mouse urine. Also acts locally as
a caustic. Burning the mouth. Itching of the
throat. Dizziness. Nausea. Tormenting thirst.
Paralysis of the sural muscles. . . . The patient
had none of these symptoms?"

He turned toward Cub Sterling questioningly.
So did every other man in the room. Cub's "No"
was verbal as well as muscular.

"You see," the leonine head rolled heavily, "one

and one-half to two grains administered hypodermically would be fatal . . . in a very short time
. . . before a patient would have the agony symptoms penetrate to the drug deadened nerve centers.
Before she could rouse herself the paralysis of the
peripheral endings of the motor nerves had set in;
also the deadening of the sensory nerves had begun.
The dominant action, however, is upon the motor
system. Death ensued from paralysis of respiration."

He stopped to draw breath and no man interrupted. Toxicology was only a branch of the science
upon which this man was an authority.

Dr. Heddis continued: "All organs appeared
normal. The stomach content, the organs rich in
blood . . . liver, spleen, kidneys, lungs . . . appeared healthy. But they . . . all . . . responded positively to the solubility, crystallization
and Melzer's tests."

Prissy could stand the tension no longer. He
screamed, "Of what plant is coniine the active principal?"

"Hemlock!"

"The fatal hemlock!" Dr. Harrison's voice was
heavy as he quoted:

" 'Then Socrates lay down upon his back and
the person who had administered the poison
went up to him and examined for a little time

his feet and legs and then squeezing his foot strongly, asked whether he felt him.' "

Dr. Heddis, who never had any trouble understanding Harrison, also knew his Plato. He nodded and continued:

" 'Socrates replied that he did not. He then did the same to his legs, and proceeding upwards in this way, showed us that he was cold and stiff, and he afterwards approached him and said to us that when the effect of the poison reached the heart Socrates would depart. . . .' "

Heddis threw out his hands helplessly.

Princeton, who was weak upon the classics, spoke.

"Sinister!" he breathed heavily.

"Used to be used for whooping cough," Cub Sterling clipped gruffly.

The information, for the shadow of a second before Dr. Heddis began speaking again, made the pupils of Hoffbein's eyes dilate slightly. Bear Sterling's eyes were pin points needling themselves past the grave figure of MacArthur and into the long face of Heddis, who continued:

"Can be prepared synthetically by means of the same cadaveric alkaloid, or ptomaine, that is formed in putrefaction of cadavers, that is, cadaverine or penta-methylene-diamine."

Hoffbein began to squirm slightly.

"The injection, $C_8 H_{16} NH$ (*Conium maculatum*), presumably combined with lactic acid is colorless and gradually turns yellow and brown in the air."

Dr. Barton rose and leaned close to Dr. Heddis' ear.

"In your opinion would the person who gave this . . . drug . . . require a knowledge of chemistry?"

Dr. Heddis pressed his plump thumb into his cheek.

"I can't say, definitely. But . . . all that a man needs to know of dynamite to destroy a city is that it will explode. Rathbone is checking supply sources, I understand. I'm not hopeful. . . ."

He shrugged his thick shoulders.

"A medical student with a flare for toxicology could have made it synthetically. Anybody with a medical background could. . . ."

"Then I suggest," Dr. Harrison's voice was patiently fighting the rising tension, "that we separate and think it over privately until after lunch. Men under a strain as long as this has been upon Ethridge and Dr. MacArthur are not at their mental best . . . you both need rest; you have borne

up magnificently. . . . Let's re-convene here at
two, gentlemen?"

Dr. Heddis turned from the door:

"If you need me, MacArthur. . . ."

Dr. Hoffbein blocked his exit. "One question before we go. Is there much hysteria on the ward?"

"Nothing visible," Cub Sterling snapped.
"There is tension of course."

A terrible desire to get away from it all for just
fifteen minutes . . . to forget! . . . to run away
and rest . . . made Cub Sterling walk through the
ground floor of his clinic and start down the accident room steps toward Otto's.

Halfway down he hesitated.

Three minutes later he walked through Ward B,
ascertained from a student nurse that Dr. James
was at lunch and Dr. Mattus still with the students. Then he opened the door of Room Two.

Rested, relaxed eyes, whose black shadows had
disappeared, whose violet shades sung against the
white pillows, turned peacefully toward his measuring brown ones.

The girl took a cigarette from between her lips
and began:

"I slept like a lamb. My leg doesn't hurt. I told
the interne a nurse brought me the cigarettes and
they quieted my nerves, so your shirt-tail is clear.
She let me keep them. . . . I've been thinking a lot.

Look here! Today is Tuesday! There is absolutely no sense keeping me here, forever. . . ."

Dr. Ethridge Sterling, Junior, closed the door sharply and strode over to the bed. His features were flattening. His dark curly hair was dishevelled. His voice had its " 'Night!" quality.

"You are my patient and you are not to get out of that bed until I say so. I know today is Tuesday just as well as you do. Possibly better! What you seem never to realize is that I am a tremendously busy man. A Physician-in-Chief works! You are not the only patient in this hospital . . . but God knows you are the most petulant! Spending all your days lying there thinking up problems to hound me with! Tying yourself in knots of complications, instead of realizing you are a damned lot luckier than you deserve!"

Her mouth had been contracting slowly. When Cub stopped for breath she opened it quickly and began:

"You may be right about the luck, Doctor Sterling. But one thing medicine has failed completely to teach you is that people without money still have pride! Do you think I've enjoyed lying here for ninety-six hours having you throw up to me that the Attorney-General will pay my bills? Do you? There is a rumor that the Attorney-General is going to be in the next Cabinet. I was riding with him to try and find out. If I had found out, I'd have

had a scoop big enough to pay all the damned-old
bills you care to sling at me. . . .

"Well . . . I didn't find out! But that doesn't
keep me from 'growing the bills.' I've got to hold
my job to meet them and I've got to get out to do
it! And all the medical hysterics you could ever
throw doesn't change the facts. I. . . ."

Her voice broke unexpectedly and she covered
her head with a pillow.

Under the sheet Cub could see her body beginning to stiffen.

He reached over gently and took the cigarette
from her fingers. Then he looked around for an
ash-tray, saw none, and vacantly placed the cigarette between his own lips. The harassment of the
morning had drained from his face. A deep concern
replaced it.

His voice was bantering and slow:

"Looks like the phlebitis is traveling to your
mind, little Salscie. Let's take it step by step. The
job; it's intact. The doctor who asked me to take
you in has been talking to the City Editor about
you every day. Mistake was I ordered no visitors
and no flowers and so you thought they had aban-
doned you. You may stay a month so far as they
are concerned. The job will be there when you get
back. If you stay a month, probably by then our
friction may have worn itself out and you'll begin
to see how nice I really am. Want to try?"

The pillow remained inert, but the feet and legs began to relax. Cub cut his eye over the body and began talking again. He decided silently that when the breasts stopped rising, he'd quit talking. . . .

He took the cigarette from his lips and moistened them:

"About the bills, I've been a rotter. I should have told you that the paper was paying them, or the hospital, or . . . but I was pushed into the situation uninformed. I didn't know whether you were the king's mistress or the governor's. I didn't care a damn! And then some terribly, horribly important situations arose in the hospital and instead of thinking the thing out, I bungled it."

The heaving in the breasts became slower, and Cub said:

"About the bills, I'll do whatever you want me to. The hospital will take your note, or I'll lend you the money myself. There is only one thing I will not do. I *will not* let you walk out of this hospital until I am absolutely sure that you are perfectly well. So make up your mind to that! I'm sorry if I've been cruel . . . I didn't mean to! Probably I'm just too stupid to be kind, Salscie!"

The heaves died completely. He sat absolutely silent.

With her left hand she caught the edge of the pillow case and pulled the pillow beside her upon the bed. Her eyes looked straight and completely into his. Her voice was contrite and admiring:

"You are the first man who ever offered to lend me money and didn't paw me at the same time!"

Cub laughed heartily, and then snapped:

"Maybe that's because I'm stupid!"

Her dimples danced and then she sobered.

"When I'm well, will you come to see me. . . ?"

Cub held her eyes to his and nodded emphatically.

"Whenever you say I may! As often as you'll let me!"

She began lowering her lids and filled the silence with words:

"Really?"

Cub sat very still and curiosity made her raise her eyes to his again. When they were safely locked, he said, slowly:

"R-e-a-l-l-y!"

The little flecks of sunlight in the room began cascading around her hair, an inside blush centered in her neck.

Cub sat perfectly still and watched her. She knew he was watching her and she also knew that something which made her sick with joy was squirming inside of her. She began speaking desperately and with frightful haste:

"We might have to hang your legs out of a window when you come to dinner. When I get a card

table up, there's not much extra space, you know
. . . but . . . oh, by the way . . . could you
steal a knife and fork from the doctors' dining
room, do you think? Not steal, but. . . ."

Cub laughed joyously.

Her face was sober.

He said, "Cigarettes, a knife and fork, . . .
anything else, Salscie?"

"Yes, Cub. What's the trouble you spoke about
in the hospital?"

The banter slipped from his features and his
left shoulder began to rise.

"Nothing for you to worry about. Just . . .
some . . . friction."

She took her right hand from under the covers
and reached over and caught his.

"Is it me?"

His eyes met hers and he increased his pressure
on the hand.

"No! You can't cause everything, Salscie!"

Then he rose abruptly.

"I'd better get back, though. Also I'll make a
survey of the knife and fork situation. That pack
of cigarettes will be gone by tonight, won't it?"

She lay back among the pillows and nodded
slowly.

Cub beat his way through the singing air and
closed the door securely behind him.

»IV«
The First Doll

Bear Sterling hurried back to take a look at his brain tumor. He had stopped for a few words with Cub, but Cub had insisted that he must get back to his clinic and relieve Mattus. So after finishing with the brain tumor, which was coming along nicely, Bear went to his own office, shut the door, lay down upon a couch and went to sleep.

There was a crisis ahead. He needed a nap.

Dr. Barton did his rounds, discussed three unusual children with his resident, did as much work and appeared as natural as possible for an hour, and then filled his pipe and began the process of elimination on the evidence.

Dr. Harrison had a fifteen minute survey with his resident; afterward locked himself up in his laboratory and settled down to a "thinking through."

Hoffbein returned to his clinic and tried to behave as though nothing had happened. His consultant and resident nearly died of excitement.

Dr. MacArthur cleared his desk and endeavored to clear his mind. He had just rung for his secretary and prepared to go upstairs and lie down in a vacant interne room and get some rest, when Prissy Paton and Princeton Peters slipped in and closed the door behind them.

"Can you give us a minute, MacArthur?" Peters' voice was sepulchral.

Prissy stood in the background and looked as if he were going to cry.

"Certainly. What's on your minds? Sit down."

They sat upon the edges of the chairs.

"Well?"

"Go on, Peters, and tell him," Prissy prompted in his treble.

Princeton's eyes took on their purple mist and he began:

"Dear MacArthur, what we are about to tell you is drawn out of us by our great love for the Elijah Wilson . . . and for you. We feel you must know, and we could not tell you in front of Bear. It would have killed him."

"What is it? Get to the point."

"Last night at midnight, Dr. Paton and I were coming up the corridor from Woman's Clinic . . . I had been to see about the eyes of the president of the Woman's College . . . sudden attack . . . and Ethridge came out of the door of Medicine Clinic just ahead of us."

Dr. MacArthur put his hands under his desk and gripped his knees. His voice, however, was perfectly calm, as he replied.

"You must have been mistaken, Dr. Peters. Ethridge said he was in his rooms."

"That is the saddest part. We heard him say it! And we could not both be mistaken about Ethridge's back. His queer walk, MacArthur. One shoulder higher than the other. . . . And we both saw it."

"But you say yourself that neither of you saw his face, Dr. Peters."

"You are quite right," Prissy purred, "we did not see his face . . . but I would swear upon my mother's Bible that it was he."

"I'll ask him," MacArthur's voice was decisive.

"Please, MacArthur, don't act hastily! It would be futile to ask *him*, and if it were not for the horrible slur upon the hospital. . . ."

Princeton's pleading was so intense that he did not note Dr. MacArthur's silent anger, but Prissy sensed it.

"You must get some rest, MacArthur," he soothed. "Come on Peters," and at the door he finished. "Great decisions must be made and we shall not meet them unprepared."

Miss Evelina Kerr, student nurse, lay prone upon her bed, sobbing bitterly, silently, rackingly

Outside her door a supervisor from Medicine Clinic, off duty at the time, sat erect in a straight back chair, reading one of Edgar Wallace's novels.

Up and down the hall of the Nurses' Home voices rose and fell. The nurses on night shift were awakening. Miss Roenna Kerr, head nurse in Medicine Clinic, sailed down the polished floor and as her reflection preceded her, a loud whisper sung.

"Foots!"

The voices ceased, and the doors filled with blond, black, straw-colored, yellow and red heads in all degrees of disarray. Thirty pairs of eyes saw her switch her stern to a halt in front of the supervisor and smile.

"Mattie! How sweet of you to stay by my child!"

Mattie said deferentially:

"Miss Kerr, anything . . . anything that I could do!"

Miss Kerr knew Mattie was playing policeman on orders from the Superintendent of Nurses, but she also knew that Mattie was accustomed to taking her own orders. Her lips drew to a beautiful firming and she said huskily:

"Having you in training and upon my staff, Mattie, has been one of the really great joys of a very trying life!"

Mattie began disintegrating, and Miss Kerr put her hand upon the knob of her niece's door and was inside before the supervisor could moisten her lips.

The room was inky, the dark blue window shade was pulled even with the sill. Miss Kerr whispered, involuntary, "Evelina!"

Two sobs inverted their explosion. The girl sat up beating the air. Miss Kerr ignored her agony and began relentlessly:

"This is no time for hysterics. Come on and tell me! What did you tell them. . . ?"

"Who, Auntie?"

"The General Staff." Each letter of each word came bitingly.

"Nothing, Aunt Eeenie!"

Miss Kerr threw out her chin, and enunciated carefully:

"No woman can talk to that many men about nothing for half an hour. You fail to realize Evelina that everything you have you owe to me. Your training, your education, your clothes, even the straightening of your teeth I paid for!"

The girl cringed in the blackness. Her voice was subservient:

"I . . . I . . . know it, Auntie. I swear . . . to God . . . I didn't tell them . . . and I never will! I'd get thrown out of training . . . before . . . I'd. . . ."

Miss Kerr's words sealed her lips. They beat into her brain:

"A private who accuses his general . . . is always court-martialed!"

Then she turned upon her heel and closed the door after her.

For ten minutes the student nurse sobbed dryly. Complete exhaustion then smothered the sobs. She fell asleep.

In the nurses' cafeteria the first group were beginning to choose their lunches. The white uniforms of the graduate nurses and the blue uniforms of the student nurses with their white collars and cuffs reflected the glare from the thin curtains at the sunlit windows.

Near a table occupied by four student nurses sat Rose Standish, head nurse in the accident room. Her small ivory face was buried in a volume of "Sonnets from the Portuguese" and she guided the teaspoons of gelatine and whipped cream into her mouth by a sense of feeling, not sight. Her outer eye was transferring to her inner one the charm of a mind drenched in the world's great love.

The student nurse with a raucous Kansas whine was saying:

"What's happened to 'Lina Kerr?"

"I don't know. Why?" responded a flat Alabama drawl.

"I saw her in the corridor with two supervisors at ten o'clock and Minnie says they've got her locked in her room and won't let anybody talk to her. She . . . she . . . looked frightful."

"Where have you been for the last week?" a Virginian purred. "Three people have died on the ward where she has night duty and they all are trying to blame it on her."

"Have you lost your mind, Lizzie?" sneered the Alabamian.

"Well, if you don't believe me, why did you ask me? They had her up before the General Staff this morning."

"Honest?"

"Yes. Honest! That's sweet for her, if you ask me."

"Jumping Jehosophat! You think she did it?"

"No. Of course not. Dr. Cub Sterling was the doctor on all of the cases."

At the mention of his name the conversation she had just been hearing re-echoed in Rose Standish's mind and she looked up just in time to catch the shrug of the girl's thin shoulders and her smirk.

"Did he?"

"How should I know?" the girl shrugged again.

Rose Standish closed her book and rose. She wanted air, and plenty of it. Ever since the second year of her training she had had a very secret passion for Cub Sterling. Ever since that time he caught her on the stairway behind the pharmacy kissing . . . she blushed when she thought about it . . . Tony Watson, one of his internes . . . and never told anybody, and then when Tony had pneumonia and died, he had let her help to nurse him and . . . be with him . . . at the last.

She reached the sun-parlor of the Nurses' Home and collapsed into a chair. After all these five years the thought of Tony could do that to her! After all these five years . . . and it was because that thought could turn her body to liquid soap that she still was so deeply grateful to Cub Sterling. He was white as chalk and always had been. Gold through and through . . . and those student nurses suspected him of murdering patients. The dirty cats! The rotten little worms! The nasty pigs!

Why, when he found her in Tony's arms halfway down that pitch-black stairway, he had pretended he didn't recognize either of them. He had laughed and said, "My mistake!"

And then when he had reached the lower door-way, before he opened it, he turned . . . she could hear his voice, even now. . . .

"It's a disease worth having. Good luck!"

Good luck . . . good luck. She was looking out of the window at the sunshine; she had long ago quit crying. The grating voice of a furious woman came up the corridor toward her:

"And I think, Miss Williams, that the nursing staff should request Dr. MacArthur to cast his at-

tention upon other departments, if you know what
I mean."

The voice reached the sun-parlor. It came from
the firm lips of Miss Roenna Kerr.

And it settled Rose Standish's fate.

She rose, respectfully slipped out of another
door and into the main corridor of the hospital.

Doctors Peters and Paton closed the door to
Dr. MacArthur's office softly behind him, and Dr.
MacArthur was too weak to get up and open it.

He felt like a man ordered to fit a jigsaw puzzle
during an earthquake.

Somewhere among the group of people he had
seen this morning there had been a liar. Out of them
some person . . . in whom the hospital had placed
a trust . . . had lied to him, face to face. Coniine. . . .

Malice and all uncharitableness, deceit and hate,
murder and meanness. Coniine. . . .

He cradled his head in his arms and moaned.
Cub Sterling, his godchild, almost his own son, and
with the exception of the old orderly William, every
witness. . . . And now two members of the staff.

How in heaven's name could Cub ever clear himself . . . now. . . .

He was so deep in his misery that he did not hear
the door open and quietly close. It was the voice
which roused him.

A small nurse with an elfin face and large gray eyes was standing beside him. She said:

"Please, Dr. MacArthur, may I speak to you, suh?"

He lifted his head and motioned her to a chair. She remained standing, her upright little body with its slim legs and small, finely arched feet, motionless.

Dr. MacArthur recognized that she had something tremendously important to tell him. He smiled.

"What can I do for you, Miss . . . er . . . ?"

"Rose Standish, suh," she supplied.

When the staff re-convened, Hoffbein was irritated. He had gone about his routine and lunched in the doctors' dining room. While he was there no other member of the staff entered and it had made him out a fool to all the internes. Looked like he wasn't "in" on the decisions. Prissy and Princeton had had ample time to repent their rash disclosure and were afraid; MacArthur might face them with it before Harrison and Bear Sterling. Dr. Harrison and Bear Sterling looked tired and uncertain. Dr. Barton's open face had assumed its judgmatical mask. Dr. MacArthur eyed each man carefully.

It was plain that all of them were ready to talk. He sat erect in his chair and prepared for battle.

The small chatter died out, and the seven men silently awaited Cub Sterling.

At four minutes past two he entered. His bushy, curly hair was rumpled, his left shoulder was hysterically high. In his right hand he carried a small doll in a pink organdie dress and bonnet that continued crying, "Ma-Ma, Ma-Ma." He seemed unaware of the noise; but it pierced the other men like a jigsaw. They all jumped and Dr. MacArthur's face for the first time appeared blank. Bear Sterling was the first to regain his equilibrium; after all he had dealt with the man as a child.

"Cub. What in the hell have you got there?" he growled.

But Cub strode obliviously past him and Dr. Barton took the doll. She stopped crying immediately. That and Dr. Barton's action brought Cub to a halt.

"Dr. MacArthur, that doll was found by Bessie Ellis upon the foot of her crib in Ward B when she awoke this morning. Evidently a present someone had put there during the night. Nobody on the ward knew anything about it. It must have been left by. . . ."

"Who is Bessie Ellis, son?" Dr. Harrison soothed.

"She's a nephritis case we have had on the ward for several months. Six years old and cute. Barton and Father know her."

"Quite a pet," Bear affirmed.

"Sinister!" Princeton Peters murmured.

"No. Real evidence," Bear's brows were thunderously low. "She must bear the finger prints of the murderer."

"Impossible," Cub barked. "She has been handled by at least ten people since Bessie found her."

And then everybody began talking at once and Dr. MacArthur rapped for silence.

"Gentlemen," his voice was commanding, "each of you has had two hours in which to think over the situation. I need not remind you that our decisions must be the sum of our wisdom, and reached without emotion. Therefore it is my suggestion that we, one at a time, state our conclusions, beginning as we are sitting. Dr. Peters what is your opinion?"

"I should rather, MacArthur, reserve. . . ."

"No. Out with it. We'll never get anywhere that way."

Princeton's lavender eyes paled with uncertainty. Cub's sensational entrance had wobbled his mind.

He moistened his thick lips and his voice lost its usual certainty. It actually contained a tremor when he began:

"I have always, as you know, gentlemen, deferred to you upon any question about which I was uncertain. I have always valued the opinion of specialists above the opinions of . . . even of friends . . . where any patient, whether dear to me or not, was involved.

"Need I say, my dear MacArthur, that the Elijah Wilson is dearer to me than a beloved patient, even? The condition is so horribly serious that I am against delay. It should be referred immediately, in my opinion, to a specialist, namely, the police. I feel it should be turned over, I repeat, immediately."

His speech fell upon them like descending plaster. Somewhere physically they all jumped. Bear grit his teeth and snorted, Harrison scowled, MacArthur gripped his knees. . . .

Nobody spoke, except Barton.

"I'm against it!"

His voice was flat and final.

"Why?" Paton purred. "I, personally, am for it. Wholeheartedly."

"Nonsense!" Dr. Harrison exploded before Dr. Barton could reply. "Sheer, childish nonsense. Are you out to kill the hospital or the murderer, Peters? I repeat, some linen is too foul to wash in public! It has taken forty years and more to build up the reputation of this place and you are planning to destroy it. . . ."

"Why, Dr. Harrison, I'm not 'planning' anything. Dr. MacArthur asked me for an opinion and I gave it. That's all!"

"Beg your pardon, Peters. No offense."

The antagonism stiffened.

Dr. MacArthur intervened, "Your opinion, Dr. Paton?"

"I agree entirely with Dr. Peters. Men trained in the detection of criminals are the men to catch murderers." Prissy folded his hands righteously and sat in a waxy pose.

Dr. MacArthur ignored his silent disapproval and passed on.

"Barton?"

"Against the police, suh. Entirely against them. Their intervention is the way, to my thinking, to muddle the whole thing . . . and take an awful chance of making the story public. Something must undoubtedly be done, and done quickly, but what, suh, I frankly do not know.

"One thing which seems to me possible is to have every person connected with the affair given a psychiatric examination by Dr. Hoffbein."

Hoffbein's back straightened and he smiled deeply.

"That's in his line, it seems," Dr. Barton finished.

"I'm against that . . . flat!" Bear Sterling mumbled. "In the first place the only hope of ever catching the murderer is to pretend we are not looking for him. At least twenty people are under suspicion as possibilities. Remove any one of those twenty people and you may be removing the murderer. Every person in connection with that ward in any capacity whatsoever must continue there until the murderer is caught. Otherwise . . . we senselessly throw our needle into a hay stack!"

"You're right, Bear," MacArthur replied. "Absolutely right!"

"What about the medical student doing routine tests on this ward?" Prissy interposed. "Dr. Heddis said anybody could, with medical knowledge. . . . What type of lad is he?"

"False clue," Cub snapped. "He's been home with the mumps for ten days. The interne on the floor has been doing his work. . . ."

"Well, what about Dr. . . . er. . . ?"

"James. Sarah James," Cub defied. "The doll rules her out of the last one, at least. She was out of town yesterday."

Dr. Barton who had been considering Bear's statement replied:

"I see your point, Dr. Sterling, and it is an excellent one . . . but I failed, evidently, to express myself clearly." His voice was perfectly even. "I was thinking of an examination of that student nurse."

Cub Sterling sat forward and clipped, "So was I."

His father turned his searching eyes into him and demanded, "What about her?"

There was a knock at the door and it opened almost immediately. The erect figure of the Chief Pharmacist shifted their attention. Baldy Rathbone held in his hand a sheaf of telegrams.

Cub Sterling's eyes followed those of the other men.

"I'm very sorry to interrupt, gentlemen, but this, Dr. MacArthur, is the report about where coniine may be obtained."

He held out the yellow sheets toward Dr. MacArthur.

"Where, Baldy?"

"It is available in gram quantities at the United Wholesale Drug Company in New York, Parke Davis in Detroit, and the Burroughs Welcome Agents in San Francisco."

"Anywhere else?"

"No, sir."

MacArthur took the telegrams. Baldy hesitated, massaged his shiny spot and finished:

"They report no recent sales, sir."

"Blind alley!" Bear Sterling grunted.

"I'm afraid so, Doctor. Anything else, Dr. MacArthur?"

Dr. MacArthur looked over his glasses and shook his head.

"Not that I can think of. Thank you for your promptness."

"Dr. Heddis asked me to say, sir, that he has just

checked the Medical Library. There have been no reference works upon the subject out for several years. He, therefore, feels that the student body is cleared."

"Thank you again, Baldy."

"May I ask a question?" Cub Sterling was clipping his words. "Will it keep long?"

"What?" Baldy was resentful of his superior tone.

"Coniine."

He turned and looked Cub Sterling full in the eye.

"I don't know, Doctor. We have never handled it in the pharmacy."

He was gone before Cub could reply; but his parting speech brought an involuntary nod from Doctors Peters and Paton, and Hoffbein pierced Cub with a barometer stare. Bear Sterling appeared to have missed the stab.

"Murderers always have motives. If we could find the motive. . . . What about that girl and Hoffbein's examining her. Where's the harm?"

"The harm, Bear," Dr. Harrison pulled his beard, "is (you will pardon me, Hoffbein, and correct me if am wrong, please?) that presuming she is the murderer, any examination different from that given any other person might frighten her into a temporary respite, but it would not put us any nearer a solution."

"That is true. Perfecly true." Hoffbein's words were enunciated with a finality, though Cub Sterling thought he hated to say them.

"And in view of the paper I found upon my desk when I returned at two o'clock such an examination would seriously hinder our apprehension of her . . . if she is the murderer."

"What paper, Dr. MacArthur?"

"Haven't I told you? I'm sorry. A typewritten sheet . . . here it is . . . which states, Dr. Hoffbein . . . that because of two low marks she received in a course in which Ethridge was lecturing last month, she has dropped from seven to seventeenth in her class and will not be in line for a staff job upon graduation. She cried straight through for three nights afterward."

The paper was still shielding the pudgy faces of Doctors Paton and Peters, so Barton, the man furthest from them asked, "Who brought it?"

"I don't know. My door was open and I found it upon my desk. It is signed . . . also upon the typewriter . . . 'A Student Nurse.' Gentlemen, we will never accomplish anything . . . unless we come to some conclusions. Will you please give us your opinion, Dr. Hoffbein?"

Dr. Hoffbein's eyes turned a liquid black. He folded his precise head on one side and each word settled itself upon the air before its successor was spoken.

"Gentlemen, I am not in favor of the police. A mental criminal is a mental case. A murder of this type is undoubtedly a mental criminal. A very clever, otherwise normal and possibly brilliant intellect. A man . . . er . . . a person quite out of scope of . . . a police."

He shrugged the police, with a final hiss, off his thin shoulders.

"What are your personal impressions, Dr. Hoff-bein?" Bear Sterling rumbled.

"I . . . I . . . er . . . as a psychiatrist . . . I cannot afford to have personal opinions, Dr. Sterling."

"Aw, for heaven's sake! What d'y'*think*?"

Dr. Hoffbein's little pigeon breast heaved. His eyes had completely lost their whites.

"I . . . I . . . I . . . think," he hesitated, and Bear cut in—

"Don't be so damn slow about it!"

At that Hoffbein flared.

"It is my impression that action . . . drastic . . . and terrible should be quickly taken to apprehend this dangerous man . . . and that action should come through the psychiatric service."

At last Bear Sterling caught the insinuations which hovered thunderously over the room. He turned too purple for speech, so Dr. Harrison laid him upon a sofa and murmured:

"Remember your heart, old timer. Remember

your heart. Nothing to be alarmed about. 'Just a symptom of your disease.' "

And then he laughed heartily, and Dr. Otto Hoffbein ducked like a beaten boxer. "A symptom of your disease" is a psychiatric term.

Cub Sterling got his father a glass of water. His hand trembled as he held it. Barton eased a pillow under his head. Peters and Paton sat like frightened schoolboys in the corner. Hoffbein was still cowed.

"Better, Bear?" Dr. MacArthur asked leaning over him. Dr. Harrison turned and said:

"Here is the situation. It has to be met. You are going to accomplish nothing by fighting. Every man in this room knows that between last night and this morning a woman was murdered in this hospital. As a result there have been some near murders since. . . ." he gave Hoffbein another look and his eye lit upon Dr. Paton and Dr. Peters. . . . "Actions speak louder than words. If you love the Elijah Wilson, as you have spent the day saying you do, then quit 'emoting' and begin to think!

"Police as a solution! Out of the question, entirely. Impossible to catch the criminal if he, she or it, knows it is shadowed, let alone what police would do to the reputation of the hospital.

"Suggestion number two. Turn the night student nurse over to psychiatrists. Impossible, for

the very good reason given by Dr. MacArthur.
Let alone the cruelty of the situation should she be
innocent.

"Suggestion number three. Turn the whole
thing over to the psychiatrists. Understand perfectly, gentlemen, that I am casting no slurs upon
psychiatry, when it stays within its limits. Hoffbein points out this is a mental criminal. That's
within its limits. Suppose we turned the whole
thing over to you, Hoffbein? Had you thought how
long it would take you and your entire force to ex-
amine twenty people? Thirty new patients a month
is all you claim you are equipped to handle and
give them the proper attention, and these twenty
which the hospital would turn over would have to
have a great deal more than just that.

"It would take you . . . every man working
day and night . . . and nobody seeing to the clinic
. . . two weeks to give us any kind of a report.
Two weeks sitting upon dynamite!

"Not on your life. Our problem is this, as I see it:

"To catch the murderer, quickly, quietly, and
without creating any suspicion whatever throughout the institution. We have got to keep our face,
or ruin the hospital.

"How to catch the murderer, I frankly do not
know. But that is the situation, as I see it now. I
suggest we take it as such and work it out
here. . . ."

Bear Sterling was sitting up again, and Dr. MacArthur was back at his desk.

"I have the solution, Harrison," he said calmly. "Put a nurse in the bed in which the three patients have been murdered."

"Are you crazy, MacArthur?" Hoffbein's voice was at last hysterical.

"No. I hope not," Dr. MacArthur's voice was deadly calm. "But today I have had the privilege of seeing such cool, calm courage exhibited by a person who really loves this hospital as to make me proud to be here . . . even . . . now.

"A nurse came to me after the meeting this morning . . . one of our graduates . . . and volunteered to go into that bed as a patient. Think it over, gentlemen. That's a solution, d'y'see?"

Dr. MacArthur's words lay over them like spring rain. Some men they heartened. Some they chilled. All they impressed.

Only Dr. Harrison spoke.

"I hope I'm a friend of hers," he said.

They were silent so long it upset Dr. Peters.

"Suppose she is murdered, Dr. MacArthur? We couldn't *allow* it!"

"Dr. Peters, this nurse knew of the murders, that is why she offered to go there. Can't you understand . . . that? I brought out that she might be murdered and she countered with" . . . he put one hand in front of his mouth . . . "that her life was a small thing compared to the reputation of the Elijah Wilson Hospital and the Medicine Clinic."

Cub Sterling lifted his wild head and snorted.

"She shouldn't take those chances . . . for us."

And then Dr. MacArthur sat perfectly straight and lied.

"She's not. She's taking them for the hospital. *She* wants to take them. Suppose we vote upon it, gentlemen?"

"Dr. Peters?"

"I am against subjecting any nurse to danger."

"Dr. Paton?"

"I . . . I . . . agree with Peters."

"Dr. Barton?"

"She seems to me . . . the solution."

"Dr. Hoffbein?"

"I should like to be allowed to give her an examination."

"Sorry. But if she goes on the ward, she must be in bed within an hour. Do I take it you favor her offer?"

Hoffbein acquiesced hesitantly.

"Dr. Harrison?"

"I regret the danger, but I agree with you, Mac-Arthur."

"Dr. Sterling?"

"I agree, MacArthur."

"Ethridge?"

"It's too much to ask. . . ."

"Nobody asked it, son. She volunteered. And with my vote, and Heddis' advice, I take it that your decision is, gentlemen, that this nurse within an hour becomes a patient in Bed 11, Ward B, of Medicine Clinic . . . and God willing . . . catches the murderer.

"Make it as natural as possible, Ethridge. Have your father and Mattus look at her."

"Any hypodermics?"

"I think not. You agree, gentlemen?"

When they had risen Princeton Peters' eyes had purpled and he asked reverently:

"Who is she, MacArthur?"

"Rose Standish, gentlemen."

Cub Sterling, who was standing in the doorway, turned as though someone had slapped him upon the back. His left shoulder was high.

»V«
A Brave Nurse

Miss KEXTER," MISS KERR STILL bore her rump and bust inflated, "this is the new patient for Ward B."

Beside her stood Rose Standish. She wore a plain blue coat suit and a small black hat pulled down to her gray eyes.

Miss Kexter turned from Miss Kerr and looked at her.

"Hullo, Miss Standish," she said. "You sick?" and reached for the small suitcase.

"Hope not . . . much," Miss Standish's ivory face was somber. "Dr. Sterling thinks I may have a bum lung. In for observation."

They walked into the ward and Miss Kerr observed, "Two vacant beds. Oh, yes, that patient in 21 went home, didn't she? Put Miss Standish in that bed."

Miss Standish looked upset. Trained nurses haven't much use for a member of their profession who has the chicken-heartedness to succumb to physical ailments. And Miss Kerr's manner plainly said so. But Rose Standish had not been head nurse in the accident room three years without being able to think quickly.

"Oh, please, Miss Kerr, mayn't I be put in that vacant bed over there, by the window?"

Miss Kerr, who had suspected something from the first and thought that the vacant bed she had forgotten had forestalled Dr. Sterling's plans, snapped:

"Certainly not. Any patient with a suspected lung should not be near a window . . . and a nurse ought to know better than to want to be."

The patients, who were too sick to be wheeled out upon the porch, looked on with interest. Mrs. Witherspoon, who spent most of her waking hours with her bed curtains drawn and upon a bed-pan, peaked out from between the curtains. She leaned too far, and then exclaimed:

"Lan' sakes, nurse! Nurse, come quick!"

Miss Kexter vanished behind the curtains and Miss Kerr stood stiffly looking out of the window, and Miss Standish placed her suitcase upon the assigned bed and prepared to open it, but footsteps . . . male footsteps . . . were coming up the corridor, so she hesitated. Dr. Mattus spoke before he was in the ward. In fact he began speaking when he saw Miss Standish standing by the bed.

"Hello! How are you feeling? Any weaker? You

are not to sleep in that bed. I want you by the window."

Then he saw Miss Kerr, and smiled. That smile always saved him verbal battles. It was delivered straightforward and deep into the eyes of the avenging female, whatever her age. Miss Kerr moistened her lips and prepared to resist it, but Miss Kexter had returned from Mrs. Witherspoon's disaster and Dr. Mattus turned to her quickly.

"Please get Miss Standish undressed immediately, I want to do a physical upon her."

"I can undress myself, Dr. Mattus."

"You cannot. Until we can definitely locate your area, the more rest, the better. Remember that, young lady, and be a good patient."

He smiled at her . . . and she returned it . . . and Miss Kerr went down the corridor and into the medicine closet door.

Dr. Mattus went for his stethoscope, Miss Kexter went to an insistent telephone and Rose Standish drew the curtains and undressed. Then she folded her best pink rayon panties and undershirt, her chiffon stockings and silk blouse with the rosepoint and her plain suit and put them into the small suitcase. On top she placed her hat and patent leather pumps. She put her hairbrush . . . the ivory one with heavy bristles which Tony had given her (he had bought it with five dollars an Italian pressed upon him when he delivered the man's wife in externe-obstetrics) . . . onto the bedside table and laid her tooth brush and paste beside it.

She re-opened the suitcase and took from a pocket in the top the same volume of Elizabeth Barrett Browning's "Sonnets from the Portuguese" she had been reading at luncheon.

She put her purse in the bedside table, closed the suitcase, dropped her black satin bedroom slippers from her feet, slipped off her black rayon kimona and got into bed.

She wore her only silk nightgown and it felt soothing upon her small round breasts. It caressed her thighs. She opened her book, pulled back the curtains and began to read.

A student nurse came on the floor and took the suitcase and brought the bed-pan for a specimen. Then she asked if there was anything else, and went away.

Mrs. Witherspoon, who had completed her operations for the moment, emerged from her curtains.

"Good evin', dearie. Hope you feelin' fair?"

"Yes, thank you. How are you feeling?"

"Better, dearie. You don't remember me, do you?" Her small murky eyes fastened themselves upon Rose's near cheek.

Rose laid down her book and smiled at her kindly.

"No, I'm sorry, but I am afraid I do not remember. I've been sick and tired and my memory isn't very good, Mrs. . . ."

"Witherspoon, honey. I come through the accident room a week ago comin' Sunday. My insulatin' was low. Too much sugar you know, honey . . . and you was so kin'. I could scarce speak and you was so kin'. I'll never forgit how kin' you was, showin' me the labatory, an' all.

"You done me so nice that I thinks I ought to tell you, dearie, 'bout thet bed. Three people . . . countin' the one . . . *they* seys was operated on . . . and Miss Kerr knows was daid . . . three patients done died in thet bed sence Thursday. Miss Frisby, an awful nice girl with a goitre, and Mrs. Overlea . . . she was a heart attacker . . . and then last night, Miss Tuck. It looks suspicious, I seys. If I was you, dearie. . . ."

She was interrupted by the reappearance of Dr. Mattus and Dr. Sarah James. They pulled the curtains to Miss Standish's bed and Mrs. Witherspoon tucked her chins into her breasts and went back to her crocheting.

Rose Standish noticed her feet felt like icicles.

When their examination was over she was frightened. You could not go over any human being that thoroughly without finding something wrong, and her nurse's disdain for a person who allowed herself to get sick disturbed her considerably. Suppose they really did find something and kept her in bed here a month? A lot more than she had bargained for . . . that!

Mrs. Witherspoon laid down her crocheting and peered at the little nurse's pale face.

"They did you up kinda bad, dearie. All them blood tests and things. Severe I calls it. A body can't even keep her corns nowadays!"

Rose Standish laughed in spite of herself.

"Oh, I didn't mind. A nurse gets used to things."

"I reckin' you right. I reckin' you right. It's pow'ful sad the amount a body can put up with, whin you is used to it. Take me, dearie. I had eleven children. Four breeches presentations, three feet, three dry, and one nat'rul. And would you believe it, the nat'rul was the wors'! It lef' me kinda flat fo' months. A body gits prepared to put up wid things . . . thet hurts . . . now things like this sugar business . . . no pain, nor nuthin' . . . you can't get resisted fur."

"Relaxation, Mrs. Witherspoon, is the best weapon with which to fight disease. I'm tired. I think I'll take a nap."

"Do you good, dearie. Excitement and all, and then puttin' you in thet bed, too. Death-beds is weakenin'. It takes a sunnin' every day and a good six months to make a mattress lose a death struggle."

Rose Standish turned her face to the window and closed her eyes, and shivered. "Lose your heart,

lose your appendix, lose anything, but don't lose
your nerves," was what Tony always said.

Ridiculous to be feeling like this. Crazy. Perhaps
if she tried to think about something else, then
her feet would quit perspiring. Think about the
way Dr. MacArthur had looked when she offered
to come . . . Galsworthy said that your mouth
was what you had become but your eyes were what
you were. . . . Dr. MacArthur's eyes were like
wave crests against a blue, blue sky. Clean and
deep and clear, when he had turned them into her,
stood up, and said:

"You have done more for me in fifteen minutes
than anybody in the hospital has ever done. You
have picked me out of despair."

She began to tremble again and then she realized
that it was the way he had looked when he said it
that made her tremble. That look was the grandest
thing that had happened to her since Tony kissed
her the day he died.

Of course she must expect to be jumpy, to feel
fidgetty, to get dry in the throat; good heavens,
all of that was perfectly natural under the circumstances! Dr. MacArthur had even told her to expect it, and he had said:

"If you get scared, shift your mind to something
else. You are like a doctor observing an operation, you are like an important actress watching a
play of which she knows all of the lines being en-

acted by amateurs. Remember what you used to do as a student nurse and see," and then he smiled wryly, "if the routine has changed one second's worth. I bet it hasn't."

She opened her eyes and felt better. She looked at her watch and found it was four forty-five. Time to bring the patients in off the porch and prepare for supper. Behind her she heard a voice and turned over. The woman, whose bed stood next to Mrs. Witherspoon's, had been rolled into place already!

She was as insignificant as a dried corn stalk. Heart case probably. That queer revived look a wilted flower has when you stick the stem in hot aspirin water. She was saying:

"The air was swell! It's comin' on cool and 'pears like we may get a thunder shower by bed-time."

Across from Rose Standish's bed had been rolled that of a tremendously fat woman. Some sort of thyroid insufficiency. The outlines of her obese legs were visible under the sheets. Rose shivered. Nice job bathing a hog like that. She had seen one in the accident room last winter with secondary burns. Fat, layers and layers and layers. Awful to operate upon!

The woman smiled at her and began speaking: "New?"

"Yes. Miss Standish," Mrs. Witherspoon supplied.

Rose bowed politely.

The fat woman whispered loudly:

"I seen her, Mrs. With'spoon!"

"Seen who?"

"Seen . . . Her . . . !"

"Y'did!"

"Who is 'Her'?" Rose asked.

The fat woman toppled with knowledge. Mrs. Witherspoon snatched the words from her parting lips.

"The patient in Room Two. They say she was hurt in a bus acci-dent. But thet was Thursday, an' she ain't daid yit. The windie shade is always drawed and the nurses acts like she ain't no sicker then the rest. . . ."

"She's awful prutty," the fat woman tried to interrupt.

Mrs. Witherspoon continued:

"Callin' thim dyin' patient rooms an' puttin' thim 'tween the ward an' the porch! I ain't no hosbittle fixer, but it 'pears to me, I'd a put 'em closen onto the nurse's dest. . . ."

Rose Standish laughed softly.

"For a dying patient, Mrs. Witherspoon, the Head Nursing Office sends a general duty nurse to do 'special charting'. So dying patients have private nurses. It doesn't matter where the rooms are."

"She ain't got no privett nurse!" the heavy woman hissed.

"Perhaps the hospital was full and they put her there when she came in and can't risk moving her. Have you been here long?" Rose said.

The woman lifted her pendulous breasts and swung them out from the body.

"Whew! Hot today! Three weeks goin' on Monday, mam. Long enough to know thet I wouldn't sleep in thet bed, you is in, not for a million dollars."

"What's the matter with it?" Rose inquired demurely.

"It's . . . it's . . ." her breasts rested upon her bed as she leaned forward, "It's a death. . . ."

But Miss Kexter's appearance on the ward brought her speech to a sudden halt. She flopped her body back upon the pillows and smiled weakly.

"When I think of all the clothes I got to wash whin I get outa here. I prides myself my chillun is the cleanest goin', and the teachers always seys so, too. In all the health campaigns at School 17, Willie is always chose. . . ."

But Rose Standish heard no more. Miss Kexter was standing beside her bed and saying, "When did you decide to be sick?" Miss Standish caught the sarcastic banter in her voice and replied lightly, "I haven't. And I hope I aren't."

Miss Kexter stood perplexedly by for a moment,

pondering that phrase. "I aren't, I am not, I aren't," she kept saying it over and over to herself. Rose Standish had been to college. She couldn't be wrong, yet that didn't sound right, somehow . . . "I aren't."

"Sorry this happened to you when the infirmary was closed. You must hate it on a ward. Hard as we work, I must say in spite of the depression, I think the nurses ought to be allowed to be sick in private, don't you?"

"Don't know," Rose's voice had taken on its accident room clip, but the tone was conversational. "Came so suddenly hadn't thought about it. Awful jolt in a way. Glad to be put anywhere, just so it's the Elijah Wilson."

"How did you find it out?" Miss Kexter's voice had lost the skepticism.

"Oh, I don't know. Been running an afternoon temperature, and then yesterday I spit a little blood, so I went to Dr. Cub Sterling." She shrugged her shoulders despairingly.

"That's a shame." Miss Kexter's voice, like her face, was shallow and flat. "You don't mind that bed, do you?"

Rose's "No. Why?" was casual.

"Oh, nothing. Just that three patients went out in it this week and they put us on the spot about it." She had leaned forward and her whisper was

She looked at her watch and smiled at the child. "Right on time, aren't you?"

The girl laughed merrily.

Rose threw her head to one side and inquired, "And supper will be along in a minute?"

"Yes, mam. I'm going to begin bringing it in, right now."

Rose sat erect and wrung her wash cloth out and ran it over her small face. The water felt good. She wrung it again and laid it behind her ears. That felt good, too. She took a small comb from her hand bag and slid it through her short black hair. Then she wrung the cloth out carefully, folded it as she had been taught to do when a pupil nurse, and brushed her teeth into the basin.

This was nice. It was fun being in bed in a ward of perfectly strange women, rather than in a stuffy infirmary with six or seven nurses talking shop and telling jokes all the time. She looked down the ward at the rows of beds, and the glass partition which separated them from the other fourteen beds; at the place where the partition stopped in the center of the ward to create an aisle and then at the white beds beyond. Through the far windows was a perfectly glorious sunset, and out of her own window just the feathery beginning of new leaves upon an old tree.

She had never seen the ward from this angle. It was really a very pretty sight, when viewed

from bed and with nothing to do. Perhaps it was
because she had been through so much emotionally
today that it looked especially pretty. Things did,
after such days.

Or perhaps it was because she wasn't rushing
to get everything in order before the duty changes,
rushing to remember this and do that. For once
her day was ending with the sun's setting.

It was a good feeling. She stretched her toes and
the covers swelled with her rising breasts. And now
in a few minutes supper would be along.

The ward was full of chatter, but she didn't hear
it. A voluptuous relaxation was upon her. In bed.
At sunset. Awaiting supper, and watching the
ugly faces of old women bloom, with the softening
light . . . and the new leaves on the tree taking
on that clear green which hurt.

"You are the last in line, so I'm a half minute
late in bringing it to you," the student nurse
apologized, poising her tray. "Want to sit up?"

"Please, nurse," Rose responded in a very helpless voice.

The nurse wound up her bed, took away the
wash basin and Rose began her supper.

It fitted in exactly with her mood, and seemed,
at the moment, much nicer than the meals she had
in the nurses' dining room.

Cream of tomato soup, and batter-bread and
liver with bacon and lots of gravy, and lettuce

Rose Standish put forward her wrist for the child to count her pulse. How young this pupil nurse looked. How young and frightened!

She was trying to think of something to say to her when the negroes on the floor above began singing. Through the melody of their voices . . . she had been in the accident room so long, she had forgotten about their singing after supper, she lost touch with the student nurse. A high soprano fluted: "Swing lo . . . o . . . Sweet Char . . . ee . . . ot."

And suddenly she knew their plaintive harmony, the admiration of the patients, the sense of work ceasing with the day, had left her tremendously happy and glad to be here. Glad she was part of the Elijah Wilson! And she was part of it! Dr. MacArthur had said:

"We are planning to enlarge the accident room. You are the first person I have told about it. And while you are lying in that bed, I want you to decide what changes you think it would be wise to make. You can be a great help to me, if you will."

A great help . . . and every head nurse in the hospital would give her eyebrows to have him say that to her! As soon as the ward quieted down, she'd have to begin to think about it . . . or perhaps it might be best to wait until tomorrow and let the singing of the negroes lull her to sleep.

She wasn't afraid any more. And anyhow Dr.

MacArthur had said, so far as evidence was concerned, she had nothing to be afraid of, except hypodermics, and she would like to see the person who could give her a hypo now! She would like to see two people try to give her. . . .

Down the corridor she caught a glimpse of Dr. Ethridge Sterling, Senior, and Dr. Sterling. Was Dr. Bear shrinking or did he just look so little and chubby because he was walking beside Dr. Cub? They both looked worried; when they entered the ward, they were smiling.

Their arrival created a nervous tension just the same. A sense of dread filled the air. Dr. Sterling began doing his rounds and talking briskly to his father about each patient. But Dr. Bear put his famous hands firmly across his back and looked solid. Rose Standish frowned. He looked just that way when a bad accident came in. Like it hurt him . . . all over . . . too.

Finally they reached her bed and Dr. Sterling barked, "Good evening, Miss Standish. Want Father to look you over. This condition sometimes comes from effusion and is operative."

The student nurse hovering in the background ran for the instrument basket, and Dr. Sterling began drawing the bed curtains.

Dr. Bear was already leaning over and looking straight into her eyes with his measuring ones.

"All right?"

Her bloodless lips turned a pinkish red. They accentuated the ivory pallor of her peaked face.

"Perfectly, thank you. But if I get examined many more times, you are bound to find something wrong, somewhere. How are you, sir?"

It was fun to be talking to Dr. Bear this way. He was accepting her as an equal, sort of. . . .

"I'm tired. Did two bad carcinomas this morning. Breasts. Two ruptured appendices, and a gallbladder, and I've a cold."

"Then why not wait and go over me in the morning, sir?"

"Because I'm the parent of an electric dynamo," he growled and the nurse and Dr. Sterling, Junior, reappeared.

"What are you waiting for?" Dr. Bear frowned at the pupil nurse.

"To hand you what you want, sir." she replied woodenly.

"You can't. What I want is rest. My son will hand me what I need. You go back to the ward."

The nurse backed out hesitantly. Miss Kerr had said every nurse in the building must permit no doctor to approach any patient without being present all of the time . . . but . . . but. . . .

Mrs. Witherspoon's, "Nurse! Tend to me . . ." and then "Hurry, nurse!" sent the girl running.

Dr. Bear put his stethoscope carefully to his ears and listened to Rose Standish's chest.

"Do everything you ought to. Don't make me ask you," he ordered.

She inflated, deflated, said "A . . . A . . . A . . ." held her breath, turned so that he could listen through her back. Repeated it all for Dr. Sterling, Junior, who listened carefully to her heart.

"Mmmmm."

Dr. Bear winked at her.

" 'Two physicians at the oar will row you to the Stygian shore,' " he quoted.

Miss Standish laughed, and Dr. Cub Sterling gave both of them a harassed stare. They sobered obediently.

The examination was thorough, painstaking and consumed almost half an hour. At its conclusion Dr. Sterling, Junior, said a very clipped, "Thank you, Miss Standish," and vanished. And Rose knew how deeply grateful he was, really.

His father lingered long enough to say:

"He'll explode some day. Thank you, my dear. Thank you very much."

He took her thin little hand in his capable one and growled:

"You are nervous, aren't you? I'm going to tell Mattus to give you a bromide, if you need it." And then he squeezed her hand gratefully and uttered, for the edification of the ward, a very professional, "Good night, Miss Standish."

"Good night, Doctor."

Her reply was professional, but she put her hand under the cover and squeezed it herself.

Dr. Bear was a darling. It had been sweet the way he had explained Dr. Sterling's attitude and then thanked her himself.

When this was all over, how many real friends she would have gained. But she mustn't forget that she was here for a purpose. Perhaps if she took a short nap now, she would be in better trim for the real thing . . . if it came. . . .

She turned over and tried to sleep, but the tension on the ward was so overpowering that she thought perhaps if she entered the conversation she might discover . . . or maybe she was just imagining things and the thunderstorm which was brewing was causing that feeling.

If only they would all begin to talk of something they were interested in and not to cover up what they were thinking.

There came a lull and she asked Mrs. Witherspoon:

"Do you think the flavor is better when you cook pork with sauerkraut, or without it?"

"Without it!" chimed in the woman with the enormous legs. "I give it to my children since they was babies and I always cooks it thorough . . . four to five hours . . . and then. . . ."

"You do?" Mrs. Witherspoon laid down her

crocheting, inserted her teeth and became emphatic.

"Thet saps all the taste. Mr. Witherspoon likes hisn so ez the pork and kraut is mixed flavored, if you know what I mean. Ain't it awful leathery, yo' way?"

"It ain't the cookin' time, as I was about to say," the fat woman drew up her chins, "it's the *cookin'* way."

"I got one of them steamer cookeths. It doz gran'," lisped the ex-circus woman.

Mrs. Witherspoon gave her a frivolous glance, and replied positively:

"I don't know nuthin' 'bout workin' them new fangled things. But I've et from them. Eddie May, Sammy's wife," both of her listeners nodded, "the one what come to see me Satd'y has one. And Mr. Witherspoon seys after we went to Sammy's Easter dinner, 'Jennie, the only way to cook victuals is to cook 'em with the eye. Baste 'em, and taste 'em, and it's jes' like stokin' an ingine,' he seys, 'you got to keep yo' eye to it.' If you know what I mean. . . ."

This precipitated a hot argument upon washing machines, with the fat woman as the defendant. So Rose Standish shifted her attention to the clouds. If the women kept up for fifteen minutes more . . . and if she knew wards they were good for hours . . . the thunderstorm would be here, and they would be quieted down for the night.

She looked at her watch. It was almost nine. Time for the night nurse to be coming along, in just a few minutes. And while she was waiting for her to come and bed the ward down, she might as well begin to think about the accident room.

Those scrub-up basins should be moved across the room and as far away as possible from the door in which the accidents were brought. And then, too, some arrangement should be made to equalize the lighting over the two tables. And also to give the nurse at the instrument table enough light to see what she was handing. And in some of the badly mangled cases, it would quicken things considerably if a passageway was built directly into the elevator corridor, so that they might be hurried up to the operating room.

Then, of course it was a little thing, but awfully important nervously: the girl who took the doctors' dictation onto the typewriter ought to have a noiseless machine. And it would be terribly hard to convince the Superintendent of Nurses, but she was going to tell Dr. MacArthur that she needed another student nurse on duty there. After a football game or a big race meet when the automobile accidents began to pour in, it was frightful. There was nobody, except the girl at the typewriter who couldn't stop, whose hands were not all gory and spotted every paper they touched.

She was distracted by a flash of lightning, Mrs.

Witherspoon's, "Lan' sake, nurse, I've wet my bed," and Miss Kerr's niece, the night student nurse leaning over her and purring:

"Miss Standish, are you better? Here's your thermometer."

Perhaps it was her voice coming so soon after the flash, but there seemed something too saccharin in its tone to Rose Standish. She shivered before she turned to take the extended thermometer.

Of course she knew Miss Kerr's niece was the night student nurse they were watching, but somehow she didn't associate the name and the girl. She had never liked this girl when she had been in the accident room. No real heart, and stubborn and cattish . . . and then her eyes were too close together. . . .

With barely a fleeting smile, Miss Kerr thrust the thermometer into Miss Standish's hand and ran to close the windows. It had begun to rain.

While the windows were being closed Bessie Ellis, the child down the ward who had received the toy in the night, began crying in her sleep. She had been disturbed by the lightning, and her moans made the women shivery.

Several of the women called out to her and Mrs. Witherspoon's lisping (her teeth again removed), "Alwite bavvy, don cwy," struck Miss Standish as highly amusing. She slipped her thermometer around and laughed. Miss Kerr, the student nurse, flopped down the last window and went to the moaning child.

While she was walking down the ward there came another flash of lightning, a sudden hissing, and the lights went out. It was followed by a panicky silence and then the hysterical laughter of Mrs. Witherspoon.

Rose Standish ducked as if she had been hit, and as she ducked something began choking her about the neck. She spit her thermometer upon the bed and began tugging at the horrible pulling. A thing, like a brick, hit her upon the head as she tried to sit up, and she thought, "it can't be the murderer, he only uses hypodermics," and the lights went up, while Mrs. Witherspoon was still laughing, and she saw Miss Kerr standing between their beds, and reaching for her thermometer.

In a moment she understood that the sash of her kimona had become twisted about her neck, and it was the book she had been reading and stuck upon the edge of her pillow which had fallen . . . and it was all absurd. All, that is, except the look in Miss Kerr's eyes.

The surprised look, when she saw Miss Standish was still alive! Her tongue was so dry she couldn't speak and a horrible nausea began rising within her, but Mrs. Witherspoon drew the girl's evil eyes when she demanded that her bed be fixed *now*.

Miss Kerr went for the sheets and Miss Standish

lay down and turned her face toward the window
and tried to forget it all. She placed one of her
thin hands at the base of her brain and began
massaging her neck. This was no way to do. Get
frightened at a little thing like a book hitting you.
A person who lost her nerve over such things
wasn't fit to look for mice in a dark pantry let
alone clear the reputation of Dr. Cub Sterling and
solve the terror of the Elijah Wilson. Forget it
all for a few minutes and remember the routine a
student nurse should be following, now.

Of course the changing of Mrs. Witherspoon's
bed was throwing everything slightly behind time,
but that should be finished in a minute, and she
turned over to watch the girl make the bed. Her
technique was excellent and she was a swift worker.
Seemed sure of herself.

Even from the back, Rose knew she didn't like
her. And never would. Miss Kerr turned to finish
the pulses. Then she began taking the flowers out
of the ward for the night. She took the pink roses
which the clowns had sent to the circus woman,
and the nasturtiums the children had brought the
fat woman, and Mrs. Witherspoon's tube rose . . .
thank goodness . . . and then she came back and
gave out the final round of bed-pans, the final
glasses of water, and went for her medicine tray.

The little girl had gone back to sleep, but down
the ward a gray old woman, whose face was like

cracked rock, was breathing with the horrible labor of a heart attack. Rose Standish started to call the student nurse and tell her to get Mattus right away, and then she decided that it was about time she began to remember that she was a patient on the ward and not a nurse.

Miss Kerr returned with the medicine tray. She gave Mrs. Witherspoon her hypodermic, and almost as a sponge does water, the withered body soaked it up, and she fell into a deep slumber. The woman with the thyroid insufficiency had her sleeping potion and began the long slow breathing of a laboring body.

The rain had broken the tension and the women were drifting off before the lights were dimmed. It, with the aid of the drugs, of course, was soothing and lulling them into oblivion. The long, slow torrents fell in strips outside the window and drowned out the labored breathing of the woman with the heart attack.

Rose lay perfectly still, so still she was almost drifting herself. Miss Kerr had reached the bed in which the heart patient lay and at last realized her condition . . . a tuned ear could have noted it down the corridor . . . she turned and walked prissily off the ward . . . not hurrying, and with her hips flat . . . and called Dr. Mattus. Rose could hear her cooing out the dying woman's condition, and gathered that he was coming up.

In a few minutes he appeared and after a quick glance began pumping digitalis into her . . . Rose could have told the nurse to do that! Then when she rallied, and after the lights had been dimmed, he came by her bed and said:

"All right, Miss Standish?"

"Perfectly. Thank you."

He took her pulse and said:

"Good heart you've got. Dr. Sterling, Senior, said you could have a sedative if you buckle. Ring for it, if you want it."

"What'll it be, doctor?"

He crinkled his long nose and sniffed, "Poison! Little nurses mustn't ask big questions! 'Night!"

His smile was broad, and forced.

By ten . . . Rose looked at her radio-light watch . . . the ward had "bedded down" and the rain had diminished to occasional drippings. Everything was cool and still. Miss Kerr had settled down to doing her fever charts at the desk. Occasionally, she turned and peered into the darkened ward, and Rose felt her looking at her bed, inquiringly.

She lay on her back, stretched her legs, put her arms at her sides, little girl fashion, and began to breathe deeply. Perhaps if she did that for thirty counts, she would drift off to sleep. If she buckled. . . . she'd show 'em. Begin to get some rest . . . plenty of it . . . it had been a long day . . . a trying evening . . . now everything was peaceful and everybody was beginning to sleep.

But if she dared to go to sleep, why couldn't the person . . . whoever it was . . . come while she was asleep and . . . and. . . .

She reached for her glass of water and took a drink. Her lips were so dry it hurt to open them. This was foolish. How was her heart doing? She took her pulse and discovered it was 106. Perhaps she had better have a potion after all.

She looked toward the desk. Miss Kerr wasn't there!

»VI«
The Second Doll

At NINE O'CLOCK DR. HARRISON EN-
tered the hospital through the accident room door
and started up the main corridor. The last of the
nurses and internes were returning from breakfast,
the morning sun as they passed the occasional windows was picking each face out of its oblivion and
then throwing it back again.

Dr. Harrison shivered. The faces looked as the
faces did upon the streets of every city in the
United States the morning after the Lindbergh
baby had been found. . . .

The cynically young, the frightened vacant, the
intelligent, the eager, the stupid, all reflected the
knowledge that Rose Standish was dead.

"A nurse died last night," the stupid faces, the
childish faces, the vacant faces reflected, and as
the intelligence increased, the horror in the eyes
grew. . . .

Upon the internes and residents they showed:
"A nurse was murdered last night."

And with an increasing frequency he saw eyes
which knew:

"She was murdered in Cub Sterling's Clinic."

He passed the entrance to his own clinic, and
then retraced his footsteps. His duty was to Mac-
Arthur, but his first duty was to suppress as much
staff hysteria as possible. With the staff in such
a condition, it was only a question of hours before
the patients, all over the hospital. . . .

His resident was standing beside the elevator
upon the first floor. He turned and Dr. Harrison
noted the first, second, and then a third horror in
his eyes.

" 'Morning, Wheeler," his voice was calm and
measured.

"Good morning, Doctor Harrison. Do you
know?"

"About the nurse? I do."

"No, sir. About Doctor Bear."

Dr. Harrison turned his searching brown eyes
into the man's gray ones.

"What?"

The resident met the glance and responded:

"Pneumonia. Bilateral. Cub is with him. Diagnosis confirmed. Brought him into hospital on a
stretcher about two hours ago. He's in Medicine
Clinic now . . . hopeless. . . ."

Dr. Harrison staggered for the first time in his
medical life.

"They murdered him! The dogs!"

He turned from the elevator and walked out of his clinic and down the corridor toward the Medicine Clinic. He walked calmly, like a man going to his execution and convinced of his innocence. . . . That heart attack was responsible, as sure as death itself, Hoffbein, Peters and Paton had killed . . . his best, his very best friend. . . .

His agony was so acute that the passing faces with their increasing hysteria seemed natural.

Turning to Mattus, Cub Sterling said:

"I'd better look in on Miss Merriweather, in case her father telephones today. Then you can find me with Dr. Sterling, if you need me."

He turned from Ward B and walked into Room Two and closed the door. That shade onto the Ward was still lowered. He had lowered it himself the first night he brought the cigarettes.

He and Sally Ferguson were completely alone.

She was smoking a cigarette. The room swam with pinking air and Cub leaned against the door jam and snapped:

"How's the leg since they took the bandages off? All right?"

She ignored the question and said:

"I just woke up! Why did you give me those pills last night?"

He walked toward the bed, and the horror of

the night receded and a wild happiness suffused his features.

"Don't you know, Salscie?"

"To make me . . . sleep?"

"Would you have slept . . . without . . . ?"

He leaned over her and kissed her twice. Completely and reachingly.

She burrowed her head between his collar and his neck and whispered:

"Did you . . . ?"

He laid the weight of his head upon hers and she moaned and brought her lips within reach again.

Cub drained them a third time and tucking his head between her breasts said:

"God I need that, darling! I've been through hell . . . hell . . . red hot hell!"

Then he jerked his head up and bored his eyes into hers. His voice was wild and heavy.

"Whatever happens, whatever anybody tells you, whatever comes . . . you must promise me, Salscie, that you'll believe in me . . . that you'll trust me . . . and know that I've wanted you all my life . . . and when all of this works out . . . I'm going to . . . live with you. . . ."

Her body stiffened and she snatched her eyes out of his. Her voice was hard and narrow.

"Cub Sterling, I wouldn't . . . ever . . . live

with you! At last I see why women have children
. . . why they want to belong. . . ."

All the angularity went out of him. He reached
over and gathered her into his arms. His voice
curled and nestled in her ear.

"You'll have them, Salscie! Lots of little Sterlings!"

Outside the loud speaker began:

"Docterr Ste-earling, Junyior, Doct-terr Eth-
err-ridge Ste-arling, Junyior. Calling Doct-
terr. . . ."

They wilted apart, but their eyes still held and
Cub said, softly and definitely:

"My father's ill. Very ill. The hospital's in a
terrible stew. I may not get to see you for a couple
of days. Be good until I do! Take care of yourself!
Don't be ferocious to anybody, Salscie! Promise?
I'll tell Mattus to let you have your clothes, and
try sitting up if you like. Think you'll need some
more pills tonight . . . darling?"

She blushed and smiled slowly. Cub took a box
from his pocket and gave her two veronal tablets.

Then he leaned over and ordered:

"Kiss me quick, Salscie! Sophie'd better kiss
me, too!"

At the door he turned and barked:

"Remember! This place is full of tales. . . .
Trust me?"

"Till death us do part, Cub darling!"

Dr. Henry MacArthur sat at his desk and awaited the arrival of the staff. He sat perfectly erect, dreadfully calm, with the hopeless heroism of the stone blind. His hands were relaxed upon his knees. Lifting them to cradle his head would require such an enormous effort . . . mentally and physically. . . .

He was as changed from the man who had lain in bed two nights before and enjoyed scotch highballs as if he had spent twenty years in Siberia. The hair at the temples looked grayer and the face was marble in its emotions. They came separately, and filled its furrows. Bitter self recrimination. He had sent a perfectly innocent woman to her death. A mere child. He had allowed her to go up, pass through hell and die . . . for his honor, Cub Sterling's reputation, and the Elijah Wilson Hospital. And to die so uselessly, so bravely, so quietly.

And the self-recrimination was followed by a nobility which made him beautiful, as the world thought King Albert beautiful while he was bleeding over Belgium.

Bleeding over the tremendous heroism of human beings. Over the cool straight bravery of quiet people. Over the fragile littleness of her still body. Over the sense of still living that her small ivory face had held when he and Cub Sterling and Dr. Bear's assistant were leaning over her body, under the glaring light of that autopsy table.

It had been like bending over a plucked magnolia blossom, on a summer morning. There was a spiritual fragrance about her as poignant as the perfume of magnolias. A feeling of sheer beauty, wasted. . . .

If he lived to be a hundred, he would never forget the exquisite curve of that child's small rounded breast and the nauseating sense of having stuck a knife in it, which came over him!

An Edith Cavell, a Florence Nightingale, a Jeanne d'Arc, and he had stood in her presence alive . . . and dead. . . .

And all of it had been so futile. But as certain as death itself was the knowledge . . . within his own mind . . . that Cub Sterling had had nothing to do with it. That Cub Sterling could not have stood beside him in that autopsy room a few scant hours ago and the sense of horror and helplessness have so entirely gripped them. And it did grip . . . both of them.

He started to telephone for Cub to come to him now and then he remembered about Bear, and his head . . . for the first time since he had been Director of the Elijah Wilson Hospital . . . fell into his cupped hands, while the door into the corridor stood wide open.

Caesar was dead, Napoleon was dead, Osler was dead, Socrates was dead, Halsted was dead and Bear Sterling was dying. . . .

Dying because of overwork and a bad heart. Sacrificed to his profession by his colleagues! That heart attack yesterday, coupled with the cold had done it.

All the great men were dead or dying. . . . Coniine. . . .

He turned over Cub Sterling's testimony concerning the death of Miss Standish, and stared vacantly at the words. Somewhere, at this very minute, there was walking, still free, about the Elijah Wilson Hospital, probably laughing and talking with other patients, a nurse, a doctor . . . a man . . . a woman . . . a murderer. . . .

Dr. MacArthur rose and walked to the far window through which the warm spring sun was shining. He must pull himself together. His duty was not to his emotional beliefs concerning men and their motives. Above all things he must be fair. His duty and theirs was to the hospital and within the next five minutes he must get himself in such perfect control that he could compel them to see it.

The opportunity of the hospital to be of benefit to humanity for the next fifty years depended entirely upon his ability to hold his staff together this morning. To force these exceptionally capable men to think calmly . . . and wisely.

He closed his eyes and allowed the sun to penetrate through the lids. A soft spring breeze floated in the opened window. A living, gentle breeze which foretold all the wealth of future living in flowers and fragrances; which expressed as clearly as Chopin might have, how he felt about the small, slim body of Rose Standish.

It seered him like a sirocco. Yesterday morning, she had stood there with just such a breeze blowing. Yesterday morning it had promised her summer, too . . . and today. . . . He turned his back resolutely to the window and still stood with his eyes closed.

The sun began relaxing the muscles at the base of his brain and then he seemed suddenly sane. Her death had been like those of the officers in the Great War who had jumped out of the trenches and walked up and down to give their men courage. . . .

He returned to his desk and calmly began planning what must be covered at this meeting, and what witnesses must be called. Cub, if he could leave his father, otherwise his testimony must suffice. The day white nurse, the night pupil nurse, Miss Kerr's niece, and Mattus' impression of the patient when he last saw her. Then it would be wise to ask Dr. Heddis to come over and report upon the autopsy findings.

The lack of sleep was telling upon him. He had entirely forgotten about questioning the orderly, William. He rang for his secretary and gave her the orders.

When Dr. Barton's squared frame filled the door it brought with it a sense of relief. Queer how sane associating with children made a man. Almost immediately he was followed by Hoffbein, Peters and Paton . . . together. They had just settled themselves when Dr. Harrison strode in. There was an armor of righteousness about him that dazzled. Dr. MacArthur had never seen Harrison this way before. Like some great patriarch of Biblical fame girded for battle.

When they were all seated, Dr. Barton and Dr. Harrison exchanged monosyllabic diagnoses upon Dr. Bear and Dr. MacArthur read their faces.

Peters, Hoffbein, and Paton missed the discussion. They were funereal, self-righteous and pious, respectively.

A nurse was dead. They had gone on record opposing placing her in the position where she might be murdered. Dr. MacArthur had sacrificed her to save Cub Sterling's reputation.

At half-past six when Dr. MacArthur had notified Dr. Peters, Dr. Peters had telephoned Dr. Paton right away and intoned "The sort of thing that purifies a man," and after that their conversation had been long, gossipy . . . and horrified. Princeton had been propped against his pillows, his feet glued to a white rubber hot water bottle and a deep purple corded silk dressing gown thrown over his still firm shoulders.

His wife was abroad with Mrs. Paton.

Prissy, whose telephone was as much a part of his bedtime equipment as his nightshirt, had lain perfectly flat upon his bed and with their decisions his "seven months gone" bay-window rose and fell. Cushioned upon what had once been his chest was a French telephone.

Their first decision had been to tell MacArthur "right out" that they had to have a private meeting without either of the Sterlings present, and decide something.

As Prissy's upper teeth and Princeton's lower ones were removed for the night, their vehemence had seemed awfully mushy to the telephone operator when she cut in for Paton's resident.

But when the discourse was resumed Princeton had said:

"I shell inten' to shay, at the meetin' we are demandin', Paton."

Prissy's front had given a proud heave.

"That we cannot have our poshishun jepodized any longer. Action" . . . the bay-window rose . . . "must be taken immediately. The powice—"

Five minutes had been lost over that word. Neither of them could persuade the telephone to accept it.

"The law to intervene," Princeton finally substituted.

"I agwee entirely, Peshurs. I'll stan' behin' you, straight through."

Prissy's offer even in the noontide sun would have come in a high treble and over the telephone and under the circumstances it didn't sound very convincing.

However, after they had both bathed, both felt her death had purified them, both inserted their teeth, both had called MacArthur and requested a meeting minus the Sterlings.

It had left them a little shaky . . . but now that Dr. MacArthur was beginning to speak, Prissy nodded to Princeton who tiptoed to the door and closed it. They felt they had been justified in the action they had taken.

Neither Sterling was present.

"Gentlemen," Dr. MacArthur's voice was measured and low, "Rose Standish is dead. She was murdered last night while a patient in Bed 11, Ward B, of Medicine Clinic. An injection of coniine. She went on that ward to save your reputation and mine. To lift the hospital out of terror . . . and she is dead, and we are. . . ."

"I was against it from the first," Princeton began clearing himself with the rapidity of a condemned schoolboy.

Nobody paid him the slightest attention. Prissy blushed, and Hoffbein squirmed.

"We are faced," Dr. MacArthur's blue eyes had taken on their fighting steeliness, "with the blackest day the Elijah Wilson has ever seen. With the fact that no patient anywhere is safe in any bed of the institution . . . with the responsibility of catching a murderer within our walls. A person who has committed two untraceable, two traceable murders. D'y'see? Gentlemen, I ask your advice."

Princeton Peters and Prissy Paton stared at Dr. Hoffbein and he nodded . . . with his eyelids, and Princeton rose.

"To put it plainly, straightly and to the point, MacArthur, it is one thing to protect your professional colleagues, but after all our Hyppocratic oath binds us *first* to the protection of our patients.

"I'm glad you called this meeting as we advised, and have given us an opportunity of speaking frankly. Murder, automatically, cancels loyalty! Call in the police immediately is the advice of myself, Dr. Paton and Dr. Hoffbein."

His peach-blossom face was brick red and it was the fury with which Dr. Harrison rose that, at a distance of ten feet, scared Dr. Peters into his chair.

"You might just as well know, Dr. Peters," his brown eyes were live coals, "that this meeting was not called without the Sterlings purposely. Barton and I were dead against it, as was MacArthur. Dr. MacArthur was intensely kind in his opening speech about the number of murders which have been committed in this hospital within the last week. They are five."

"Stop, Harrison. Please stop!" Dr. MacArthur had risen from his chair, but he might have been a fly upon the distant mantelpiece for the effect he produced.

"Sorry. I can't stop. They might just as well know it! Call in your police! Call them in now! And as sure as Christ was crucified I'll swear out a warrant for each of you, Hoffbein, Peters and Paton, for the murder of Bear Sterling, now dying of pneumonia complicated by the heart attack which you, famous colleagues and a world-renowned psychiatrist caused by your foul insinuations yesterday.

"If you value your international reputations as much as your self-exhibitions in the last fifteen years indicate, the police are out of the question.

"Now let's get down to business."

For fully four minutes after he had finished no man in the room spoke. No man could. For fifteen, twenty, perhaps thirty years none of them had ever heard Dr. Harrison raise his voice above a conversational tone, never had seen him for one-quarter of a split second lose complete control of himself or of a situation, never had heard him judge a man without charity.

And the three he condemned were too seared to be angry, too frightened to be resentful, too dazed to be amazed.

He had spoken the truth . . . and they knew it.

Dr. Barton, as a nurse might work upon children upset by an explosion, took his pipe from his mouth, and began speaking. He said:

"Dr. MacArthur, I think it is your advice that we need, suh."

The thing that cowed Dr. Peters, Paton and Hoffbein, was that Dr. Harrison had suffered no relapse. He sat firmly stroking his beard and looking alternately at each of them.

Dr. MacArthur, his blue eyes firmly defiant, began:

"The hospital has never been in so delicate a situation. I repeat that the matter must be handled with secrecy, tact, and sanity.

"You see, gentlemen, this hospital was endowed, it has been perpetuated for, and is famous as, a great teaching institution. When through any clumsiness of ours we have more beds than patients the hospital is doomed. Its great advantage has always been more patients than beds. D'y'see?"

Prissy's green, Princeton's lavender and Hoffbein's liquid eyes were glued upon his face. Dr. Barton's shoulders were hunched attentively.

"Now if we were to turn this situation over to the police, regardless of Dr. Harrison's statements, we would automatically spread into every ward of every department, every newspaper in the country, the superstition of every negro within a thousand miles, the means of ruining, absolutely, your work, mine and that of all the medical men now resident and student here.

"Murder is a very horrible situation, but dooming the future of at least a thousand capable men is, in my opinion, worse, all oaths, notwithstanding D'y'see?

"Whatever hysteria is manifested must not come from the staff, nor the blunders which so horrible an occurrence makes us likely to fall into."

"You're absolutely right, Mac!" Dr. Harrison's voice was placid, and Prissy and Princeton automatically exhaled the breath they had been inhaling preparatory to argument.

Dr. Harrison said:

"Do you know how many rabbit feet I've seen on dispensary patients in the last six months? Sixty-three! The cancer cases love 'em. How many patients we've lost because they moved when another negro sprinkled salt upon their doorsteps? Eighty-one! Within three blocks of here I've counted fifteen chiropractors, ten optometrists, five osteopaths, and seventeen midwives.

"Superstition, witchcraft, voodoo, dynamite!

We've *got* to keep our face no matter if all of us are murdered. Matter with you three is just a touch of hysteria."

Hoffbein squirmed and replied:

"Fear psychosis is a most contagious disease, but like all contagious diseases most debilitating. It has only one cure: to remove the cause of the fear."

His voice was precise and his words, he felt, showed how he stood and yet were dignified.

"From which I understand you are suggesting we scrap Cub Sterling," MacArthur's angry eyes bore into him like a hot poker, and his mouth drew to a tight line as he slapped his hand upon his desk and stated, "I won't do it without *ample, complete* and *convincing evidence*. Have you any to offer?"

Hoffbein squirmed acutely and he replied evasively:

"Nothing . . . tangible. . . . Only those small and very personal signs which to a man in my branch are so revealing. His hands, the hysterical set of his left shoulder, the peculiar light which comes into his eyes. . . ."

"That'll do!" Dr. Harrison barked. "If I knew any of you had cancer, I'd tell you so to your face. If Bear Sterling had found any man here suffering from an incurable brain tumor, he would have told that man. We are not asking you for symptoms, Hoffbein. Have you any evidence, yes or no?"

Hoffbein's eyes lost their whites. "No."

"Then let's get on to people who have. Read Ethridge's testimony, please, MacArthur."

Dr. MacArthur picked up the long white sheet of paper and began in an even voice:

"Complying with the decision of the General Staff of the Elijah Wilson Hospital, I admitted Rose Standish, graduate nurse of this institution, as a patient in Medicine Clinic, Ward B, Bed 11, yesterday afternoon. The diagnosis, for the benefit of the nursing staff, being a possible tubercular effusion.

"She received a routine examination from the house staff and from seven-ten until seven-thirty last evening my father, Dr. Sterling, and I went over her. We found her lungs in excellent shape, her heart slightly enlarged, but not seriously so, her general physical condition splendid, with the exception of the fact that she was somewhat thin and underweight. There were no signs of any malady of any kind whatever. Her temperature was normal, her pulse good, though a little rapid, which, considering the circumstances was not surprising, and her spirits commendably calm.

"We both felt most reassured by her mental and physical condition, though my father, Dr. Sterling, in case she might discover herself too fatigued to sleep advised a sedative. We told

Miss Standish of the order and suggested she call for the potion if she felt the necessity.

"There was some vague hysteria in the ward, which both Miss Standish and ourselves sensed, and I understand from the seven-to-nine-student nurses that she calmed it by conversation.

"The prescription for the potion was, later, removed from Miss Standish's chart and is in the possession of Dr. MacArthur, as is, also, the testimony of a patient who claimed to have seen Miss Kerr, student nurse, standing over Miss Standish's bed for several seconds during the thunderstorm which extinguished the lights at nine-forty.

"From the time we walked off the ward at seven-thirty, until Mattus notified me of Rose Standish's death at one-ten, I did not see Miss Standish. Mattus saw her around ten and reported her in practically the same condition in which Father and I had left her.

"After seeing my father, Dr. Sterling, to his car at seven-thirty, I went to dinner in the doctors' dining room, took a short walk, and was in bed by eleven-thirty.

"When Mattus notified me of Miss Standish's death at one-ten, I immediately called Dr. MacArthur who ordered an autopsy, tried to get my father and learned that the cold he had complained of was settling in his chest and his temperature was 101. At his orders I got his assistant, Dr. Withers, who in the presence of Dr. MacArthur, Mattus and myself, performed the autopsy, the findings of which will be given by Dr. Heddis, who came in when it was half finished and later took the organs for examination.

"Because of the excellent forethought of Mattus, we borrowed an operative patient from Surgical Clinic and rolled her bed into the place where Rose Standish's had stood and left orders to say to the patients that Miss Standish had hemorrhaged and been put in a private room. From the time the ward awoke until the operation was called, the new patient was in the process of preparation and did not realize the change.

"From the time of the discovery of Rose Standish's corpse, until Mattus and I had rolled the bed toward the elevator, the deportment of William, the orderly, was most praiseworthy and the demeanor of Miss Evelina Kerr astonishingly calm.

"While the autopsy was still in progress, my mother called to say that Dr. Sterling's temperature had risen to 103, his breathing was labored and he was requesting I come to him. Dr. MacArthur insisted that I go. I found him with a definite case of pneumonia, both lungs seriously involved, pulse irregular, and breathing labored, semi-delirious. I immediately called an ambulance and brought him into the hospital for oxygen.

"The response is disheartening. His heart is weakening. I have remained by his bedside, again through the advice of Dr. MacArthur.

"Dictated to Dr. MacArthur's secretary, outside room 511, Medicine Clinic, at 8:30 A. M. Wednesday, May 18th.

"(Signed) : Ethridge Sterling, Jr., M.D.
            Physician-in-Chief (Pro-tem),
            The Elijah Wilson Hospital."

Dr. MacArthur laid the paper down and looked from the window.

"Questions?" his voice was old and heavy, and he brought his eyes back to the men with an effort.

Dr. Harrison shot a glance around the room and insisted:

"Let's continue with the evidence."

Dr. MacArthur pushed a button upon his desk, the door into the corridor opened and Miss Evelina Kerr, night student nurse on Ward B, entered.

It was Princeton Peters who escorted her to the chair beside Dr. MacArthur's and Dr. Hoffbein who would have liked to question her, had he not felt Dr. Harrison's eyes judging his every thought; so Dr. MacArthur turned to her and said:

"You have been through another dreadful night. I'm sorry. Please tell about it carefully."

She sat as she had sat yesterday, her hands primly in her lap and her flat feet carefully together, her stubborn defiance breaking through her voice.

She looked carefully around the large room before she began to speak, and to Dr. MacArthur, Dr. Harrison, and Dr. Barton, there flashed a realization that her eyes were still too close together, and that somehow she was enjoying her importance.

But her survey did not escape Dr. Harrison.

He barked, "Dr. Sterling is not here because his father is desperately ill. Will you be so kind as to tell your story, now?"

"Yes, Dr. Harrison, I will." The stupid definiteness in her voice was maddening. She turned her eyes upon Dr. Hoffbein and told her story to him. She said:

"When I went on duty at nine I found Miss Standish a patient in Bed 11, Ward B. She said Dr. Sterling thought she might have a tubercular effusion and she was in for observation. I gave her her thermometer and ran to close the windows as the rain had started."

"And when the lights went out, you were standing by her bed, Miss Kerr," Dr. Barton announced pointedly.

Her eyes did not leave Dr. Hoffbein, and she replied:

"I had come back for the thermometer."

The answer crashed like a broken plate, and Dr. Harrison insisted:

"And then?"

"Then I counted her pulse," her voice was wooden, "gave my medicines. Put out the flowers and called Dr. Mattus about a woman with a heart attack."

"Why didn't you give Miss Standish her sleeping potion, when you were distributing medicines?"

"Because, Dr. Barton, Dr. Mattus came up to the heart case and said not to give it to Miss Standish unless she called for it.

"After he went, I dimmed the lights, went to work on my fever charts, made up the midnight medicines, and began studying my nursing manual. William, the orderly, came up the hall twice to ask me about some dishes and the breakfast trays, and then about eleven-thirty, Miss Standish rang and asked for her sleeping potion, and I gave it to her."

"Are you sure you gave her the right prescription?" Dr. Harrison's eyes had bored past Dr. Hoffbein and into her.

She pouted her thick lips and lifted her ugly chin.

"Yes, sir, I'm positive. She went to sleep right away. You don't think, Dr. Harrison . . .?"

"What I think does not concern your story, Miss Kerr. Please continue."

There was a slight tightening of her jaw, and had she had sense enough to cry then, every man in the room would have felt beaten. She continued woodenly:

"After I gave Miss Standish her medicine, the next patient had to have her linen changed, and when I had finished with that, Miss Standish was asleep. I could tell by her breathing.

"It was then almost midnight and I went to boil my syringes for the midnight hypodermics, and while I was boiling them Mrs. Witherspoon, the patient whose bed I had just changed, rang again, and I ran to see about her.

"And as I reached her bed, I found Dr. Cub Sterling leaning over Miss Standish. He looked up and nodded, and. . . ."

"Repeat your last three sentences, Miss Kerr. Repeat them twice! And look at me while you do it." Dr. Hoffbein's voice was mesmeric.

Miss Kerr repeated them . . . twice. . . .

They filled the room and permeated the senses of every man present like poison gas.

Dr. Harrison shot his gimlet-like brown eyes into the narrow, close ones of the student nurse.

"You are wrong, Miss Kerr. Dr. Ethridge Sterling, Junior, was in his rooms."

"I'm not! He was bending over Miss Standish. I

know it. His bushy hair, his funny shoulder. . . ."

"Did he speak?"

"No, Dr. Harrison. He just nodded. Like he always does."

"Why didn't you *make* him speak?"

"I couldn't stop to. We had no more clean linen and I had to run for a bed-pan for Mrs. Witherspoon."

MacArthur's hand beat upon his desk . . . hopelessly. . . .

"Go on, Miss Kerr." His voice was like a death-knell.

"And when I came back he was gone. He had hurried off the ward while I was getting the bed-pan. And I went to Miss Standish as soon as I could. She was still asleep. And I ran to William. He was asleep. And then I started to 'phone the night supervisor, but it was time to give my medicines . . . and Aunt Roenna always told us even if the building were burning down, the medical patients must have their medicines on time. So I began giving them their hypodermics. And when I could, I went to look at Miss Standish. She was still sleeping.

"And then I finished the medicines and fever charts and called in the rounds . . . I forgot to mention about Dr. Sterling because the supervisor rung off so quickly . . . and I had to hurry from the 'phone to give out three bed-pans. When I had

finished the bed-pans I went to look at Miss Standish again and she was dead . . . and so I called
Aunt Roenna. . . ."

"Why?" Dr. Harrison's word hit her like a
brick.

"Because she had told me to."

"When?"

"Last night before she went off duty."

"What did she say?"

"She said, 'All right, I'll come over.' "

"Then you both *expected* Rose Standish to die,
Miss Kerr?"

All of this dialogue had gone on so swiftly that
the girl had failed to make her brain control her
speech. It had come out . . . spontaneously. . . .

"We didn't either, only. . . ."

Dr. Harrison decided that this was not the time
for the truth. He passed off her reply with, "What
happened next?"

"I called the night supervisor and Dr. Mattus,
and waited until they came. And then. . . ."

"From that point forward we have several eye-
witnesses." Dr. MacArthur interrupted. "Thank
you, Miss Kerr."

He picked up his telephone and asked:

"Nursing office, please. Miss Merrill, will you
please come for Miss Kerr, student nurse, and put
her to bed, and follow the orders given you this
morning. Thank you."

The girl turned to speak and Dr. Harrison motioned to Dr. Peters to open the door. He did so, as Miss Merrill appeared.

"Before we discuss this, let's have the other witnesses," Dr. Harrison's voice was relentless. But it failed to puncture the self-righteous-I-told-you-so posture of Doctors Peters, Paton and Hoffbein.

Dr. MacArthur said, "I think we might dispense with the orderly, William, and with the day white nurse. According to the testimony of everybody William slept through the murder. He is useless either to condemn or confirm the girl's statement. And the day white nurse seems to me completely out of it. Here are Dr. Heddis and Rathbone."

They entered and sat down quietly. The mental heat of the room stifled them. They drew their handkerchiefs quickly and Dr. Heddis mopped his leonine head and Rathone his bald head furiously. Dr. Heddis felt himself sinking into the tension. He spoke immediately:

"The findings upon the organs of Rose Standish, gentlemen, are that she was murdered by coniine in such a quantity that it took effect in about thirty to forty minutes. The left arm bore a hypodermic puncture; the injection was larger than that administered in the other traceable case. Her liver, spleen, lungs and stomach were suffused with the odor and the substance. Because of the enormity of the dose, indications are that the death was painless. She died of the customary respiratory paralysis."

At least the testimony of these two men was definite and sane. The staff sat forward attentively. Dr. Harrison asked:

"Ethridge mentions a sleeping potion in his report . . .?

Dr. Heddis turned toward Peter Rathbone. Baldy's wide straight shoulders squared. His delivery was impressive:

"The potion was . . . bread pills. Dr. Sterling, Senior, came by the pharmacy, around six, and left the order himself. It was his idea that if the student nurse was doing the murdering and administered the potion, without knowing its content (the copy upon Miss Standish's chart was for an intricate formula), she would create a trap for herself."

MacArthur groaned, involuntarily. Hoffbein stated:

"He overlooked the psychic effect upon the patient."

"It seems so, Doctor." Rathbone's words were slow and measured: "Dr. Heddis is unable to trace a potion in the system, and I understand the student nurse insists she administered the potion, so the obvious assumption is that she is telling the truth and the effect was psychic. . . . "

"Bear's endeavor to prove his son. . . ." Barton ventured and Hoffbein realized suddenly that he had been in temporary acquiescence with the theory of Cub Sterling's innocence, and hastened to add:

"Who, Baldy . . . er, Rathbone, except yourself and Dr. Sterling, Senior, knew of the contents of the potion?"

"I can't say, Doctor." Rathbone's mouth closed tightly, and Heddis lifted his heavy body, as Barton inquired:

"With our methods of cadaver handling is putrefaction possible?"

Rathbone repeated the question to Dr. Heddis, who answered:

"Perfectly. Clip off a small portion of an arm or leg, before embalming, and keep it. . . ." He threw out his hand, "To a toxicologist the synthetic possibility seems increasingly unfeasible. Formulas are too intricate, and the discovery of the murderer that way would be worse than looking for a penny in quicksand. Mean checking every organ of every cadaver. . . .

"Look for the administrator, not the manufacturer. Someone with access to the patients in that bed. Time enough after that person is found to find out. . . ."

He turned to Dr. MacArthur and said, "Any hour night or day, Mac. . . ."

Rathbone, too, rose; his clear baritone filled the room:

"The medicine closets of all floors of Medicine Clinic were searched again today. They reveal no coniine. The syringes check as to number but are useless; the routine boiling eliminates any hope of tracing that way. Is there anything else we can do, sir?"

"No, Rathbone," MacArthur's voice was hopeless and affectionate. "I wish there were. Thank both of you, gentlemen."

They were followed by Dr. Mattus, who came, as Cub had done the day before with a doll tucked under his arm. This time the dolly wore a blue dress and frilled bonnet and said, "Pa-pa. Pa-pa."

Every man in the room shivered.

"For heaven's sake turn that damn thing over!" Dr. MacArthur ordered. "Where did you get it?"

"Found it in the desk of Miss Roenna Kerr."

"Whew!" It was Dr. Barton who expressed the combined sentiments.

"When?" Dr. Harrison's face was eerie with hope.

"When she was at Head Nurse Conference, and I went into her office looking for some case reports."

"Did you face her with it?"

"No, Dr. MacArthur, I did not. I brought it to you. Only first, I happened, casually, to learn that her niece won a similar doll at a street fair last week. She went with a party of nurses during her P. M."

Dr. Harrison's fringe of white hair haloed his face. He looked like a man coming out of torture.

"Tell what you know about last night, Mattus."

"Dr. James, interne, and I examined Miss Standish yesterday afternoon. Found her normal in every respect and in good spirits. By Jove . . . when I came on the ward, Miss Roenna Kerr was trying to put her in another bed . . . and I ordered her into Bed 11. Did not see Miss Standish again until around ten when I was called to the ward for a heart case. She was still awake and cheerful; told her Dr. Bear had ordered a sleeping potion and to call for it if she needed it."

"What was the potion?" Dr. MacArthur interrupted.

"Veronal, sir. He handed me the prescription as he left Medicine Clinic, sir."

The men stirred and Mattus continued:

"When I saw Miss Standish again, she was dead."

"Did you see Miss Roenna Kerr on the ward after the murder?"

"Yes, sir. She arrived soon after I did and I presumed Dr. Sterling, Junior, had sent for her. That's all I know, sir. Except that Cub, Dr. Sterling, Junior, left his father and made rounds on that ward to calm the hysteria this morning about nine and had the heaven-sent sense to say his father was ill. The women are wallowing in sympathy and have almost forgotten the death of Miss Standish.

"Dr. Bear is sinking, gentlemen."

When he was gone, Dr. Peters suggested calling Miss Roenna Kerr, but Dr. Harrison opposed it.

"Not on your life. You are out to convict Cub Sterling. I'm out to save him. Let's have it out in plain words. Bear is on his deathbed."

Princeton interrupted abruptly, "Harrison, isn't there some hope? Dear Bear's physique. . . ."

Dr. Harrison turned on him coldly.

"No. No, dear Peters. His eyes will not be better, tomorrow. They will be closed!"

"Then don't you think we had better wait until after the funeral?" Prissy intervened.

"Hell, no!" Harrison snorted. "Bear Sterling is the best friend I ever had. He dragged me out of the gutter and made a doctor of me. Either his son is cleared, or I'll not be caught at his funeral with you skunks!"

His anger was so intense that nobody dared object. Princeton wiped his brow clean with a lavender silk handkerchief and Harrison continued:

"He cannot defend his son who by his own murderers is accused of murdering patients. Well, I know his son is innocent!"

"How do you know it?" Hoffbein hypodermicked.

"By a method that none of you three could ever comprehend. Because I trust the man. Now let's get down to tacks. If Ethridge is innocent he ought to be cleared before sunset. If he is guilty he ought to be hanged before then. Clearing him or convicting him with the police is out of the question. But cleared he has got to be, and therefore I propose that we instruct MacArthur to hire the best private detectives in the United States to become patients on B Ward and orderlies throughout the building, with the right to question any or all of us. . . ."

"But why . . . why . . . Harrison" . . .?

"Shut up, Princeton. . . . I beg your pardon, Peters. . . . How do MacArthur and I know that Miss Roenna Kerr and her niece are not working as accomplices for you or Hoffbein in murdering patients in Ethridge Sterling's clinic?"

"Oh, oh, oh! Harrison you *don't* mean that!"

"I do, Peters."

"You can't realize what you are saying, man," Hoffbein was soothingly calm.

"I do, Hoffbein! I realize quite thoroughly that Bear Sterling's son's reputation is as dear to Dr. Barton and Dr. MacArthur and to myself as that of any world-famous man who ever had a patient in the Elijah Wilson Hospital. I would sooner, much sooner, see the reputations of you three scraped in the mire and flung away across the world by the tabloids than to see the name of a man who cannot be present to protect himself slurred by your nasty insinuations.

"His good name is just as valuable to us as yours are . . . more so . . . and so far as we are concerned your honor needs cleansing a great deal more than his does. The only way to cleanse any of our reputations *now* is to quit treating every person . . . *whatever his rank* . . . involved in this matter . . . as innocent, and consider all of us guilty until the criminal is caught.

"Do any of you suspect MacArthur? Well, that's something in your favor. MacArthur, you hire the detectives, and instruct them to consider all of us guilty . . . until we are proved innocent. . . .

"And in case any of you have any scruples whatever about talking I wish you to remember that Barton's brother is the Attorney-General of this state and at one word from MacArthur he will have all of you *made* to talk . . . to save your own reputations, let alone that of the blessed hospital.

"Miss Roenna Kerr, working through her niece as accomplice, outside of Ethridge Sterling, Junior, is the other suspect. She has been a patient of every man sitting in this room with the exception of Dr. Barton, Dr. MacArthur and myself. Consider your position, gentlemen. . . ."

»VII«
The New Patient in Bed Eleven

D R. MACARTHUR FLAPPED THE YEL-low telegram helplessly and wondered how to face them. Through some pull or other they had made the mail plane from New York and would be in his office in fifteen minutes.

Two men and a woman. Three detectives; and he had never faced a detective in his life. How did a man treat detectives? Must one defer, or order?

Probably Harrison would know. A urologist had every profession in his grip sooner or later. He reached for the telephone. Dr. Harrison laughed at the question. It was the first time he had laughed since entering the hospital that morning, learning of Rose Standish's death and realizing that Bear Sterling's was only a matter of sixty or seventy hours.

"You are tired, aren't you, Mac? Give 'em some infant feeding and a dose of paregoric once around! Buck up, old man! I suggest you tell the truth, the whole truth, and let them create their own suspicions.

"Remember they were hand-picked by the Rock-efeller Foundation. They are intelligent. News-paper reporters grown up . . . and you're a whiz with newspaper reporters. Call me if you need me. 'By!"

Dr. MacArthur was reassured. Like an oak, Harrison! Tried, staunch and straight!

His secretary entered and said, "Two men and a woman to see you, sir."

"Show them in, please."

The two men were carrying handbags and over-coats. The first was tall and dignified. He had a long square body. Everything about him was mus-cular, under perfect control and heavy-set. His eyes, suit, overcoat, and hair were gray. His teeth were strong and even. His eyes showed the same steely calm that Bear Sterling's had. Judgmatical. The enemy was death; the man you were after, or yours. So far he had been lucky, and he had a lucky man's nonchalance.

"Dr. MacArthur? Matthew Higgins is my name."

His voice was deep and buoyant.

His handclasp was like a vice. It steadied Dr. MacArthur like a cup of strong coffee.

The voice continued:

"Mr. Smooty, Dr. MacArthur."

Smooty was slight. His body and face were completely relaxed and pastel. Green eyes melted into mild cheeks. He had the utter inactivity and extreme alertness of a clown and the fading quality of a chameleon.

His grip was like that of a contortionist. One had to find it.

His voice was colorless.

"Delighted to know you, Doctor."

Mr. Higgins turned to the woman and said:

"I beg your pardon, Miss Parkins. I should have introduced you first, but air-travel leaves me woozy. Miss Parkins, Dr. MacArthur."

MacArthur was her kind and she sensed it. She stretched her capable hand and smiled. Their summary was like sun on metal.

One could never lose memory of her physically. She was tall, square-shouldered, with the long, slender legs of a gracefully tall woman. Her face was ugly and expressive. The nose was too short, the mouth too wide, but the flashes were sudden and revealing. They were as vivid, highly original and occasionally blank as heat lightning. And massed in with her extreme directness was a wistful, childlike appeal.

Her limpid eyes flashed into life as Dr. MacArthur carefully seated her, took her coat and motioned the men to chairs.

"A pleasant trip, I hope?"

His voice was old and courteous.

"Very," the gray man was the spokesman. "This

letter," he drew a thick envelope from his inside coat pocket and handed it to MacArthur, "we were instructed, Doctor, to request that you read it immediately upon our arrival."

Dr. MacArthur took the letter and carefully tore the flap.

"Thank you," he said looking up. Then he rose and offered the men and the woman cigarettes, struck a match and extended it to the woman. He always offered newspaper reporters cigarettes, and Harrison had said detectives were. . . .

Miss Parkins smiled, took the match, lighted, and passed it.

Dr. MacArthur returned to his chair and began reading and she said, "Three on a match. Unlucky!"

Then they were silent. The air was full of estimation. The letter was long, and evidently from the head of the detective agency. It was addressed to Dr. MacArthur and said:

"Mr. Higgins has been in our employ about fifteen years and handled many executive jobs. Your request was for a man capable of impersonating a well-to-do patient, or a member of the administrative staff of a distant hospital; a man who may be given full run of the hospital and thereby an opportunity, we gather, to question, without creating suspicion, in every department. We have recently had Mr. Higgins upon a job necessitating the trapping of an embezzler within one of our largest New York hospitals. He has our complete confidence, a world-wide experience with people, and an excellent judgment of men. We have found him especially successful in catching mental criminals, and from Dr. Bridgman of the Rockefeller, we judge that is your problem.

"Mr. Smooty has long experience in impersonations. He has done confidence work in Sing-Sing, department stores, and as a hotel detective; also we have used him in the Pennsylvania Station. His nondescript appearance is an excellent foil for his capabilities. You asked for a man who might be placed as a menial.

"He and Mr. Higgins have worked together for many years and are among the first ranking detectives in America. Mr. Smooty is originally an Englishman and has also done work for Scotland Yard and in the British Intelligence."

Dr. MacArthur took his handkerchief from his pocket and blew his nose. This was the first time, to his knowledge, he had ever sat in the presence of a Scotland Yard man. And as a little boy, next to being a dogcatcher, to belong to Scotland Yard. . . . It left him rather awed. Maybe the woman was a Russian Grand Duchess!

He returned his attention, his eyes had never left it, to the letter and read:

"Miss Parkins has done international and character work for us for about five years. She, in our opinion, is capable of any situation where courage, brains, and mixing abilities are required. Within the last year we have had her upon one of the big liners between New York and Cherbourg, on the road with the circus, and living as an immigrant on the East Side. During the war, she worked for the Government in Mexico. She, we understand, you desire as a patient on a ward of medical women. She has an unfortunate, and slight, heart ailment, which will serve to divert the suspicion of even your staff.

"The terrible delicacy with which the situation must be handled has occasioned our sending what we consider the three most able people in New York. Miss Parkins was taken off political work today at the insistence of Dr. Bridgman, through whom we were contacted, and who seems to feel that the patient in the ward of medical women is the key person. All three people were interviewed by and met with the approval of Dr. Bridgman.

"Our terms, which at his suggestion we state, are $2000.00 per week and maintenance.

"Awaiting your orders,

"We are. . . ."

Dr. MacArthur carefully folded the letter and decided to take Harrison's advice. Two thousand dollars a week . . . it took brains and plenty of them to be able to demand that!

The late afternoon sun had left the room. He looked up and discovered the room was semi-dark, and the three people were sitting motionless. The door into the corridor was still open; he had been too rattled to close it when they entered. The measured and constant footfalls of the thousands of feet had padded into his consciousness so long that he didn't sense it, but they must.

He rose, closed the door, turned up the lights and said, as he walked toward the windows to lower the shades, "Sorry to subject you to all of that racket. Time for duty changes. Hospitals are noisy places."

Mr. Higgins had risen and was pulling down the shades, too.

"So is New York, Doctor."

Dr. MacArthur nodded and returned to his desk. He looked at his wrist watch and said:

"Miss Parkins, Mr. Higgins and Mr. Smooty, if we are to get Miss Parkins on Ward B as a patient tonight, my résumé must necessarily be shorter than I should desire.

"You were sent for because there have been committed in the Elijah Wilson Hospital within the last week two traceable murders, proved by autopsy findings, and two deaths . . . in the same bed. The deaths (we presume them murders also) preceded the murders. The last person murdered was a nurse who volunteered to go into the bed in an effort to solve the mystery."

Mr. Higgins moved restlessly.

"I know we have been slow in calling you in, Mr. Higgins. But this decision was only reached after a series of long and irascible conferences, and frankly I was against it, until the nurse was murdered.

"A hospital, you see . . . a great hospital . . . lives, breathes, exists, as a fountain of hope. It is trusted by *everybody*. For more than forty years the Elijah Wilson has lived up to that trust. We have received endowments, and large ones, to add units to our plant for the teaching of medical students. We were started, have been perpetuated, and are famous as a great teaching hospital.

"Now a teaching hospital, Miss Parkins, exists upon the fact that it has more patients than beds. When you have that situation reversed, the hospital is doomed. D'y'see?"

The three people nodded, and Dr. MacArthur continued:

"If any of you three walked out of this room and gave to the press of this country the information I have just given you in the last five minutes, you would automatically ruin the future of every medi-

cal man, resident, student and interne here, the
hope of renewed health in a very large portion of
suffering humanity, the years and painstaking
labor of many famous men, now dead, whose lives
were given, as bricks are given, to the building of
this hospital's justified fame.

"It has been upon the complete realization of
that grave responsibility that our hesitation was
based. I admit that we were mistaken, but our situation was so unexpected, so unparalleled, and so
terrifying, that we dared not alter one straw for
fear of losing our needle in this great haystack.
There are at least fifteen people who may have
been guilty of this crime. If they suspect . . . ?"

"Have you any suspects, sir?"

"Yes, Mr. Higgins. That was why I finally succumbed to sending for the best detectives that this
country has to offer. My nursing and medical staffs
are beginning to suspect themselves . . . and each
other. . . ."

"I see! I see, Doctor."

"All four patients were nursed and attended by
the same staff members?"

"Yes, Miss Parkins."

"Then I suggest, in fact, request, sir," Mr. Higgins intervened, "that you do not tell us who your
suspects are. It will cloud our work. An open mind
and a lack of tradition. . . . Oh, no. Doctor, . . .
we are completely aware of that and will guard it,

sir, with our lives. . . . I am referring to personal tradition with reference to staff members. . . .

"A lack of belief in the honesty of any man we contact because he is famous, or brilliant, or noted, will be one of the most invaluable things we can have.

"Now to return to the murders. What do the autopsy findings show, exactly?"

"That they were committed with the same drug. Coniine, the active principal of hemlock. Administered hypodermically and in the first case which took effect in a little over an hour and in the second case within less than forty minutes. The second dose, that given the nurse was much larger. Our chief pharmacist has checked the supply sources. We have never had any coniine in the hospital, and it can be secured from only three houses in the country. None of them reports recent sales. We have wired all three.

"Who, qualified to administer a hypodermic, had access to the patients?" Mr. Higgins' voice was low and sudden.

Dr. MacArthur's was clear and calm.

"The entire nursing and medical staff practicing upon that floor."

Mr. Smooty sat blankly by. Miss Parkins took her second cigarette from her mouth and asked:

"Are the hypodermics compounded in the pharmacy?"

"No. On the floor. By the nurse on duty, acting only upon prescription from the attending physician. The medicine closets on the ward . . . and every floor of that building . . . have been searched after each murder. They reveal nothing."

"When were the murders discovered?"

"At night, Miss Parkins. After midnight rounds made by the student nurse. Perhaps I had better give you a full picture. The ward contains thirty beds, in four rows, each seven being separated by a glass partition. The two extra beds are in rooms for dying patients. Each ward has a day white (graduate) nurse, and four student nurses on duty. Their duty changes as to hours are not important to this case.

"The white nurse goes off duty for the night at seven, and leaves her instructions with two student nurses who prepare the ward for the night, and go off duty at nine, when a single student nurse (bringing the total of student nurses to five) usually a pupil within the last six months of training, comes on and "beds the ward down" for the night and remains on duty until seven the following morning. It is her business to give all night hypodermics and medicines, and make regular rounds upon the patients to see how they are. On the ward with her is an orderly, who runs any sudden errands and helps with any manual labor. He usually remains in the ward-kitchen washing dishes and preparing

the breakfast trays and cleaning the ward corridors, etc. The orderly on this ward has been there
twenty years, and is not capable of any remarkable murder. A trusted menial. He has been ordered
into bed, as a suspected typhoid carrier, tonight,
and it is his position which you are to fill, Mr.
Smooty."

An imperceptible nod was Mr. Smooty's only
acknowledgment.

Dr. MacArthur continued:

"Over the entire building at night there is a night
supervisor who makes floor rounds upon the student
nurses in charge and is available in case they get
into difficulties."

"Where was she during the murders, Doctor?"

"During the first one, in the lavatory, Miss
Parkins, and during the second her telephone did
not answer and she was making rounds in the
building."

"I see. The student nurse. . . ?"

"Don't go into her," Mr. Higgins ordered.
"Take her with an open mind. You and Smooty
tell us about her tomorrow."

Higgins leaned forward and asked:

"Any way to enter the ward, except by the corridor?"

Dr. MacArthur hesitated a moment; his eyes
narrowed suddenly.

"I hadn't thought of it, sir, but there is. In the

rebuilding, the porch of each floor, upon which the convalescent patients are rolled, is connected with the porch of the floor below by a narrow concrete stairway. Wide enough to permit a stretcher, as a matter of fact. Satisfies fire regulations and does away with fire-escapes."

Higgins nodded.

MacArthur continued:

"But the door to that porch is always locked at night. The key is on the inside. All of our combined evidence points to an entry via the ward corridor."

Higgins nodded again.

Then to Dr. MacArthur he said:

"Outside of the autopsy findings are there any pieces of evidence which re-occur after the murders, Doctor?"

"Yes. After the first, the student nurse claimed that she felt someone on the floor, but was boiling a syringe and could not leave and that a patient said it was. . . ."

Mr. Higgins stopped him.

"That is just what I do not want to know."

"Anything else?" Miss Parkins insisted.

"For six months, Mr. Higgins, we have had on that ward a little girl, a chronic nephritis . . ." he looked over his glasses and explained to Miss Parkins, "a kidney ailment of a very stubborn sort. . . . She is really pretty and quite a favorite throughout the hospital. Upon her crib, the morning after the first traceable murder she found a doll."

He opened his desk drawer and took out the Ma-ma doll. Miss Parkins reached for it to straighten the bonnet, and it howled. She turned it over quickly and Mr. Smooty said, "Jesus Christ!"

It was the first response he had made to any of the information. Mr. Higgins ignored it and said, "Finger-prints?"

"It had been handled by many people when we got it, sir."

"Yes. Of course. After the second murder, Doctor?"

"There was no doll upon her bed, but this doll was found. . . ." and he reached for the Pa-pa doll and handed it to Mr. Smooty, whose green eyes were like pin points.

"Where, Doctor?" his voice was again colorless.

But his interest was so concentrated that he forgot and turned the doll over and it whined, "Pa-pa."

Everybody jumped and Mr. Higgins reached for both of them and laid them on the mahogany table upon their backs. They closed their eyes and Miss Parkins looked at the crisp bonnets, dresses and panties and shivered.

Two dolls. Two murders.

"I think we should know where it was found, Doctor," Mr. Higgins' voice was firm.

"In the desk of the Head Nurse of Medicine Clinic, sir. A doctor looking for case charts discovered it, accidentally."

"Is she friendly with the night student nurse?" It was Smooty who spoke.

"She is her aunt, gentlemen," and then Dr. MacArthur cleared his throat and continued, "She was one of the first head nurses when the hospital was young. Her work has always been well executed. A very trusted woman."

"Especially antagonistic to any doctor?"

"Yes."

"Whom?"

"The head of the clinic, Dr. Ethridge Sterling, Junior, affectionately known as "Cub" Sterling. He is on probation, very confidentially, as head. The physician-in-chief died of a heart attack last spring, and Dr. Sterling, who has done very brilliant work, has temporarily his chief's place. His father is Dr. Ethridge Sterling, possibly you have heard . . . ?"

"The surgeon. Bear Sterling! I should say so!" Higgins responded. "Why is the head nurse antagonistic?"

"I do not know. Perhaps because she is getting old and is afraid of retirement if Sterling remains in charge."

"I see. Pretty ugly situation you have been in, sir."

"It isn't I, it's the hospital. Dr. Ethridge Sterling, Senior, is dying of a heart attack complicated by pneumonia brought on by this situation. One of our graduate nurses has been murdered. . . . Frankly, your coming shifts a great weight from my shoulders. And I should like to say if I have failed to make anything clear, question me. We are all a bit shell-shocked, I dare say."

"Yes, there is, Doctor. Did Dr. Sterling, Senior, see all of the murdered patients, too?"

"He did. He performed the autopsies on all except the last one. The nurse."

"Has any person been murdered since he has been out of the picture?"

Mr. Higgins' weight was behind his words.

"I don't believe I understand you, Mr. Higgins," Dr. MacArthur gripped his chair arms, and his sensitive mouth looked like blistered flesh.

Mr. Higgins ignored that and attacked his eyes.

"Sorry, Doctor, but that is exactly the reason you sent for us. To understand things. Please answer my question."

"He was taken with double pneumonia last night, and Rose Standish was murdered last night. The bed is empty now."

"But he saw her and left a sleeping potion of which you told Dr. Bridgman over the 'phone and after that was administered she was murdered?"

"Please, Mr. Higgins," Dr. MacArthur's knuckles were white against the desk, "I have learned that potion was . . . bread-pills. . . . He had hoped to calm her nerves and yet leave her capable of catching. . . . I would swear before God that Dr. Sterling. . . ."

"Of course you would, sir," there was admiration in Mr. Higgins' response, "but painful operations are often necessary, and since he is the only person who has retired from the case, since the beginning, I am obliged to know what developments have taken place since his retirement. It's like chess, Doctor, your moves depend upon your position."

Dr. MacArthur had regained complete control of himself and Miss Parkins had risen and poured out a glass of water from a thermos bottle upon the mantelpiece which she was holding out to him. She smiled and said:

"It's been a long strain and you have stood it magnificently. Is there anything else you wish to tell us before Smooty and I go?"

Her strength passed through him and he straightened himself, and Mr. Higgins said:

"If brought in as an accident, what are the chances of Miss Parkins being put in this bed . . . number . . . ?"

"Eleven."

The eyes of the other three people were upon Higgins, inquiringly.

"Why?"

"Because, Doctor, in view of the information I now have in hand relative to the head nurse and her niece . . . by the way, what are their names?"

"Kerr. K-e-r-r."

Only Mr. Smooty's lips fought to remain a straight line. The concentration of the other three was too intense to notice the expression.

Mr. Higgins placed his gray eyes upon Dr. MacArthur's blue ones and continued:

"If Miss Parkins goes on the ward in a routine way as a patient, she will automatically be suspected by them and therefore become less valuable to us. But if she falls upon the street with a heart attack within four blocks of the hospital, arrives at the accident room entrance in an ambulance, and is admitted to Ward B, Bed 11. . . . You see?"

"Perfectly."

"Can we be sure that she will be placed in Bed 11, sir? That the staff in the accident room will admit her for medical treatment and that she will be sent to that floor and put in that bed?"

"A moment and I'll see." Dr. MacArthur reached for his telephone and said:

"Superintendent of nurses, please. Miss Carruthers? Dr. MacArthur. Will you please ascertain for your *own* information the vacant beds in

Medicine Clinic and their location, and call me back immediately? Thank you."

He turned to Miss Parkins and said:

"What kind of ailment is it? How bad?"

"It's a false angina, and during the attacks causes extreme palpitation. By intense excitement I can create a definite change in my heart action, and the other symptoms are permanent."

"I see. Given you much trouble?" MacArthur was solicitous.

The telephone interrupted.

He answered and took his pencil, wrote upon a memorandum pad and repeated:

"Medicine, Ward A—7 & 8, Ward B—11, and 5th floor, rooms 502 & 514. Thank you."

"An unknown accident case, with a heart ailment, Mr. Higgins, picked up on the street and admitted through the accident room, would undoubtedly be placed in Bed 11, Ward B. Ward A, which has two vacant beds, is medical men, and floor five is private rooms. You are too well-dressed, though, Miss Parkins."

"If her pocketbook contained only one dollar and she had no addresses upon her person, Doctor?"

"They would not take a chance on someone paying for a private room, Mr. Higgins. You are right. The only chance is whether she can pass the accident staff, as I see it."

"That is a chance we have to take," Mr. Higgins decided.

He looked at his wrist watch and said:

"One more question, Doctor, and then, with your permission I should like to have some private place where I may talk to Mr. Smooty and Miss Parkins before we turn Miss Parkins out upon the street and you take Mr. Smooty to the head orderly.

"Two more questions, now I think of it. The first: How is the hysteria throughout the hospital? The second: You expect, of course, that Mr. Smooty will be suspected as a detective?"

"Since the last question has the shortest answer, I will go to that first. That seems to me unavoidable, Mr. Higgins, and perhaps will work to our advantage. It will focus attention, from the nursing, medical and menial staffs, upon one person.

"As to the hysteria in the hospital. It is at a dangerous level and rising hourly. Not among the patients, yet . . . Thank God! . . . with the exception of the patients on Ward B and they have been told that Miss Standish, the nurse, hemorrhaged (we put her in as a tubercular suspect) and although they probably believe her dead, they have no proof. And their attention has been diverted by the terrible condition of Dr. Sterling, Senior. He has always been a great favorite throughout the wards. Patients love him. The other patients, on the other wards are too segregated and many of them too dangerously ill to be excited or aware of the situation.

"According to Miss Carruthers, our superintendent of nurses, to whom I was just talking, the hysteria among the nursing staff is serious. Before the death of the nurse they took the excitement mildly, with the exception of the people in Medicine Clinic who were questioned.

"With the exception of the General Staff, the toxicologist, the chief pharmacist, and the staff of Medical Clinic, no persons in the hospital have any definite knowledge as to whether these patients are murders or fadeouts.

"Perhaps it is that lack of knowledge which has so increased the fever heat among the medical staffs. They suspect, but they *do not know*. And half knowledge, and especially around a hospital. . . ."

He threw his hands out hopelessly.

"Since the death of the nurse, the entire medical and nursing services have been at a breaking point. Their internal pressure can be felt in every dining room. Something must be done and done immediately. That is one of the reasons I approve of the word getting around that a detective has been put on Ward B at night. . . ."

"A wise attitude, Doctor. Now if you will be so kind as to give us a private room and a few minutes?"

"I suggest you use my office and allow me to retire. After Miss Parkins has gone, I will show you a room in which you and Mr. Smooty may meet, when you desire. A laboratory in an unfrequented part of the hospital."

He rose wearily and passed out of the door and closed it carefully behind him.

Mr. Higgins lit a cigarette and turned to the other two.

"What do you make of it?"

He questioned both of them in one sentence.

Miss Parkins answered, "He's square. But he is shielding someone."

Mr. Smooty inserted his sentence at the end of hers. "Honest as the King. But worried sick. There is somebody he considers innocent, that the others have dots on. All I got to say is somebody around here is crazy as hell."

Mr. Higgins, who had never been sick a day in his life and never slept in a hospital even so much as one night, had a healthy man's antagonism for the medical profession.

"Toughest job we've ever had. He's square all right, but how the hell can you catch a murderer in a hospital? You are right, Snod. Somebody around here is crazy as a tick. And lots of people are lying. One thing you got to remember is you are up against professional liars. All nurses and doctors are professional liars. Didn't one tell me my mother was 'doing nicely' when she had been dead an hour? So watch everybody in the same way you watch a spy.

"He's also covering somebody that everybody else believes guilty. I think I know whom he is covering. But that'll wait. He suspects that head nurse and her niece. That's plain as day. And he didn't tell the truth about why he thinks she is doing it. There's somebody behind them, in his mind."

He stopped for a moment to draw breath and Miss Parkins flipped her cigarette and said:

"Matt, I'd like a gun, if you don't mind?"

"You scared, Lil?"

"No. I'm never scared. Especially when I have a gun."

"Don't be a fool, Lil." He put his big square hand over her capable one.

"They'll strip you to the bone when you go through that accident racket. A gun is out of the question. You'll have Snod." He motioned to Mr. Smooty.

She smiled but she wasn't reassured.

"He is slow as hell about wiping dishes when you are having a Sunday night supper. I couldn't get him out of that kitchen till I'd been dead hours."

Smooty's green eyes took on life for the first time since he had entered the room. He said.

"A hospital's duty is to protect everybody. I'll

be a member of a hospital staff in twenty minutes,
Lil."

She shrugged her square shoulders and her
limpid eyes begged.

"The murderer is a member of the hospital staff,
Snod. He'll beat you to it."

Higgins intervened.

"For God's sake, Lil! Hold on to yourself!"

"It's those damn dolls," she laughed.

Higgins smiled strongly into her eyes and threw
his overcoat over the dolls. "There's enough hysteria around here as it is. Don't add to it. Unless
Snod has something to say I guess you might just
as well sneak out and do your fainting fit. Want
me to send you flowers when you get sick, little
girl?"

"Hush, Matt. Flowers are not funny in this
case."

She opened her handbag and took out three
hundred dollars in fifty dollar bills and counted
them carefully. Beside them she laid the cards of
a speakeasy on West 11th Street and of one on
44th. She opened the zipper center of the black
alligator bag and took from it her identification
card with the agency and the picture of a man
in an officer's uniform of the British Intelligence.
Near these she spread a large white silk handkerchief into which she scooped the outlay, and then
removed from her wrist a large sapphire and dia-

mond wrist watch. She closed the bag, first counting the money remaining. One dollar bill and three
dimes and a nickel. Then she tied the contents of
the bag in the large silk handkerchief and handed
it to Higgins.

He took it carefully and put it in his coat pocket.

"Going, Lil?" His gray eyes looked up into her
limpid ones confidently.

"Now. See you later."

She opened the door and disappeared.

Miss Evelina Kerr, student night nurse on Ward
B, Medicine Clinic, shook down the thermometer
and inserted it into the mouth of the new patient
in Bed 11, with an air of relief, and just a touch
of condescension.

"Good evening. Have you remembered your
name?"

Miss Lillian Parkins weakly shook her head
and her eyes were sad.

Miss Kerr, who had been over the clothes in the
locker, knew that the coat was expensive and the
fur good, but that she had no money, so gave her
her "free patient" smile and passed on.

Lillian Parkins lay inert and tried to clear her
mind. A long plane trip, then the terrible strain
of appearing ill before the prying eyes of two
internes and that little Jewish resident doctor had
left her weak as dishwater. A touch of straight

scotch was what she needed. . . . It was damn hard to relax and veil your eyes and yet see everything. Still that was the game, that was what made the job so . . . fascinating!

That girl's eyes were too close, and there was an ugly sense of triumph when she had found her in the bed, and a nasty condescension, and a dead voice, creepy kind of! Somewhere she had seen a woman who moved like that with a voice like that, a stubborn little mind like that who . . . who . . . hands like snakes, or bananas, who . . . was it?

She closed her eyes to keep the life out of them, and began to check cases. On the Leviathan last year, in that Welfare Island group in May, doing that route collecting for pimps on the Southern circuit? No! None of those, but somewhere within the last eighteen months. . . .

Ah, she had it. That medium who worked for the hypnotist in the side-show and peddled dope in the circus. That vicious little adder who had tried to throw acid in her eyes when she caught her with the goods. Whew! Lord!

The goose-flesh began to stand out on her arms and legs. That's who she was, the same automaton voice, the same kind of little snake, out working for a python and she had to face her without so much as an automatic and go to sleep while she was doing it. Not go to sleep. Not on your life. Feign sleep! Feign sleep for ten hours, and then somehow manage not to have a real heart attack and pass out honest!

Swell job this was! Lots of fun! If she could get her hands on Matt Higgins now! Somehow she had to have a word with Snod. And quick!

Around her the monotonous conversation of the ward was droning, but since she was supposed to be too weak to talk, she closed her mind to it. Except for the realization that these women were afraid of the night. Had stood the day, but were afraid of the night and wanted to tell her about the bed. Wanted desperately to warn her . . . somehow. The lapping conversation and her own preoccupation made her unaware of Miss Kerr's return, until she felt the thermometer eased from her lips, and shivered.

Reptile who moved like that would have a hypodermic in you before you knew it.

She kept her eyes closed and pretended complete fatigue. Miss Kerr's pleasure at her presence seemed to increase. She said briskly and jubilantly:

"You'll be around before you know it. Your pulse and temperature are pretty good, considering. Your medicine will be along in a minute and then you can have a good night's sleep."

Miss Parkins opened her eyes feebly and gave her the fading lily smile. Miss Kerr returned it with the "miserable object" expression.

But had Miss Lillian Parkins been less of the

consummate actress, the glimpse of Snod Smooty, late of Scotland Yard and the British Intelligence, now arrayed in the nondescript white coat of a hospital orderly, and carrying, as a hotel porter might bags, an assortment of bed-pans, would have shattered her facial control.

He was on the ward before Miss Kerr had seen him. His face was as vacant as a concrete highway and his voice was as deferential as a butler's.

"Here you are, Miss."

The laughter of the women made Miss Kerr ease around, and when her slow eyes had taken in the situation, her routine mind exploded into wrath, remarkably spontaneous.

"Who told you to do that? You are not supposed to bring the bed-pans on the ward. I . . . I. . . ."

Smooty swallowed like a hurt child and one pan started slipping toward the floor. Miss Kerr slunk forward and caught it.

Mrs. Witherspoon spoke up:

"Don't be upset, Miss Kerr. We understands. And now thet he's here. . . ."

Miss Kerr looked appraisingly toward Mrs. Witherspoon and tried to deny her.

A very insistent telephone commanded her attention and threw her routine existence out of whack. She was told to prepare for a new patient and spent five minutes explaining to the night superintendent that the bed was already given to an accident room case and the patient would have to. . . .

The orderly took advantage of the opportunity and began handing out pans along the side of the ward where Miss Parkins lay. It was Mrs. Witherspoon's, "Pull the curtains. Pull the curtains. Quick!" which gave him an opportunity to speak to Miss Parkins unobserved.

He said, "How are you?"

"Scared."

"I'll watch her, close."

"Stick to her, Snod. For God's sake!"

His eyes came to life and strengthened her.

"She won't do anything tonight. She won't get around an old pan-handler like me. If you are scared as you say you are, you must have the. . . . Here's a pan!"

He thrust one at her and moved on.

Miss Kerr re-entered the ward and said crisply, "William."

"Horace, mam," he corrected as he handed the circus performer her pan.

The girl was disconcerted by the correction.

"Well, it doesn't matter, really. The thing that matters is that you are to stay off this ward unless I call you. There is plenty of work for you in the kitchen. Go down to Ward A and get me a syringe.

I've already called Miss Wilson about your coming."

Snod Smooty looked blankly up at the nurse.

"A hypo syringe?"

"Yes. Of course. Why?"

He thought he detected a slight dilation of her pupils, and replied carelessly:

"You see, Miss, at St. Giles, in London, we always called enemas syringes. I jus' needs to know, you see."

"Were you there, Horace?"

"I ain't braggin' Miss, but I was an orderly there four years. That's how come I brought the bed-pans; we done it that way!"

He threw his helpless hands out in an explanatory gesture and shambled down the corridor.

Miss Evelina Kerr sat down at her desk to regain her control. She should have gone on with the routine. But she sat down. Things weren't going so well. That man was a detective as sure as life and he was lying, and Aunt Roenna ought to know. . . .

She picked up the telephone and started to take the receiver from the hook, and then she jumped up and somehow smothered a scream.

Standing over her, peering down into her little, piggish eyes with his steel-gray slits was a tall, fat man, in a blue uniform with brass buttons. In his right hand he held a bunch of red American

Beauty roses, and the other was in a side pocket.

Miss Kerr thought he was a policeman and the left hand was upon his pistol holster. He carefully placed the roses in the elbow of the left arm, and with his right hand drew her out into the ward. His grip was strong and heavy.

By that time Miss Kerr had regained her breath. She tried to snatch her arm away and cringed when she failed.

"What do you want?"

"To shee the night nurse on Ward B."

"I'm the night nurse." Her voice still quaked.

Gripping her like a vice, he stuck his thick face into hers and the stench of his breath reached the whole ward.

"Y're not Rhosh Standziz! Where is Rosh?"

Then swaying as a top-heavy steamer might when tied to a brittle mooring, he turned to the ward and announced:

"I'se bin in luz wiz Rosh, scincz . . . sincz . . . sincz . . ." he shook his head helplessly and the motion seemed to straighten his tongue, temporarily . . . "I just came back from China Station. They said over the 'phone last night Rose was on Ward B." His voice clouded again. "Sho I brought her shum r . . . r . . . rhozes."

He laid the flowers upon a bed and took Miss Kerr's face in both of his hands. By that time every woman on the ward was sitting bolt upright regardless of her condition. A fly would have sounded like an airplane.

Crushing her face with his hands, he demanded: "Swhere iz Rosh? Zhu! Phoo! Zhu ain't Rosh!" and then his voice took on a hide-and-seek tenor.

And he crushed with more force, and they both swayed.

"Swherah . . . iz . . . Rosh?"

Lillian Parkins sat like a race horse at the starter. Every time he crushed the nurse, she thanked him . . . silently. . . .

He swayed horribly and they staggered.

He increased his grip and his voice was brutal.

"Stell me! St-ell me! Swhere iz Rosh?"

"Rose is dead!" Miss Kerr's voice had taken on life at last. Every woman in the ward heard her remark.

And it was Mrs. Witherspoon's horrible, scrunching scream that came like the brakes of a truck after an accident, which shocked the other women into silence and brought Horace, the new orderly, up the corridor on the run.

And with that scream the brain of Lieutenant Brady, U.S.N. disintegrated. He loosened his grip upon the student nurse and flung her to the floor.

"Rosh iz dead! Dead in a hoshbittle!"

He began skipping around as a child might and singing monotonously, "Ring aroun' de Roshy! Rosh's dead. Rosh's dead. Ring aroun' de Roshy."

Then he caught the approaching Horace out of the corner of his eye and laughed hollowly.

"Cash me!"

He began rolling under the patients' beds, playing a literal hide-and-seek with both the student nurse, who had staggered to her feet, and the nimble orderly who was saying in a loud voice.

"You are dead drunk! You . . . fool!"

The final scramble took place under the bed of Lillian Parkins and Miss Kerr ran to the telephone to call the night superintendent.

As Snod Smooty caught one foot of the big man and began pulling, Lillian Parkins leaned over the side of her bed and hissed:

"Don't let that bitch get within fifteen feet of me! Tell Matt that examination was worse than being looked over for a harem. If he doesn't get me out of here by tomorrow night, I'll walk out. Get the sailor out quietly, Snod. He loved that dead nurse."

Apparently paying no attention, Snod Smooty managed to keep the scramble loud enough to cover Miss Parkins' remarks.

He gave the sailor a little jujutsu and had him swaying down the corridor before Miss Kerr had found the night superintendent. They disappeared to the sailor's monotone which had sunk to the note of a child trying to lull himself to sleep.

"Ring aroun' de Roshy! Rosh's dead. Rosh's dead. Ring aroun' de Roshy!"

Snod Smooty carried him over his shoulder down the stairs and out of the side entrance. Upon the curb stone he stood him against a parked automobile and then socked him under the jaw. As he fell, Snod opened the automobile door and laid him out upon the back seat to sleep it off.

Snod's colorless face was tender and old. He wanted a cigarette. Worst scene he had ever witnessed and he'd seen some hellbenders in his day. But Lil was as hysterical as any of them.

He shrugged his shoulders and re-entered the building. That was the trouble with women. They made good detectives, where men were to be caught, but with women . . . !

It was Mrs. Witherspoon's second and blood freezing scream that made Dr. Mattus close his mind to his own bad heart and forget to button his fly.

The piercing horror of her high agonized wail hung over the corridor like poison gas. He tore through it and the effort made his knees tremble.

What was it? What terror had entered her soul?

When he reached her, she was sitting bolt upright, her weak eyes ablaze, and gazing with fixed horror at a large bunch of American Beauty roses which lay upon the foot of her bed.

»VIII«
The Control

MATTHEW HIGGINS LAID DOWN *The Morning Call* and smiled vaguely. It had been a long time since he was in the Middle West, and you got out of the way of remembering it. He finished his coffee, motioned for his check, paid it, leaned over the bar and said:

"That's the best coffee roll I ever had outside of Paul's."

Otto beamed and cocked his head slowly.

"Fank you! Fen I fus cum to dis country, I vork in Paul's. Two vyears."

Matt put his weight in his shoulders and his voice was admiring.

"Why did you come West?"

Otto began wringing his towel helplessly.

"Vell, my vivfe vus humsic, so I tried to make into a Jerman settl'ment . . . an'. . . ."

He stood silent a moment. All of his verve wilted.

Higgins interposed, "Any news around town?"

Otto peered over his glasses pleasantly.

"Ve reever made four inchers, las' night. Eif

she continuers. . . ." He threw out his hands. His face flashed sober and he drew his hands over his abdomen and said carefully:

"Docturr Bearr Sterlink is . . . dyin . . k."

Matt squared his shoulders and sat straight on the stool. He stretched his torso upward.

"Great man I guess . . . that Bear Sterling! Saved the lives of lots of people. . . !"

Otto reached over the counter and began carefully balancing the dishes and his words.

"Yess. Lots. Lots of people. But even great men half der veak spots. . . ."

Matt Higgins poised a spoon upon the saucer of the cup Otto was lifting.

"What do you mean . . . 'weak spots'. . . ?"

"Vell . . . ," Otto's conscience and his philosophy collided. He peered over his glasses again.

"Du . . . did you kno', Docturr Bearr Sterlink?"

Matt Higgins shook his head definitely.

"By reputation, only. What's his weak spot?"

Otto closed his lips completely and turned his back. When the dishes were safely deposited, he said:

"Sum men are veak vid de knife, sum aroun' de heart, sum like me, aroun' de stumack. . . ! Sum ven ve are young. . . . Sum ven ve are students. . . . Sum ven ve are in bed. . . ." He whirled quickly and threw out his hands. His head nodded the periods to his sentences.

"Ve all haf dem!"

An interne burst through the door and begged:

"Otto, gimme some coffee quick! Quick, Otto! Black!"

Matt Higgins noted the boy's blanched face and shaking hands.

Otto soothed:

"Fut vus hit, Docturr?"

The interne gulped the coffee and shook his head pleadingly.

Otto leaned across the counter and ordered:

"Fut . . . frightened you, Docturr?"

The boy put down the cup.

"Hell!" he strode toward the door, "I ain't frightened. It was a nigger baby with a severed head. It just got my guts . . . that's all. . . !"

When he was gone Otto turned to Matt Higgins, shrugged and smiled.

"Hiss iss . . . fear!" he said.

Then leaning upon the counter he asked:

"Vy did *you* cum Vest?"

Matt looked him straight in the eyes and replied:

"I'm a New York gangster, on vacation, come to see my kid brother interning at the hospital."

Otto perked his head.

"Maybe . . . I know him."

Matt Higgins shook his head.

"No. You couldn't know him. He's high-hat as hell. Only lets me see him half a day every six months. . . . He's my . . . weak spot!"

He slid from the stool and stepped aside. Four medical students jostled through the door.

Otto mopped his counter, slowly, thoughtfully, painstakingly.

Matt Higgins tipped his gray hat over his narrowed eyes, and went through the door.

That man knew something . . . but there was no use trying to get him to . . . .

He turned down Beeker Street and made his way over to Wilson Boulevard, one end of which was façaded by the Elijah Wilson group; the other was bounded by the River. He looked back over his shoulder to see if he could get a glimpse of anything denoting the river. Only a curling line of smoke from a ferry-boat.

The air was clear, still and comforting and the people all walked like New Yorkers. But the women didn't amount to much. No good legs. No poise. No New York verve.

He looked at his watch as he entered the tall iron gate and approached the main entrance. It was eight forty-five.

At the main entrance he took off his gray overcoat and stood back to let two nurses pass. They weren't much.

He passed the statue of Elijah Wilson, went on into the main corridor and turned to the left. He walked with the air of a man who knows where he is going and is not to be stopped by trifles. Long experience had taught him that demeanor could get one almost anywhere. Especially in a hospital.

Nurses and doctors passed, returning from breakfast. The faces of the lovelorn and the love-lettered were revealed by every passing window. Intermingled with all of these were a group of abnormally sad faces, and then he remembered that today was the day of that nurse's funeral. She'd been a pretty little thing, too. Her fragile little corpse had skipped rope in all of his dreams last night! He quickened his pace and his hairy hands were clenched in his pockets.

Halfway down the main corridor he stopped ostensibly to look from a window at the back garden of the hospital. He took in the approaching people in both directions at a glance. They were all of them distant enough to risk it.

He walked several feet further, began walking close to the wall, and faded into a door. The door opened into what had been the old laboratory building, and with the renovating of the hospital had been left vacant. The corridor was lighted by a series of tall windows at the far end. The brilliant morning sun sifted through them vaguely. The grime and dust of the panes and of the intervening corridor made its trickle thin and eerie.

Matthew Higgins closed the door softly and stood silently against it for a second, listening. Then he accustomed his eyes to the light and looked at the floor. In the center were the tracks he and Dr. MacArthur and Snod had made last night. On the far side were the tracks which he and Snod had agreed Snod should make this morning.

He shifted his hat upon the back of his head and began walking up the corridor next to Snod's morning tracks. Halfway up, he stopped and listened. Then he threw his overcoat over his shoulder and approached, cautiously, the door of the laboratory they had decided upon. On tiptoe. Silently. His weight was thrown forward with the expert training of a toe-dancer. Slowly, melting into it as he did so, he pushed open the door of the laboratory.

It was darker than the corridor. The outside window blinds had been closed for several years. He stood silently several seconds and then decided to chance a match. He took off his hat and struck it carefully in the shadow the hat provided. Then when it was well-lighted he lifted it and surveyed the room.

The dusty lab sinks, the rotting rubber hose, the two stools with their cane bottoms gone, and upon a bamboo couch in the corner Snod Smooty, his face totally devoid of expression, sleeping with the abandon of an infant.

As the match burned low in his fingers Matthew Higgins leaned over and watched Snod Smooty sleep. This was the first time in ten years he had known Snod to sleep with someone watching him.

The night must have been a swell affair! The smell of smoke reached Smooty's consciousness; he turned over suddenly and opened his eyes completely. His face was still blank with an effort to see in the darkness, and his voice came huskily:

"Matt?"

The answer was in keeping with the dimness. The match had burned out and Matt Higgins was killing it on the floor with his toe.

"Yeah. Wake up! Any news?"

Snod Smooty raised his slim body to a sitting posture and slung his thin feet to the grimy floor. He ran his left hand through his colorless hair and wiped out his eyes with the right palm.

"Cigarette?"

Matt Higgins took *The Morning Call* from his overcoat pocket and placed it over the hole in one of the stools. Over that he folded his overcoat and raised himself onto the stool.

"Better not. Watchmen or something. How was the night?"

Smooty put the unlit cigarette sullenly in his hip pocket and said sweetly:

"Hell all the time . . . and then some. . . . 'Bout ten a drunk naval officer-beau of the dead nurse brought her a bouquet of red roses, darling. Thought she was doing duty on the ward. Didn't know about her death. Shook the guts outa that student nurse when she told him and then began playing hide-and-seek under the patients' beds with me."

"The devil!"

"Yeah, himself! I got him outa the hospital, socked him, and tucked him into a parked car to sleep it off. Went over him first, though. William Brady, U. S. N. Loot. J. G.

"Then I went back to the ward. And he had left the roses on the bed of one old blattering fool and she took it that she's next to go and can she scream! So loud the others couldn't make a squeak. Well, the Jew doctor got there and a mess of nurses and hen medics and give them all a bromide and then they needed bed-pans again . . . and then . . . they had to have a drink of water. And then another bed-pan around. Like salt and pepper, you know. Now I see why the Waldorf makes money. Pay toilets for ladies."

"And Lil?" Matt's voice was demanding.

"Lil's lost her nerve, Matt. Swears if you don't get her outa there by this afternoon, she's going to walk out. Says the examination she had to get in that damn bed was just like being frisked naked.

During pan-rounds we had some conversation.

"She's took it into her head that that student nurse, the niece of the head nurse, is doing the murders. She's took it that the girl is like that moll she caught in the circus last spring (she says you know which one) working for a hypnotist and selling dope. Damn if Lil ain't decided that the head nurse of the clinic, Miss Kerr, who got her stout old tail up there before it was all over, ain't making her niece work for somebody . . . ain't both of them working for some control . . . who is having them murder patients."

"Lord God! That ties up, too. . . . Go on . . . finish your story."

"It's Lil's idea, Matt, that they are doing it because they hate young Sterling and are trying to ruin him, and get him out . . . and nothing I could say . . . between bed-pans and glasses of water . . . could change her mind a nits worth. When Lil is out of reach . . . you know what I mean . . . she's hard to reason with.

"And she's got the creeps bad as the rest of them, now, and told me if I let that little bitch come within fifteen feet of her the rest of the night she'd . . . .

"So after we'd gotten all them females quieted inside and out, I had to spend till seven this A. M. doing things that would keep me where I could see the nurse. Sweeping corridors and asking ques-

tions and messing up the guts of the electric refrigerator and, you know . . . having the hell of a
good time. . . ."

He threw out his hands futilely.

"Women who can walk and talk is bad enough,
but when they ain't got nothing to do, except lay
out in bed . . . thirty strong . . . I ain't been
this tired since I worked in a prison camp in Ger-
many in '16.

"That student nurse and her aunt suspect me,
too. And I had to put up some alibi about having
been a hospital orderly in London and when I was
always in the place I was told not to be, that was
the way . . . you know. . . . Lil says if I ain't
back on the ward by three this afternoon, time the
aunt usually makes floor rounds, pretending to be
learning the ways from the day orderly, she will
be outa there . . . and . . . you know. . . ."

"Good work, Snod." Higgins complimented, and
then ordered, "Good idea. Be back on by three.
Sleep here this morning. After last night, the
murderer will either strike quick, or lay off for
some time. I'll wire for another man this morning; but he may not get here until tomorrow. . . .
We'll have to do double time all around. . . ."

Snod's voice was flat and caustic.

"Yeah."

Higgins ignored it and said:

"After you went on, MacArthur and I had an-

other talk, and he took me to see the nurse's body.
Lovely thing. Seems this coniine can be prepared
synthetically but the toxicologist laughs off the
idea that it was. Too hard to do. And I brought
out that however prepared the first thing to do
was to stop the 'shots'. MacArthur agrees, but he
won't commit anybody. You were right. I told him
it's a crazy nurse or doctor and he had apoplexy.
He's straight. I like him. I'm to see the heads of
all departments today and see what I can find out,
unobserved. And I'll meet you here again at two-
forty, before you go back on the ward.

"If Lil's right, they are working for the psychiatrist, and if she's not, then it's the man Mac-
Arthur is shielding. See anybody last night took
your eye?"

"No. They were all too shocked. The murderer
wasn't there." Smooty, who had a habit of talking
"in character" was too interested to "think" as an
orderly. "The person in authority was the Jew and
he's white. Jew doctors are! Those Kerr women,
head nurse and student, took it too calmly."

"Want any breakfast?" Higgins asked from the
door.

"No. Just a bed-pan, please!"

Snod's voice fluted after him.

With the overcoat, Snod Smooty made himself
a pillow, and was asleep before Mr. Higgins had
retraced his steps halfway up the corridor.

When Higgins reached the place where the basement steps came up into the corridor of the vacant building, he struck another match, again under the protection of his hat and looked for the tracks he and Dr. MacArthur had made last night. Then he descended the steps and stood in the dark basement corridor. He stood erect, with his shoulders thrown back, listening. When the silence assured his mind and hurt his eardrums he began walking up the basement corridor, toward the entrance into the main service corridor, which ran directly under the main hospital corridor. He and Dr. Mac-Arthur had decided the best way to get out of the lab building would be through the service corridor, the door of which had a spring lock, and then up the service elevator to the main floor of the Administration Building.

The basement corridor was black as night, but totally dead. The worn-out odor of old chemicals mingled with that of damp plaster. The smell began to permeate his nostrils and made each creak of the sagging floor hit his brain like a pistol shot. The soft blackness closed in like a sweating fog.

He began to feel as a swimmer feels against strong tides. The door at the end of the corridor was diminishing as the door in *Alice in Wonderland*, or had it been Alice who diminished? He had just convinced himself that the last sound and the newest smell were caused by a leaking water tap and an escaping gas jet, when something struck his foot, ran up his pants' leg to his waist, and down the other side.

Rats!

He jumped with the agility of a fencing expert into an open door and threw up his arm automatically. He stood with his muscles flexed, listening and beginning to feel the beads of perspiration starting under his arms and trickling down his thighs.

And then he laughed at himself and tried to lower his arm. It wouldn't come. He tugged and he could feel his coat sleeve beginning to give. The tap continued its regular drip, drip, and his nerves became strung and he reached his free hand in his pocket and drew out a match and lit it upon the seat of his pants, regardless.

Then he saw the trouble instantly. His arm was caught by a long iron hook suspended from the ceiling. He looked around and saw the room was full of such hooks.

"Wuuh!"

The ejaculation came naturally. He was in the room where they had once hung the cadavers. His coat was caught upon a cadaver hook! And with the realization his reflexes began working automatically. He leaped and freed his arm and struck his head upon the ceiling.

Then he leaned against the wall and shivered.

The feel of the burning match against his flesh brought him to, like a pain.

"Fool!" he muttered reprovingly and his perspiring body was seared dry by a consuming shame. "Lighting matches in a basement with escaping gas and getting hysterical over rats. Get out of here!"

He regained the corridor and proceeded quickly in the direction of the door. When his hand was upon the handle he stopped for a moment to consider and get himself together.

Was Snod safe in this building? Had those feelings he had just been through been entirely hysterical or were they partly occasioned by the presence of the murderer, somewhere, in that basement?

He checked over it all step by step and decided that they were pure . . . might as well admit it . . . pure hysteria. An innate fear of dead people, which he knew perfectly well he had had ever since that boy in Mexico took so long to die when he shot him fifteen years ago. And he had glassed his eyes on him when he finally did go.

Nobody but Snod was in this building. A murderer left tracks just like any other man and he had examined all of the tracks.

You had to take a chance. . . .

He snapped the spring lock and stepped out into the service corridor. The door slammed behind him and he looked both ways.

The corridor was whitewashed and brilliantly lighted with electric lights, like a subway station. In the distance were two orderlies pushing two large laundry bins. They had their backs to him. In the other direction were three maids standing around a woman who was talking hurriedly and gesticulating wildly. They were standing in a knot and did not see him. He started to walk and as he lifted his foot it caught upon something. He looked down.

He had kicked a huge bunch of American Beauty roses from in front of the door. Somehow he side-stepped them and began making his feet rise, fall, and move.

Should he go back? Should he go on? Should he pick them up? The great thing was to keep moving . . . the great thing, and by the time he had begun moving he had decided to ignore the flowers . . . temporarily . . . and try to remember Mac-Arthur's directions. Past the print shop, past the laundry entrance, and then the first door to the left. . . .

He had accomplished the print shop when he discovered that walking beside him was a small faded woman, and she was carrying the roses. And then he decided to find out.

"Is this the main corridor of the hospital?" He had removed his hat and was giving her the "somebody's mother" treatment. "Pretty flowers!"

She began to gasp out respectfully:

"No, sir. Take the elevator there, Doctor," she pointed. "Pretty, ain't they? Miss Kerr told that maid," she pointed again toward a retreating figure, "to bring them over to the Nurses' Home for Miss Standish's funeral (she was of that simple class which believes everybody knows her acquaintances) and an orderly in the corridor told the maid. . . ."

The elevator door opened and Matt Higgins had learned all he needed to know, immediately.

He gave the woman his "silver threads among the gold" smile and asked the elevator boy:

"Is the main corridor above this?"

"Yes, sir. Lost? It's easy to get lost around here."

They reached the main floor and Matt Higgins stepped from the elevator and began walking toward the entrance from the main corridor to the Administration Building.

He was dead tired. . . .

But when he saw Dr. Henry MacArthur, through the open door of his office, he knew that whatever he had just been through he must hide.

The last man he had seen with that look of steely panic was the president of the bank in Wall Street during the first days of the 1929 collapse. That kind of panic was followed by icicles of fear in the brain and after that . . . .

"Good morning, Doctor," his voice was calm and confident.

With its tone, MacArthur's courtesy revived, but it was automatic. He rose with an obvious effort and motioned the detective to a chair, closed the door into the corridor, and offered Higgins a cigarette.

"Thanks."

Neither of them noted the brilliant sun upon the mahogany director's table, nor the glint it gave the diamond upon the finger of Elijah Wilson in the portrait hanging behind MacArthur's desk.

MacArthur re-seated himself, rubbed his eyelids listlessly and then, his blue eyes upon Higgins' gray ones, asked:

"You know about last night?"

Higgins nodded and replied:

"We must do something, Doctor. After that the murderer will either strike immediately, or wait indefinitely. In either case, we need a man on the ward day as well as night. May I call the agency now?"

"Why not use a local man?"

Higgins shook his head decisively.

"Too much depends on the man to take someone I am not sure of. With your permission?"

He reached for the telephone and MacArthur said, "You have it."

"New York. Digby 4-3872. Mr. Anderson.

James P. Anderson. Put it through right away, please."

He held the receiver and put his hand over the mouthpiece. Dr. MacArthur began pacing the room. He carried himself with a brittle straightness, and Higgins watched him closely while the girls were saying, "Indianapolis? Chicago? Hello Buffalo?" . . . and then . . . "New York?" and then Anderson's voice.

"Anderson?" Higgins knew the voice immediately. "Higgins. Can you get Rogers on the Westbound mail plane in twenty minutes? Then the other plane and he'll have to change at Chicago, or charter a plane from there. Yes, shaping up. No news yet. Good! O.K."

MacArthur wheeled.

"He will be here this afternoon?"

Higgins pushed the telephone over upon the desk.

"If he makes the plane leaving in twenty minutes. Otherwise about eight tonight. Next to Smooty I'd rather have him than any man on the force.

"Smooty passed himself off as an orderly from a London hospital and will go back on at three to watch things and learn the Elijah Wilson routine from the day orderly. So you can rest easily, as to the vigilance, Doctor."

His voice, like his person, was strong and commanding.

Dr. MacArthur slackened his pace and Higgins continued:

"Doctor, Miss Parkins thinks that the head nurse and her niece are mediums murdering for some control . . . some doctor. . . ."

Dr. MacArthur sat down suddenly and an imperceptible shadow of relief passed over his graven face.

Last night he would have exploded at the mere mention of such an idea, while this morning. . . .

His voice was old and unconvinced.

"I don't believe it, Higgins. I have known doctors by the thousand. Good. Bad. And indifferent. But I do not believe any doctor. . . ."

"A crazy doctor?"

MacArthur threw up his hands helplessly.

"A crazy somebody, yes. But not a doctor. . . ."

Higgins decided to pass up the point and continued:

"Whoever it is must be caught quickly. I suggest we give up the idea of putting me through as a patient. Last night it appeared feasible but I spent most of the night thinking, and I feel certain, Doctor MacArthur, that after the episode on the ward, we must hasten everything. Put me through the hospital as a member of the administrative staff of some distant hospital. Thereby I get a chance to see the heads of every department, including the Psychiatrist, and the Physician-in-Chief. . . ."

Dr. MacArthur winced. Then that was the man! Higgins continued, placidly, "And decide who I must question, and also permit me . . . if necessary . . . to get about the hospital suddenly. After last night. . . ."

Dr. MacArthur interrupted him. His panic was welling up.

"I'll agree to anything . . . almost, Mr. Higgins. After last night action is vital. Tomorrow is visiting day throughout the hospital. By tomorrow night relatives of every patient on that ward will know that Rose Standish was murdered! And we cannot avoid their knowing it. If we close the ward to visitors . . . we have never in all the years the hospital has been in existence done . . . that! Public confidence is our greatest asset. Has been. What shall we do? The newspapers, the police, the reputation of the hospital, d'y'see?"

"Too well, sir."

But the tension was wearing itself out in speech and Dr. MacArthur went on:

"The hysteria among the nursing and medical staffs was bad enough, God knows, but before today is over, we must face the hysteria manifesting itself among the menial staff. How can a hospital run without orderlies, electricians, cooks? If the menials become hysterical . . .?"

"They already are, Doctor. When I came out of the basement entrance of the old lab building into the service corridor fifteen minutes ago, my feet caught upon a bunch of red roses."

"What?"

"I said, sir, my feet caught . . ."

"I heard you. Where did they come from?"

"They had been dropped, Doctor, by a maid who had been ordered by Miss Kerr, the head nurse in Medicine Clinic, to take them over to the Nurses' Home for the funeral of Miss Standish. An orderly told the maid where they came from. . . ."

"God!"

The panic re-entered Dr. MacArthur's eyes and Higgins took advantage of it.

"You are right about time, Doctor. It's everything. To save time I must have every atom of knowledge which you have. Last night I hoped to work independently, but now. . . ."

He leaned forward and shot his gimlet gray eyes into the horror stricken ones of MacArthur.

"Is the man everybody but you suspects, young Sterling?"

MacArthur's groan was evidence.

"Well, I thought so. Last night you suggested I question him last on account of his father."

MacArthur's fight seemed suddenly to return and he shot back:

"This morning I demand it. His father will be

dead by midnight. I appreciate your position, but I must ask you to respect my wishes. Have you given up the idea that Bear Sterling is implicated?"

"No, sir. But we cannot await another murder to clear him."

"Precisely. Nor anybody else, Mr. Higgins. I see that. But I also see that if Cub Sterling does not leave his father's side today and is not questioned until after his death, supposing . . . the other . . . to be correct . . . you will have not lost anything. They must all be checked, automatically, since you believe the murderer is a crazy doctor. Check them today, Mr. Higgins. And if. . . ."

He rose and began to pace the floor, and his figure was more than erect. It was almost illuminated.

"You belong, sir, to that type of man which can appreciate trust between strong men. Between Cub Sterling and his father such a trust has always existed. Within twenty hours it will be broken and . . . why, Mr. Higgins, if you wish, I shall sit outside the door of the room in which he is fighting for Bear's life, from now until you release me. . . . But my position . . . d'y'see?"

"I do, and I respect you for it, Doctor. But the two men who have attended all of the dead patients were the Doctors Sterling. Regarding the ques-

tioning, I shall do as you desire, provided, sir, that
when the superintendent of nurses takes me to
Medicine Clinic, you will insist that Dr. Cub Sterling accompany us over the clinic, in precisely the
same manner in which the other men are to do.
Thereby I can at least judge the man. Otherwise
I throw up the case, here and now. My position
would be hopeless, if I were to be denied at least
a summary . . . not made through the eyes of
personal esteem and family fame . . . of one of
the two chief suspects. Perhaps it is brutal to put
it so, but the chief suspect in the eyes of the nursing
and menial staffs."

"I know it, Higgins. I'll do as you wish."

His voice and his face were parched and sad.

Their eyes locked again and Higgins said:

"You brought me here to find the criminal. In
many things we shall have to fight each other.
Mainly because all evidence points to a crazy doctor and you cannot accept the evidence. Somehow
I'm glad you can't, Doctor."

Higgins stretched out his large hairy hand and
Dr. MacArthur gripped it firmly.

Then MacArthur looked at his watch and
reached for the telephone.

"Superintendent of nurses, please."

"Miss Carruthers? Dr. MacArthur. Will you
please come over to my office immediately?"

As he hung up, he seemed to have regained his old authoritative manner.

"About Miss Standish's funeral. Do you think it worth your while to attend? Would a murderer of this type go to the funeral of a person he had murdered?"

"Hardly, Doctor. What time is it?"

"Four-fifteen."

"The Kerrs?"

"Have both asked to come."

"Then I will."

They were interrupted by a knock upon the door and the figure of Miss Carruthers.

Dr. MacArthur rose and smiled her into a chair.

"May I present Mr. Immerheld, Miss Carruthers. He is on the administrative staff of the Cornell Medical Centre, and I want him to see the Elijah Wilson. He came unexpectedly and this morning I am upset about Dr. Sterling. Mr. Immerheld used to know Dr. Sterling . . . and understands. . . . Will you please take him around, and see that he sees the heads of all clinics? Cornell has been very kind about approving our rebuilding plans and Mr. Immerheld has been a great prop . . . to the hospital. His advice. . . ."

Miss Carruthers smiled politely at Matthew Higgins, and rose.

"I shall be delighted, Dr. MacArthur."

Her voice, body and face were brittle, and at

the same time authoritative. She was the spun-glass skeleton of what had been a buxomly commanding woman.

"May I leave my hat, Doctor?"

Higgins rose and stood beside Miss Carruthers; as he opened the door, he gave her the "silver threads among the gold" look and she took it as sand does water.

Dr. MacArthur's voice halted their pleasant unity.

"By the way, Miss Carruthers. Will you be so good as to telephone Miss Kerr just before you go to Medicine Clinic? I am especially anxious for Mr. Immerheld to meet Ethridge Sterling. Go over the building with him. He knew Dr. Bear when he was . . . ."

His voice faded and hers filled the gap.

"Certainly, Dr. MacArthur."

And as they started up the corridor, her words floated back:

"As a great teaching hospital, Mr. Immerheld, the Elijah Wilson has always . . . ."

"Been free from crazy doctors." Dr. MacAuthur thought and his hands pounded his desk . . . hopelessly.

"What are you smoothing my bed for?" Lil Parkins' voice was irritable. She had been awake for twenty hours now and her nerves were fraying.

"Rounds." Miss Kexter, the day white nurse, was brisk and snappish. These murders were beginning to get on her nerves. Not that she was scary. Or that she had liked Rose Standish. But just the same, those roses against her face, when she had gone to breakfast, and gone up to "look at her," left the stomach kind of. . . . And then "Foots" Kerr was trying to behave. . . .

Lil Parkins looked her over casually and decided that she was out of it. Spineless as a stick of cooked macaroni and . . . and . . . .

The conversation in the ward had died and all of the women were either sitting or lying respectfully still. Dr. Cub Sterling, Dr. Mattus had telephoned, was going to leave his dying father and come down to see how they were.

The lull was welcome to Lil Parkins and she felt, suddenly, for a few hours at least, she was safe and free to just relax a little.

She awoke to find a tall, angular man with bushy hair leaning over her and saying, "Pretty fair. Considering. Strengthened in the night?"

The Jew doctor, who had admitted her, stood beside the tall man whose left shoulder was cocked at a queer angle.

"Good bit, Dr. Sterling. When she came in . . ." he slid off into medical terms and Lil Parkins' face took on one of its flashes of sudden intensity and Cub Sterling's responded. His response was slow and he was tired, but his eyes were gorgeous and his hands were soothing.

"Pretty tired, weren't you?"

The question was put in the voice one used with a social equal and Lil Parkins knew she really liked him. He recognized that she wasn't just "another free patient."

"Has your name come back?"

He had straightened up and stood at the foot of her bed looking kindly into her eyes. With a supreme effort, Lil knew that she must manage to act, really act!

She shook her head slowly, and her face faded blank again.

"It will," he said confidently. "What you needed was rest. How did you get that scar?"

He pointed to one halfway up her left forearm and Lil, mesmerized by his eyes, actually told the truth.

"In the circus. Trapeze work."

"With that heart!" his voice carried both reprimand and admiration, "What circus?"

"Ringling Brothers."

"You did!"

The heart case two beds up was sitting boldly erect. "You don't say? An old trouper! Well, I'll be doggone! Ringling Brothers, too! Top-notcher ain't you, kid? Is Fred Bradna still ringmaster? How far out did you get last year? Playing Texas this spring? Is Old Bill, the bull elephant, you know . . . still alive. . . .?"

Dr. Cub Sterling laughed spontaneously and every woman in the ward smiled.

"You'll have to wait till she's better. And then she'll remember everything."

His voice was crisp and final. The other doctors had passed on and were discussing Mrs. Witherspoon's condition. Cub Sterling joined them, but he turned suddenly and smiled into the limpid, waiting eyes of Lil Parkins.

"Go to sleep!"

His lips formed the words noiselessly, and her tension snapped and her eyes began to close, listlessly.

Cub started toward Room Two. Mattus' voice halted his steps. Mattus said:

"She's all right, Doctor! Slept clear through it! I just saw her ten minutes ago. Your father's latest tank of oxygen is half gone, sir. Do you wish me . . .?

Cub nodded silently and walked down the corridor toward the waiting elevator.

»IX«
The Third Doll

"Roll 'em up, Snod! Time to get up!"

Snod opened his eyelids narrowly and then closed them again. He began experimenting slowly with his head, burying his chin in his long neck and stretching his shoulder muscles.

"Any news?" his voice was still somnambulant.

"Lots! Got your wits about you?" Matt Higgins began pulling himself up on one of the stools and his voice was grating. The old deserted laboratory building was on the side of the hospital where no afternoon sun ever penetrated. It was now inky black in the room.

"Where do you think my wits would be? In this feather bed?" Snod replied sarcastically, raising himself to a sitting posture, and rubbing his aching neck with his hands.

"Stinks like a skunk in here!" Snod stood up carefully and walked toward one of the dusty lab sinks. He turned on the tap and stuck his head under it.

"Men have it over women in lots of ways," he

said as he took his handkerchief from his pocket and wiped his dripping face. "What's the dope, Matt?"

"After you went back to sleep I went to Mac-Arthur and he was as frightened as an old maid in a harem. All up in the air . . . hundreds of feet. Said tomorrow is visiting day throughout the hospital and that it will be all over town by tomorrow night about the nurse being murdered and that after last night . . . you know . . . the-you-you-must-do-something line. . . .

"So I made him come across with all he knew and sent for Rogers. He'll be here by six on the mail plane or eight via Chicago.

"The man everybody but MacArthur suspects is young Sterling."

"The hell you say!" Snod continued placidly waving his wet handkerchief in the dead air.

"Yep. I've seen him and he's not guilty."

"Huh? Howd'y'know?"

"Nothing concrete. Except he took me over his building. Left his dying father at MacArthur's request, because I was supposed to be a friend of the old man. He's worried, jumpy, nervous as a cat locked up, but he's square or I'm a ninny."

"You've been one a long time, Matt. Still, if he's where we can keep an eye on him, just in case a real unbiased detective, like me, for instance, should disagree with you, I suppose we'd better not tell

Lil. If she ain't improved since this morning, she might do a real fade-out, and then where'd we be, with MacArthur pressing for immediate action? In hell! Who else charmed the pants off you, mister?"

"Shut up, Snod. We've only twenty minutes before you go back on!"

Snod groaned deeply. "A light luncheon, before I again enter the dominion of women?"

"Eat out of the ward refrigerator and shut up!

"MacArthur gave me the head of all nurses, the leavings of a general gone senile, and she took me to all of the clinics. So I could look the doctors over. Administrator from a distant hospital line, you know. . . . I've hammered into MacArthur that it's a crazy doctor."

"Could you find one, Sherlock?"

"Didn't see anything else! Crazy ain't the beginning of it! First we took in the Eye Clinic, all the wards dark and dismal and the air full of un-uttered screams, and people putting their hands up close to their faces to see if they are better.

"That's run by an old soft soap artist with hair and complexion like the guts of a soft-boiled egg. Pure and precious. Pat the tail off a shetland pony and grab out your eye 'fore you knew it. Peters. Doctah Petahhs. Princeton '92 and Sons of Cincinnati rosette."

"Your control?" Snod's voice was casual and

flat. "Snappin' out eyes gets a man in the habit of murdering, Mr. Higgins."

"Aw hush, you little pan-toter. He'd run from a Pansy in a dark alley."

"So would I."

"From there," Higgins' voice was stern, "we went on to see the kids. The pediatrician's square. Eyes like a searchlight. Kids play around him. Kids and dogs know. He does not suspect Sterling, and he knew I was a detective. He didn't say either."

"Didn't anybody utter a word this morning?"

"Snod! Gimme a chance!"

"Birds of a feather . . . you sound as loony as the rest, Matt!"

Matthew Higgins flew off the handle. The darkness concealed his steely eyes, but his voice was clear and hard.

"Are you telling me, or am I telling you? Ever been in a slaughter house where they were doing everything from little pigs . . . on up?"

"Sorry, Matt. Might have known it would get you! The trouble with you is you are up against the medical profession, and the medical profession is composed of men who wait until you are down to hit you, and you ain't used to. . . ."

"Ain't they queer, Snod? I didn't see but two he-men this morning, and I saw at least ten doctors, and about half of that ten, I'd be damned if I could tell you what they was."

"Statistics show that one-third of the silk underwear sold in the United States is bought by doctors." Snod was grave and authoritative.

"I believe you, kid!"

"They buy it for the nurses!" Snod continued monotonously.

"Aw . . . dry up! . . . From the kids we went to the Maternity Clinic, and speaking of he-she things! Well he wore pants and a vest, but he talked like a nervous wife of fifty and his hands were always twisting. . . ."

"I know. A rat catcher!"

"They call him Prissy. How did you know?"

"And he believes Sterling is the murderer," Snod announced.

"Say, you been sleeping all morning?"

"Yeah. But I'm a real detective. An obstetrician is the busiest animal on God's earth. He don't have time to change his undershirt. Any woman can call him at any hour, and what do you expect from a man in that fix but gossip, mister? 'Spose you spent your life. . . ."

"Aw, naw!" Matt's response was definite. "He and Peters are buddies."

"Sissies. It takes guts to fight death, and skill to be a doctor. Guts is masculine, skill is feminine. They're sissies."

"It takes more than that to be a urologist, Snod. The one here holds out in a clinic where you see men . . . Jesus! . . . The damnedest looking liquids suspended over the beds hitched under the sheets with rubber tubing and patients who curse your soul black if you so much as sneeze as you pass them!"

"After the ball is over," Snod inserted flatly.

"Well, believe me, that doctor is all man."

"Have to be. Urologists rule men and men rule the world, Mr. Higgins."

"Yeah? He believes young Sterling is innocent, and he knew I was 'a dick' the minute he laid eyes on me."

"And how do you know that? Personal charm? Or just 'two strong men face to face'?"

Higgins ignored the remark and continued:

"Offered me a good cigar, and looked me smack in the eye, and then says, 'A friend of Doctor Mac-Arthur and Dr. Bear Sterling is always welcome in my clinic, sir.' He's the bird made MacArthur hire us against the opposition, or I'm a green one."

"You are that, too. But you are right about him. Everything comes to a G. U. including 'dicks'."

"How do you know?"

"My grandmother told me. What about the psychiatrist?"

"Ever faced one of those birds?"

Snod had felt his way back to the couch and sat down.

"Nope, but I seen 'em telling fortunes at Coney Island."

"You crazy? This fellow here is 'bout ten thousand jumps from a tent. Got a building with swimming pools, and roof gardens and woodwork painted green and locks on all the doors. . . ."

"And a staff of old maid nurses and unmarried women doctors, who are always telling you 'sex done it.' Night-prowling alley cats, at heart. What about him?"

"His name is Hoffbein, and he's got a little body like the tripod of a camera, without the stiffening, holding up his mentality. Got a head like a German. All front, with oriental black eyes, a controlled sissy mouth, a beaky nose, and no back.

"He slithered all over the clinic with us, and God that was gruesome! Perfectly healthy people, eating saltpetre in their food and wondering how long before they'd be nuts! And him saying, 'Routine, as you of course know, is the basis of all recovery.' And way down below a voice wailing 'Rock-a-bye-baby.'

"He ain't a man, he ain't just a sissy, he ain't even a human being. If you put a bullet through him, it wouldn't even kill him.

"And he's the thing we got to catch. He's it!

"He's so crazy that you ain't sure whether he's

crazy or not. He's the control. He's the person who
is working the Kerr women and Lil is right. And
he knows I know it, too."

"Charm it out of you?"

"After I'd seen the Surgical Clinic, and was always trying to ask intelligent questions about costs
and that kind of thing to the man who is Bear Sterling's assistant, Miss Carruthers took me to Cub
Sterling and I told you about him. But I saw the
Head Nurse, Miss Kerr, too. And then I knew I
was right. Seen her?"

"Last night. During the Battle of Roses." Snod's
reply came through the darkness with confirma-
tion.

"Then I ditched Miss Carruthers and went back
to the Psychiatric Clinic and into Hoffbein's office
before anybody realized I was there. He was sitting in a room with bare walls, at a bare desk, and
when he looked up and saw me, he almost lost his
'control.'

"He looks up and his eyes lost their whites like
a horse, and he says slow, 'So.'

" 'Yep!' I said, 'You're right.'

"Then I walked over and sat down in a chair
beside his desk, and we looked at each other and he
tried to make me feel like the furniture in the room
was melting and running together and so I says:

" 'I know the multiplication tables well as Kim
did, Doc. The last person who tried that hypnotiz-

ing stunt on me was the head of a snowbird ring at
Atlantic City. She is making dresses in the Federal
Pen in Atlanta, now. What about Miss Kerr?'

"He turned red like a cooked beet and then he
switched his head like a sparrow and says:

" 'Miss Kerr is a nurse in this hospital and a very
trusted person. Your name? Real name?'

" 'Don't matter a tinker's damn, Doc! Miss Kerr
was a patient of yours some years ago and you used
to hypnotize her to put her to sleep and this doll,
the doll which is always left by the murderer in
Medicine Clinic, was found in her desk and you
knew it yesterday. What about Miss Kerr?' "

"He looked kind of scared a minute and then he
turned on me confidentially and says:

" 'If you want my opinion, Mr. . . , these unfortunate occurrences are the work of Dr. Sterling,
Junior. An excellent example of a man who has
devoted the best years of his active life entirely to
his profession. To speak plainly, sexual abstinence
has caused an inversion of that natural energy by
which a man obtains his balance, and is responsible
for his aberration. When a man devotes himself
entirely to any profession he in time becomes somewhat unbalanced. If you understand . . . ?'

" 'You bet I do, Dr. Hoffbein. You are in a rotten position, and all the evidence you have been
trying to build up against young Sterling in every
staff meeting for a week won't hold water *fifteen*

minutes if you can't explain to me by four o'clock about the doll. . . .'

"He stiffened and replied: 'I'm going to Miss Standish's funeral.'

" 'See you there, then,' I said, rising.

"At the door I turned and his eyes were spraying venom on me like a snake's fangs, and he says:

" 'What patients tell me in confidence, I will never . . .'

" 'Reveal on the gallows,' I finished slowly. 'Think it over, Doctor! You'll be guarded till you make up your mind.'

"Then I shut the door, hard, and came here."

"Who is watching him?"

"A local man the dick at the Roosevelt got me. It's five to three. You'd better be moving. . . ."

Snod rose slowly. "Where are you going? What shall I tell Lil?"

"To scare the guts out of the Kerr women. Tell Lil she's right."

Snod left the building by the basement door and started up the service corridor toward the Medicine Clinic. Matt Higgins rolled his overcoat carefully in the crumpled copy of *The Morning Call*, hid it in a corner of the room and left the building by the main corridor door. Since it was three o'clock and the duty changes were at two and five, he took a chance. . . .

By two-thirty the patients on Ward B had been bedded down for their afternoon nap. Two student nurses were on duty. Miss Kexter was off for the afternoon.

Sally Ferguson lay in her bed, her arms locked above her head, her knees crossed and making a tent of the covers. She was smoking her last cigarette, inhaling slowly and gazing from the window. She had slept all night, a loggy black sleep, and was fatigued and internally trembly. A boredom, a lassitude and a loneliness were descending.

An overpowering desire to see Cub, backed by a hundred residents and internes, if necessary . . . just to watch his eyes change and slip over hers . . . to see again, even at a distance, the nice way the black hair grew below his white cuffs and over the knuckles of his fingers . . . to hear from his own lips that, "Doctor Bear Sterling is doing nicely, thank you" . . . instead of having it smirked by prim nurses. . . .

The ash-laden tip fell upon the covers. She flounced them and decided even if his father died, even if *The Call* was bombed, she had Cub forever and he had her and they both knew it, and life was going to be complete . . . yet!

The door to her room breathed gently inward. A man wiggled through and closed it. For a moment he stood entirely silent, then his beady black eyes snapped and his bumpy body relaxed.

The rush of asthmatic air made Sally slide her eyes and gasp:

"Jumbo! Where did you come from?"

Her voice relaxed into amusement and continued:

"You are an angel from God. Give me a cigarette!"

Without withdrawing his thumbs from his vest armholes, he pushed two fingers into a pocket and flipped his cigarette case onto the bed.

Sally's eyes narrowed. Jumbo had a spell of his "scoop hysterics." Something was up! She lit the new cigarette and remained silent.

The words splashed out of the man.

"Hell of a time getting in. No visitors. You ain't lookin' sick, Ferg. Sneaked up the porch stairs. Half hour stomach travel and five minutes walking. I ain't got time to ask polite questions.

"Listen, Ferg. You been here long enough to get the dope. What is it? Come on, kid! What about this Cub Sterling? Bucks wants to. . . ."

Sally kept his eyes on her body and fought for time.

"What? Who?"

"Bucks. In case you've forgot, Ferg, he's City Editor of *The Call* and saving six columns on the front page for this Sterling story."

Sally took the cigarette from her lips and said crisply:

"Why don't you quit bubbling, Jumbo, and tell me what it's all about?"

"About. Je-sus Christ, Ferg. About! It's about this guy Sterling murdering patients in that ward out there. Bucks says you've had time to get 'in' and it's up to you to get the dots on him. Four people gone out in the same bed since Thursday. All patients of his. Done between eleven and twelve at night. He jabbed 'em with a hypodermic. For four days we've known hell had burst loose up here, but we couldn't squeeze blood from no tick. Then this morning a woman dropped a bunch of red roses in the service corridor and we got a tip.

"The Attorney-General's trying to get the Governor to 'hush' it . . . but Bucks says he can fry his tail in hell. It's the biggest story west of the Mississippi in twenty years and he ain't goin' to lock those presses 'till ten tonight. In the meantime you got to. . . ."

As usual when excited, Jumbo walked up and down and did not look at the person he was addressing. That habit gave Sally time to take the shock before he turned.

She held the cigarette between her lips to keep them from trembling. Her feet were flat upon the mattress, pressing against each other desperately. Her voice was hail-fellow and confident. She said:

"Thanks for the chance you and Bucks are giving me. It's white! Darned white! And lucky, too,

Jumbo. He's my doctor. Due to come to see me in about half an hour. You go back and tell Bucks to give me till five. It's now a quarter to three. I'll get the story! Gimme a pencil and some paper. Beat it, before somebody comes in. . . !"

"But Bucks said. . . ."

"You tell Bucks Hammond if he wants this story, he'll get it . . . provided he gives me a little time. I know the ropes around here. I know the man. The only way to muff it is for you to stand there till you're caught! Quit sucking your tongue like a lolly-pop and beat it. If you are not back by five I'll wrap my story in a cake of soap and sling it out that window!"

Jumbo tripped to the door, turned and said:

"You're a swell kid, Ferg! Everybody's missin' you!"

"Been one twenty-four years! Tell 'em hello, Jumbo!"

After he was gone Sally Ferguson pulled the sheets over her head and sobbed dryly for five minutes. Then she tiptoed over to the washbasin, put cold water under her eyes and got back into bed.

Her mouth was set. Her head was very high.

He was as innocent as she was and . . . by God . . . she'd prove it. But you couldn't prove anything lying here being policed every pulse counting. You had to get out and think and. . . .

She rang her bell; when the student nurse came, she smiled wanly and said:

"Dr. Mattus and Dr. Sterling said I might get up for a while this afternoon. Will you bring me my clothes now? They said from three to five."

The girl drank the smile. When she returned with the clothes she apologized:

"Can you manage alone, Miss Merriweather? The other nurse has the cramps and doesn't want to report off duty, less she has to. So I'm doing most of . . . ?"

"Sure," Sally smiled. "Poor kid!"

The girl turned from the door and said, "Ring if you need me!"

A terrible strength began to flow through Sally. A strength which centered just under the skin and left her vitals hollow and quivering. It took ten precious minutes to dress. Inside, and with every motion of pulling on stockings, adjusting garters, smoothing her hair, inside, deep inside, her consciousness sang:

"Cub Sterling, you are not! You are not! Cub darling, I love you! I love you!"

The deep singing was like a walking cane as she started across the room for the door. She pulled the knob, hesitantly, ascertained the student nurse was out of sight, and gathering all of her strength, ran the few feet to the screen porch door. When her knees gave way she was on the concrete steps, halfway down to Ward A, and Ward A was the ground floor.

A wild mental clearing made her understand that with or without strength, she had to reach that porch off Ward A, get over the railing and drop to the ground, before the nurses began rolling the patients out for their afternoon airing.

Ten minutes later, a young girl, walking with an erectness every motion of which hurt, entered Otto's restaurant and leaned against the deserted bar.

She fastened her violet eyes into Otto and said:

"I love Cub Sterling as much as you do. I think I can save him . . . if you'll lend me a dollar for two hours. . . ."

The money was in her hand before Otto could open his lips. When he did open them, the girl was already in a taxi-cab, and the cab was coasting down the hill from the hospital.

When Miss Carruthers, in response to a telephone call, brought Evelina Kerr, student nurse, to Dr. MacArthur's office, Matt Higgins rose from a chair and said:

"Miss Carruthers, Dr. MacArthur just stepped out a minute. . . . He asked me to wait until he returned and ask you to please let this nurse. . . ?"

His "silver threads" smile brought an immediate

acquiescence. The old lady smiled, backed out, and Higgins offered the student nurse a chair.

She sat upon the edge, her narrow feet together and the bony ankles pressing against each other. Higgins offered her a cigarette. Her refusal was jerky.

"Excuse me," he said walking toward the door. "My mistake. I don't want to get you thrown out."

She flinched slightly and her round chin tried for a well-bred hauteur. It missed.

When the door was closed, Higgins looked squarely, slowly, with open summary, at the girl. She thought he was flirting. When his eyes began their spreading lid trick, she felt as though he were pointing the muzzle of a pistol toward her. She tried to fight his silence with words.

"Who are you? Why are you looking at me that way?"

Higgins laid his head against the door. His lids continued widening.

Her words beat the air:

"Stop looking at me! Stop it!"

His words were like an ice cloth against her brain:

"Why don't you quit lying, girlie?"

The battle was uneven. Perfect physical control against shattered nerves. Her close-set eyes began to ferret. She made a last effort to hide behind her sex.

"I'm not lying. I don't know what you are talking about! You are crazy!"

Matt's eyes stayed steadfast. He said very slowly:

"No . . . it's your aunt who is crazy!"

Her beaten nerves threw the battle back to her body. She leaped to her feet.

"She's not. She's not! I swear to God she's not!"

Higgins walked over and clenched his hands into her shoulders.

"Look at me!"

She fought to get loose.

He increased, gradually, his hold.

"Look . . . at . . . me. . . !"

Her piglike eyes cringed before his steel ones.

Quickly, unexpectedly, he released his hold and smiled at her. His voice was deep.

"Kiddo, I'm sorry for you. Sit down!"

She fell into a chair and began dry-sobbing. He filled a glass from the thermos jug on the mantel and placed it against her lips. And while she drank, with his free hand he soothed her ugly little forehead as one soothes a terrified child.

Kindness was the one thing the girl had never known. She couldn't fence against it.

Higgins' reasoning voice suggested:

"Tell me about it, won't you?"

He took the glass and sat it upon the table. Then

he took her sweating hand and held it protectingly in his.

The words cascaded out of her:

"She's not killing them! I swear to God she's not! She's . . . she's . . . I can't tell you . . . she'll have me thrown out. . . . I can't! I can't!"

Higgins put his other hand beneath the hand he was already holding.

"Go on!" he ordered in a monotone. . . . "She's . . . ?"

His eyes picked into the shady depths of her close-set ones. He smiled again. . . .

The girl's terror fell away. She whispered:

"She's . . . taking . . . morphia-off-the-ward-I'm-on-in-her-clinic. At night. Between the supervisor's rounds!"

Neither the pressure of his hands nor his voice changed.

"For herself?"

"Yes!"

"Is she an . . . ?"

The girl's whisper was almost inaudible. . . .

"I . . . I . . . think . . . so. . . ."

Higgins' voice became stern.

"Then how do you know she's not . . . the murderer?"

The girl shot back instantly:

"Because she . . . didn't come until I notified

her . . . the   night . . . the   nurse . . . went
out!"

"Maybe you didn't see her."

Her words came in gasps:

"I . . . I . . . counted-the-tablets . . . when-
I-came-on . . . duty . . . and-when-I-went-off.
They . . . checked. . . !"

"Perhaps she didn't take any to throw you off
the track. Had you thought of . . . ?"

The terror in her eyes and voice made Matt
shiver.

"No. . . !"

The word was a wail.

He changed his tactics immediately.

"That's not likely, though. When the urge is
'on', nothing . . . not even murder . . . can stop
it."

He had risen while he was talking and opened
the door into the corridor. Ten minutes had passed.
Dr. MacArthur entered. Higgins said to the girl:

"You have nothing more to worry about. Dr.
MacArthur and Miss Carruthers will stand behind
you . . . till you graduate!"

Then he went out of the Administration Building, down the main corridor of the hospital. The
corridor was nearly empty. In the distance five pro-
bationers, with new text books under their arms,
were coming toward him, but they were the only
people in sight. The wards had settled down for

the afternoon, the white nurses were off duty, and
two student nurses on each floor and the head nurse
of each building were on duty. The internes and
resident were doing lab or case studies.

After he rounded the corner and started toward
Medicine Clinic, he met more people and an air
of increased tension. The tension was especially
plain in the orderlies and maids. He remembered
that he had forgotten to tell Snod about the roses,
and considered going up to Ward B after he entered Medicine Clinic, then decided to let it slip.
That would be dangerous. Even though he had his
group cornered there was no reason to take unnec-
essary chances.

Good thing he had spent part of last evening
checking up on Miss Kerr's past. Now that he had
the dope information. . . .

Lil Parkins was the best woman he had ever
worked with. She smelt people like a dog. Kind of
sixth sense and she never missed. Her hunches had
made his reputation.

The explosive air hung over him like a pall.
Through an open door he could see Miss Roenna
Kerr, her flat feet primly under her desk, her white
pompadour overhanging her lean face. . . .

He walked straight into her office and closed the
door behind him. Her pen dropped from her fingers
and she turned her long head. Then her face became as devoid of expression as a mule's. Panicky

and blank with fear. But her long years of training came briskly to her aid.

"What can I do for you? Is there something in the Clinic that you failed to see, Mr. Immerheld?"

"I'm not Mr. Immerheld of Cornell Medical Center, Miss Kerr. I am from New York, though, and you can be so good as to tell me," his gray eyes narrowed and tried to make her china blue ones rise above his necktie, "how you happened to have this?"

He drew from his back pocket the doll in the blue dress and frilled bonnet, that Mattus had found in Miss Kerr's desk, and turned it over on its stomach.

The raucous, "Pa-pa! Pa-pa! Pa-pa!" kept repeating itself slowly and insistently.

"Turn it over! Turn it over! I'll tell you," there was relief in her voice.

"My niece had a P. M. several . . . about . . . a week ago . . . and went to a street fair and won it. She brought it to me. . . ."

Higgins seated himself carefully in a chair beside her desk and said:

"Half an hour ago the doll that your niece won was lying in her top bureau drawer!"

Without intending to do so, her china blue eyes raised to his and he shot past her protective covering into her unprepared ear:

"Is morphia quicker than cocaine?"

From inside, without intention, she answered:
"Yes. Much."

Then she realized what she had said and opened
her lips to make a statement about "depending
upon the condition of the patient. . . ."

Higgins did not allow her to utter the words.
Once an addict has acknowledged the habit, he
knew she was powerless to refrain from talking
about it.

"What's the shot you use?"

"An eighth used to do. It's a half now. . . ."

Her hands began to flutter wildly. Higgins
turned the doll over again. Its nasal whining raised
the electric tension.

His voice cut through the whining. He said:

"It was clever of you not to take any tablets the
night you did the nurse. . . ."

"I didn't! Before God, I *didn't do*. . . ."

"You don't like Cub Sterling, do you?"

The question shot at her like a bullet. She staggered internally.

"Dr. Hoffbein doesn't like him, either! Dr. Hoffbein used to put you to sleep after . . . !"

"After what?" she defied and cowered at the
same time.

"After that woman doctor you lived with died."

"That's not so. How do you know that?"

"Dr. Hoffbein."

"He didn't tell you either. He just called me. . . ."

"Maybe it's in your case history, then. . . ." He leaned quickly forward. "Why did you hide the doll?"

"To protect my niece."

He changed his tactics:

"Did you use your own syringe on the nurse?"

The old woman's facial muscles contracted. Her yellow teeth laid bare against her purpling lips. Her bust relaxed hopelessly and then she began to talk, openly, helplessly:

"I didn't do the nurse. Really, I didn't. I didn't do any of them! . . . I . . . I . . . was . . . there . . . Monday . . . but. . . ."

"Who did . . . them . . . if you didn't?"

Her china eyes protruded.

"One . . . one of . . . the Cub Sterlings!!!"

"What?"

The words bit through her old teeth:

"There are two of them! . . . Two . . . ! . . . Two Cub Sterlings . . .! I *saw* them that night . . . of the first traceable murder Monday night! . . . I was coming out of the Medicine Closet with my . . . and one of them was bending over the patient in Bed 11, and one of them was shadowed against the window shade bending over the patient in Room Two.

"And the one . . . bending over the patient in

Bed 11 . . ." her words began to burst . . . "*saw
me*! I know *he saw me*! . . ."

Higgins cut in sternly:

"It was your duty to . . . investigate. . . ."

Her hands began to pick her bosom wildly.

"I couldn't. . . . I couldn't. . . . Don't you
see I couldn't?"

"Why didn't you tell Dr. Hoffbein. . . ?"

"Because . . . because . . . he had said if
. . . I ever went back . . . to my . . . habit
. . . on duty. . . ."

Higgins nodded grimly and hunched forward.

"Who around this hospital looks like Cub Sterling?"

"Nobody! I swear nobody! Oh, God, I've been
over every single face since then . . . in my mind
. . . and on sight. . . . Nobody!"

"One of those Cub Sterlings was a man who knew
you were taking dope, Miss Kerr . . . who knew
that when you saw him . . . you'd keep your
mouth shut. Who knew . . . ?"

"Nobody but . . . my . . . niece! That's why
I took the doll. To keep the Staff from . . . grill-
ing her . . . I was afraid. . . ."

"You are missing out somewhere. Who checks
the dope?"

"The floor nurse, once a month. She gives the
sheet to me and I turn the clinic sheets over to the
pharmacy. . . ."

"Ah, the pharmacy! They knew, Miss Kerr!"

"No! No! They didn't know. I . . . I . . . changed . . . the sheet from Ward B . . . the day I turned it in . . . so as to cover. . . ."

"When did you turn it in?"

"The day of the first traceable murder."

"Take your telephone, Miss Kerr, and ask the white nurse from Ward B if the pharmacy called her to check her figures."

"She's off duty now."

"Get her in her room!"

The old nurse hesitated and cringed.

Higgins' voice cut her into action.

"If you want to save your own neck . . . take it!"

When Miss Kerr hung the recevier back upon the hook she whispered:

"They did. She . . . read them . . . her pencil memorandum . . . on Monday. . . ."

Higgins rose steadily and said carefully:

"If you go on as though nothing has happened, you may get off . . . scott free. As soon as I step from this door, until I return, there will always be somebody watching you. Is the pharmacy next to the Administration Building?"

Her wilted voice responded:

"Yes. It is off the main corridor . . . but I can't go on! I *can't*!"

He stood against the closed door and snapped:

"Would you rather have a chance to resign . . . or spend the rest of your life in the pen?"

"Resign!"

"You are not off duty until seven! Understand?"

The old pompadour shook carelessly.

Higgins opened the door and started through the lobby and up the main corridor toward the pharmacy. His brain was reeling. He was dizzy.

Two Cub Sterlings! God Almighty! Suppose she was lying? Suppose? . . . She was too frightened to leave, though. . . . The best thing to do was sit tight and look over the pharmacy staff.

When Snod Smooty came back on Ward B, he found two student nurses on duty and the women remarkably quiet. They were still subdued by the grandness of Dr. Cub Sterling's leaving his dying father to come to see about them. They were excited over his furrowed face and his sudden ageing. They didn't call it that, but they felt it, profoundly. To the funeral-wake-type, death is always as exciting as birth, and the death of a famous doctor. . . .

Snod tiptoed up to lower a window shade near Lil Parkins' bed. She was sleeping peacefully and contentedly. The same feeling of admiration which the other women had experienced for Cub Sterling had taken the form of protective relaxation in Lil Parkins. He would see that nothing happened to her. He had told her to go to sleep.

And expression of sudden warmth lay over the colorless features of Snod Smooty as he looked at Lil. A grand girl, Lil! And a swell detective! Do anything for a pal. Nursed him through pneumonia last fall, just because he was her friend. . . .

The day orderly beckoned to him and he went back to washing dishes. They worked quietly and with the doors closed. One of the nurses came to say she was going off the floor a minute.

The day orderly was a squashy fellow who talked all the time. Snod had known it soon as he set eyes on him. He finished the saucers and left the man still talking. His garrulousness had put Snod's nerves on the jump and he was hungry, too.

Three-thirty and the fool wouldn't leave him long enough to get even a bottle of cream outa the ice box! Maybe a cigarette would help. . . .

Snod eased over toward the door and through it. Halfway up the ward corridor, he caught sight of chubby Bessie Ellis sitting up in her crib and playing with a doll . . . exactly like the two Dr. Mac-Arthur had shown them yesterday.

He ran noiselessly to her crib and smiled at her. They were friends immediately. As he passed the medicine closet he saw the single student nurse coming out of the nurses' lavatory.

When he smiled at Bessie he took hold of the foot-board of the crib to steady himself. She was

six, and the pink dress of the doll looked pretty
against her brown curls and eyes.

It was the hardest job he had ever tackled. He
said slowly, and his face was innocent and friendly:

"Where did you get that new dollie Baby?"

"Dr. Cub jes' gave her to me. . . ."

Snod reeled from the bed and staggered toward
that of Lil Parkins. The other women were still
asleep. Some of them were snoring. He leaned over
and peered behind the drawn curtain.

Lil's eyes were wild with fear and her face began to contract.

"Stop it!" Snod's voice was harsh and heavy.
"Tell me! You all right?"

She nodded weakly and her intense features began kaleidoscoping her thoughts:

"God Almighty! It's Dr. Cub Sterling. I
trapped him . . . cold. . . . He thought I was
asleep and when he leaned over me . . . with the
hypodermic . . ." her profile shadow convulsed
against the white pillow, "I . . . opened . . . my
eyes. He had pulled the curtains to . . . get
me. . . !

"I said, 'You!' and started to scream . . . and
he drew back and his eyes, Snod. Oh, God . . . run
mad, together. Crazy! And then he cocked his left
shoulder, shrugged, lowered his curly head and
bowed himself . . . out.

"It's spells, Snod. He wasn't that way this morning. His eyes! I couldn't scream. My heart. . . ."

"Rest it, kiddo, till I get Matt."

Snod coiled around and his eyes with the sudden sharpness of great stress saw the tall figure with the high shoulder walk out of the linen closet and enter the elevator.

And then swiftly, noiselessly, and panther-like he followed.

The elevator door closed just as he reached it.

Three minutes later Snod Smooty slouched up the main corridor. Nobody was in sight, either way, except in the distance was a man. The man wore a white hospital coat, and Snod eyed him hopelessly; then Snod's eyes narrowed.

The man's left shoulder had lifted and from the left patch pocket there was dangling a frilled pink organdie doll bonnet!

Snod gathered his muscles and began to run. . . .

He was almost up with the man when a panicky woman opened a side door and halted his progress.

She fell into his arms, before he could sidestep her, and the agony of her face made him involuntarily support her.

"The Maternity Clinic. Quick! For God's sake, quick!"

Snod looked both ways. Only the tall figure was visible.

"For God's sake, hurry!"

He gathered the tortured body of the woman into his long arms and began running with his back to the retreating figure.

Nature had tripped him, and he knew it.

When he had helped the orderly inside the door of the Maternity Clinic, who awaited such emergencies, to get the panic-stricken woman onto a handy stretcher, Snod turned swiftly and started slowly back toward the Administration Building.

MacArthur would know where Matt was. No use trying to locate him through Miss Kerr.

God in Heaven! Young Sterling! And they had been so damn near framing three innocent people! Within that space of a hundred yards, he must readjust his mind.

His ineffectual thin body shambled innocuously along. . . .

Behind him there burst upon the air the perfect trilling of a robin. Snod slid over to a window and looked stupidly at the grass in the back garden.

Matt Higgins drew alongside and asked loudly:

"Beg your pardon, but could you tell me the way . . . ?"

Snod began pointing through the window at the different buildings. His eyes followed his fingers. His voice, once it had formulated an action, was like a scimiter blade. It shimmered:

"Where's MacArthur?"

Higgins was harassed and hot. He was measuring his forefinger against the left thumb.

"Gone to train to meet dead nurse's mother. There are two Cub Sterlings, old Kerr says. Just confessed. Claims she's seen 'em. On my way now. . . .

Snod's loose hands continued their flappings.

"Kerr's innocent. Two? Jes-sus! One Cub Sterling just tried to murder Lil. She frightened him off!"

Higgins face grayed.

"W-h-a-t?"

Snod snapped, "I nearly caught him. Had a doll bonnet hanging from his pocket, walking up this corridor five minutes ago. Pregnant woman. . . ."

A smile almost split Matt's lips. Words knocked it off:

"I'll call MacArthur at the station. Have him get the sheriff to send a warrant immediately. No! I'll get the kids' man. His brother is Attorney-General. He can act quicker. Then I'll watch Cub Sterling, until they come. Give me time to think. Something don't click. I still don't believe it. . . ! You go to the pharmacy before you go back to Lil . . . over there . . . and see if the pharmacist is in . . . if he is watch him until I come. . . ."

Snod's hands continued their waving. But his eye was cut upon the corridor. He hissed:

"A running man. . . . Turn around, Matt!"

Matt whirled. Ahead, almost through the door into the Administration Building, and round the statue of Elijah Wilson, careened Cub Sterling.

Higgins' legs were in motion and his words shot back:

"I'll follow this one. You watch out for Lil! The other may try again. . . ."

Snod's face remained blank. His biscuit watch was in his hand. Four doctors were coming up the corridor. His deferential voice followed Higgins:

"You have five minutes to make that train, sir."

»X«
The Cupola

As THE TAXI WOGGLED DOWNHILL,
Jumbo's words pushed past the busy clicking of the
meter into Sally's weary brain. Once inside her
consciousness, they rolled around like brightly
colored Christmas tree balls, and butted into each
other and crashed. Far down beneath the shatter-
ing concussions her mind began reverberating:

"Think it over, think it over, think it over."

Twice she decided to go to Bucks and then she
knew it would be hopeless. They couldn't help if a
big story broke. They didn't make the news. They
. . . they were like buzzards . . . and she must
do something to keep them . . . from. . . .

Murdering patients. . . . Oh God! Oh God!
. . . No! . . . They are wrong!

She pushed her curly bright hair back from her
sweating forehead, and at *The Call* building gave
the driver the dollar, and slipped unnoticed into a
crowded elevator and out again in the main hallway
of the sixth floor.

This wouldn't do. Somebody might come along.

She leaned against the wall for a moment, then decided to walk up to the seventh floor. There was a vacant suite of offices on the corner; perhaps if she went where there was plenty of room her brain would get . . . wider. . . .

Half way up the marble stairs began rising and hitting her in the face, and then slipping back so that she couldn't quite reach them when she stepped. She slumped and rested.

If Cub's arms were only around her now. How many murders had there been? Four! Jumbo had said four, and the last a nurse. The night he brought the last cigarettes. She hadn't seen him since the morning after . . . the nurse. . . . Not since Dr. Bear began dying . . . but she knew! She knew!

Oh God! God! It wasn't Cub! It wasn't! A murderer couldn't kiss you so that your soul ran up and spread out flat under his lips. . . . A murderer couldn't look at you so that you said you were sorry, even when you tried not to be. . . . A murderer's hair wouldn't fold into little waves where it spread under the curve at the back of his neck.

But how could you tell a paper that? How could you make a city editor understand . . . when you had no proof . . . that a man was innocent and framed?

There must be some way! You had to think clearly to see it, and the place to think was upstairs with the whole world spread out below in orderly rows and streets. Just as the sun spread over the city, and strengthened it, so control made it possible. . . . Two hours! Less than that now. . . .

She clenched her fists tightly and rose with studied steadiness. Necessity cleared the brain. Working in a newspaper office taught that the best ideas came under pressure. She had gone out on enough murder stories to know the person who worked his brain . . . could beat anything . . . even newspaper reporters and . . . police.

By the time Sally reached the door of the vacant suite, the seams of her stockings were straightened and her reddening eyes carefully and painstakingly dry. There was an air of jauntiness about her small figure.

She had a head and was going to use it!

Her violet eyes had changed to the deep purple and iridescent white of orchids. She closed the door and stood against it. Then her irises focused.

A stooped, intent figure was silhouetted between the rows of windows and the long city vistas below. For a second her artistic sense forebade speech.

Like an apple tree, knarled and buffeted by too much winter, the thin shoulders, flat chest, beak nose, and long hands ribboned with purple veins, strained after the peering eyes which were hidden by a pair of binoculars. The dirty white hair drawn into a tightly furled knot, on the upper front of the head, helped Sally recognize the next-to-the-oldest-employe of *The Morning Call*. She momentarily forgot Cub Sterling.

"Emma! What are you doing?"

Emma wheeled around, and the binoculars fell from her hands. Sally moved with extended palms to catch them.

"Oh, it's you!" Emma's voice was pleased and birdlike. "They don't drop, Miss Ferguson. Mr. Bucks told me you was on vacation. Did you have a nice time, dearie?" She reached toward the long leather thong which held the binoculars around her scrawny neck and then embarrassment replaced pleasure.

"What *are* you doing?"

"Well, I tell you, dearie. Whin I can't git inta th' offices on six ri-away, I jes' comes here for a little while and takes in the city . . . kinda. It helps a lot, sometimes, for bein' lonesum, Miss Ferguson."

The news-story instinct welled up. Sally eased down into a window sill. Perhaps, if you shifted the mind completely. . . .

"Where did you get them?"

"Well, dearie, it's like this: My boy . . . you know . . . what was killed at the Argonah, had 'em." Emma's lower jaw dropped. "His buddy . . . my boy had got 'em off'n a dead German General, and you kno' what fine things Germans makes

. . . well, his buddy took 'em off'n my boy's body after . . . and brought 'em back to me. And, Miss Ferguson, he seys whin he give 'em to me, he seys, 'These is t'gif ye a chancst t'see life.'

"Ain't that sweet, dearie? And they'se bin the greates' consterashun thu m'sorrow. Whin I gits t'thinkin' 'bout my boy and wishin' f'gran'chillrin . . . you kno' . . . I jes' comes up here and takes in a few lifes."

A swell newspaper story! "Vicarious living," Sally muttered.

Emma, heard it and protested:

"No mam! Nuthin' like that! I never looks beyond Second Street, Miss Ferguson. Two blocks this side of Beeker Street is an awful nice I-talyan neighb-hood. It's sweet t'see th'women nursin' babies on do'steps. That's helped me an awful lot . . . sometimes. . . .

"Wouldn't you like to take a look, dearie?"

Emma removed the thong from her neck with the care a concert master saves for his violin. Her face had now a deep, sweet warmth. Miss Ferguson had given her five dollars at Easter and at Christmas and this was a chancst. . . .

Sally saw the look and rose. The folds of her blue crepe dress molded the curve of her slender thighs as she lifted the thong carefully over her head, adroitly around her white cowl collar, and walked toward the window.

Emma stood proudly by and suggested:

"If you look tword the sout'wes' down by Sears, Roebuck, you kin' jes' catch a piece of the bridge 'roun' th'corner buildin'. It's awful prutty at sunset."

Sally, who was something of a football fan, realized these were eight-power Zeiss binoculars. They brought the city out with startling clearness. She looked for the University, and on out toward Sears, Roebuck and across the river. Then she began picking out the Italian district near Beeker Street and the speakeasy just around the corner near Pershing Road.

"They're wond-er-ful, Emma!"

"Ain't they gran'?"

Suddenly she remembered about Cub, and trained the glasses upon the Elijah Wilson four blocks uphill. Cub was over there . . . somewhere. . . . Cub was. . . .

She began going over the building carefully. How pink the bricks were in the afternoon sun! The trees up Wilson Boulevard looked so green and feathery! How. . . .

Her eyes found the cupola upon the top of the Administration Building. She had always wanted to see what was in that cupola! She unscrewed the lenses to their full power. They came into focus. One of the grimy windows was open. How lucky! She trained them into it.

Scissored against the far white wall was Cub Sterling sitting at a small table. His hand held a hypodermic syringe. He was laughing. . . .

God Almighty!

Sally staggered as if she had been struck. Emma, supporting her, soothed:

"I orta told you, dearie. If you looks too much you gits dizzy."

"Emma," her tone was parched and pleading, "look through these at the cupola of the Elijah Wilson Hospital and tell me what you see."

The old woman took the binoculars, readjusted them . . . it seemed to Sally that she used a thousand years . . . and said:

"Shucks, honey, I don't see nuthin' but a curly-headed man settin' at a little table writin' in a book . . . H'm . . . he's awful nice lookin'!, too. . . ."

Sally snatched the glasses and spread her feet to prop herself while she projected them. Her eyes, as she stiffly moved the dials, were filmy, but within seconds she had the lenses magnifying the cupola and as a man might repeat by rote what he knew by heart, she forced her horror-stricken eyes to focus again.

What they saw was Cub Sterling sitting at the same small table, a pen in his hand, writing swiftly and absorbedly in a small book. Behind him was the same big red splotch . . . as if a bucket of blood

had been thrown against the wall . . . the same
. . . small medicine case between two of the sooty
windows.

But before him, upon the table, was the hypodermic syringe. Her eyes kept coming back to it
over, over and over, as the eyes of a bird fascinated
come back to a snake. And upon his face, as he
wrote, was the awful look which she had never seen
there, until he held that syringe up and laughed.

As she gazed, like an echo in the distance, little
things about him began to be unfamiliar. There
wasn't so much distance under his ear and collar,
where she had buried her nose. And his hair wasn't
that long . . . not nearly. . . . He had just had
his hair cut . . . Tuesday. . . .

Maybe that was somebody else. . . . Maybe. . . .

The glasses began slipping from her hands and
while they fell, with the rapidity of a panic-
stricken brain, she decided.

If it was Cub and she telephoned him and told
him she needed him terribly and to come right away
and he came, then it wasn't Cub. And if he didn't
come, but stayed right there in that chair all the
time. . . .

Well, you had to know . . . sometime. . . .

"Emma," her voice was crisp and had lost its
note of friendly equality, "put those binoculars to
your eyes and watch that man in the top of the

hospital till I come back. . . . Don't take your
eyes off of him *for one second*. It's . . . it's . . .
whether I'm ever happy depends on his sitting in
that chair till I come back."

The bent old woman took the glasses, trem-
blingly, and Sally was halfway down the hall of the
seventh floor before the cupola was in focus again.

As she ran she debated whether to take a chance
and call from the newspaper office. The open door
of a suite of legal offices flashed by. She wheeled
and entered. None of the stenographers was in the
outer office.

Steadying herself against a typewriter desk she
snatched up the telephone:

"Wilson 2000. Hurry, please!"

She had called it two weeks ago for a news story!

In response to the hospital operator's, "Lijah-
wilsin," she said:

"Dr. Ethridge Sterling, Junior."

The voice died away and then came back:

"Dr. Sterling's 'phone doesn't answer."

"Call him on the loud speaker, please. It's terribly important."

She could hear the weary, raucous rasping, which
was penetrating every corridor of the whole hospital:

"Docterr Ste-earling. Doct-terr Eth-err-ridge
Ste-earling-Junyior. . . ."

Every day of the month on the calendar tacked

to the far wall hit her in the face . . . Monday,
the ninth . . . Monday, the sixteenth . . . before she heard Cub's:

"Dr. Ethridge Sterling, speaking."

"Cub . . . can you come to room 708 in *The
Call* building, right away. . . ?"

"What? . . . Salscie. . . ? Where are you?
How did you . . . ?"

A terrible calm invaded her.

"It's me, Cub! I walked out of the hospital. I
had to. . . ! Something awful . . . !"

"What?" the rising concern of his voice seemed
to be put on, and then his, "I can't leave Father.
He's. . . ."

She braced herself for a final effort and begged:

"I know. But I'm in *terrible* . . . I need you,
darling!"

"But, Salscie. . . ."

"Room 708, Cub! . . ."

She threw the telephone from her and reeled into
the hall and toward the vacant suite. Her eyes were
right! Cub was not coming. Cub was . . . was . . .

With a listlessness which portrayed great physical effort, she pushed the door open and looked
toward the stooped back of Emma; then she swayed
steadily toward a low window sill and sat down. Her
eyes were the color of clouds before a thunder storm
and she leaned her head against the casing.

Then with that funny clearness which is always

part of terror, she began to count the carpet tacks on both sides of two planks in the floor. One, two . . . his voice was foggy and distant . . . six, seven, eight . . . he was irritated. . . . "I can't come. I can't come!" . . . Cub Sterling was a murderer . . . a maniac. . . .

As the thought began forming in her mind she revolted, and the revolt brought energy. Within half a minute after entering the room, she was at Emma's side, begging:

"He didn't move, did he? He didn't move, Emma?"

"Not as I seen, but twicest I sneezed and los' him, Miss Ferguson. But whin I got him back in, agin, he was settin' jes the'same and writin' away . . . liken he is. . . ."

Sally grabbed the binoculars and twisted them painstakingly as she placed the strap over her head. If he hadn't moved, then perhaps . . . but he might have heard the loud speaker and gone to a 'phone while Emma was sneezing . . . would the loud speaker penetrate into that cupola. . . ?

When she focused the figure again she began scrutinizing it. He had turned. Only his back and high shoulder . . . but the distance from his ear to his collar wasn't wasn't. . . .

Nobody but Cub had shoulders like that! Nobody except Cub sat that way. . . .

There was only one Cub Sterling in the world

and in spite of every little thing which wasn't right
this was he. And if he sat in that chair another ten
minutes she would never walk and talk again . . .
and if he didn't sit there but came to her. . . .

She staggered back at that thought and Emma
ran to her.

"Don't git yourself so excited, dearie. What's
that big-headed man to you? He ain't nuthin' but
a doctor's helper, doin' his regular. . . ."

Sally kept the glasses carefully focused and
said, quite calmly:

"Did you ever seen him before, Emma?"

"Not as I kin recklek. But thin I ain't no jedge.
I ain't no crazier 'bout lookin' at hossbittles thin
I is 'bout bein' in thim, Miss Ferguson. I tell you
lots of my frin's done gone up to thet hossbittle and
ain't never bin heard frum since. Ef a body's goin'
to die, he's goin' die, hossbittle or no hossbittle, I
says. Look at my boy en the Argonah! I recklek
whin he got hurt in a football scrimpage, over at
Western High and they tried to take him to. . . ."

Her chatter, like water in a distant bathtub during a bad dream, splashed past Sally's brain. Then
it ceased to register, for the man at the table had
risen and was opening a drawer in the medicine
cabinet.

And hope sprang suddenly high in Sally's
heart. His shoulders squared and were flat! Cub
stooped. . . .

But the shape of the head and the way the hair curled at the back of the neck sickened her, horribly. It was only when he reached in a hip pocket and drew out a handkerchief . . . Cub carried his in his white coat breast pocket. . . .

Then he reached back toward the table for the hypodermic syringe, and held it up to the light again. . . . And his left shoulder rose . . . and Sally Ferguson's eyes floated hopelessly, the stiff tensity of her body began to relax . . . she staggered forward. . . .

Coming up the hall was the sound of running feet and they sounded like the feet of running men. . . .

The door swung open. The note of relief in Cub Sterling's voice as he said "Salscie!" stiffened her relaxing muscles and gave her the power to turn.

Matthew Higgins had come out of the Administration Building as the long, lank body of Cub Sterling shot into a taxi at the stand.

Higgins had jumped another cab.

Sally Ferguson turned and swayed toward Sterling as Matthew Higgins stepped inside the door and it was he who caught the incredulity, the anguish, the blind hope of her voice.

"Cub! Are you *really* Cub?"

As Sterling reached her his voice was stern.

"What is it? You *must* tell me," his eyes cut into

her clouding ones and Matthew Higgins stepped alongside and said curtly:

"Poison her too?"

Sally Ferguson's lids began lowering and she gasped, holding up the glasses with her ebbing strength:

"Look, Cub! The cu-po-la!"

The words faded with her closing eyes, and the final horror in them made Cub Sterling lay her head against his chest, place his long arms under her breasts and raise the binoculars, which were still suspended around her neck.

"Lan' sakes. It's only a man. Jes, a doctor's helper. And I seys. . . ." Emma had found her voice at last, but Cub Sterling cut in:

"God Almighty! Look! And tell me what you. . . ."

His words were directed toward Emma.

Matthew Higgins took the glasses from Cub's hands and Sally's neck before Cub said, "Tell me. . . ." The expression on his face had convinced Higgins that he saw . . . something . . . vile.

A silence, like the high hysteria after a buoy-bell, spread over the waiting doctor. His eyes, livid with fear, turned upon the florid, gray figure of Matthew Higgins. And it was Higgins' voice that brought Sally Ferguson out of her purple palaces.

Its steadiness was more hysterical than any word that had been uttered.

"A man with his head turned away from me . . . sitting at a small table writing in a book, his left shoulder is . . . he is reaching for a hypodermic syringe and holding it up and. . . . The murderer! . . . The murderer! The crazy doctor! The other Cub Sterling!"

The glasses hit the floor with a thud and Matthew Higgins started down the hallway before Cub Sterling and Sally Ferguson turned around. He must reach Snod . . . reach Snod. In the same legal offices from which Sally had telephoned he grabbed the receiver and ordered:

"Elijah Wilson Hospital, immediately!"

"Number? Number? Number?"

"Give it to me. I don't know it."

Sally reached the doorway and sighed:

"Wilson 2000."

When the connection was through Higgins rasped:

"Dr. Henry MacArthur."

The nasal whine of the placid operator came back:

"Dr. MacArthur's 'phone doesn't answer."

"Then give me Ward B, Medicine Clinic."

"We never connect 'outside' with the wards."

"To hell with you!" Higgins threw the 'phone from him and followed the running figure of Cub

Sterling toward the elevator shaft. Sally Ferguson
eased in as the door slipped to, and said to the operator:

"Will, non-stop one. For God's sake, quick!"

Higgins' head cleared. "Who is he?" Cub nodded
vacantly.

As they ran from the building Cub Sterling
jumped in beside the driver of a cruising taxi and
ordered:

"Elijah Wilson. To hell with traffic lights! Five
dollars if you do it in two minutes!"

Matt Higgins pulled Sally Ferguson into the
back seat and slammed the door.

They began their wild, uphill snaking in and
out.

Mat Higgins said:

"If we are not there in seconds, that devil will
be. . . . Who is it, Sterling?"

Cub took his panic-stricken eyes from the approaching hospital and said:

"I don't know, Mr. Immer. . . ."

"Higgins. Hired by Dr. MacArthur to . . . a
New York dick, doc."

Sally's "Oh" was spontaneous.

Higgins turned and smiled.

"But it took a lady . . . !"

The cab drew up at the hospital. Cub Sterling
was out and up the steps before the driver applied
the brakes. Matt Higgins tossed him the money

and he and Sally caught Cub before he was halfway
up the main staircase in the Administration Building. They reached the second floor and ran around
the octagonal railing, through which Sally caught
a glimpse of the statue of Elijah Wilson, far below, and on to the third floor. There Cub turned,
wild eyed.

"Damn it!"

"Which way?" Higgins demanded.

"I don't know. . . . I've never been. . . ."

Higgins began systematically opening doors
and looking for an outlet. Little streams of late
afternoon sun filtered through the cracks. The hospital was deathly still. All of the people off duty
were preparing to go to Rose Standish's funeral.

Sally's hands continued wringing themselves,
and she begged:

"Cub, isn't there some way . . . another stairs,
Cub?"

He swirled without a word and ran down to the
second floor again. Higgins and Sally followed,
hopefully.

Another stairs . . . behind the pharmacy . . .
where Rose Standish had kissed his interne . . .
perhaps that went up as well as down. . . .

They reached the door that opened onto the en-
closed stairway. Cub pulled the knob savagely.
The door flew open. He peered into the darkness.
Matthew Higgins thick body brushed him aside.

The detective pushed onto the narrow landing and struck a match. Caticornered from the stairway that led down to the pharmacy, a rusty door-knob caught the reflection.

"Locked!" his discovery was like a curse.

Sally stood in the doorway that led to the second floor and moaned. Fatigue. Blinding fatigue was beginning to. . . .

Cub Sterling moved over to Higgins' side and said "Let's bust it!"

They propped their feet upon the opposite wall and laid their shoulders against the flimsy panels. The match was out and the veins in their necks began choking them.

Far down below Sally heard the clanking bell of an approaching ambulance; it hid the scrunching of the wood from her ears.

She stepped onto the landing and tried to see. Before her eyes were accustomed to the dark, the heavy breathing of the two men seeped into her like a narcotic. She lay weakly against the wall.

The breathing had ceased for half a second before she opened her eyes. Through the final screech of the bulging door she heard Higgins' voice.

"Footprints!"

He and Cub were through the hole and halfway up the narrow, winding stairway. She could see Higgins' match ahead as she scrambled through the jagged panelling.

The steps were high and horrible. She lost all light when Higgins rounded the turn. When she staggered up, again, Higgins had his hand upon a knob and was ordering, in the heavy darkness:

"Stand over there, Sterling!" and then, "It opens out and is. . . ."

He turned the knob, and a rush of yellow sunlight filled the twisting stairs. They pushed on into it. The last three steps extended past the cupola door and into the octagonal room.

Higgins, Cub and Sally stood upon these steps and looked.

Their gray, brown and violet eyes mirrored beside the white medicine case, a raised glass in hand, the counterpart of Cub Sterling . . . gone insane.

The late afternoon sun played upon the bushy hair upon the similar, yet dissimilar faces. It caught each feature, as it catches mountain crags and emphasized it. The same white coat, the same carriage, but not the same eyes.

It was the eyes which froze all three spectators into a paralyzed horror. They were the color of Cub Sterling's, except that they centered upon his own eyes with a blistering, venomous, consuming hate, and that hate was confirmed in the crooked, violent twist of the almost rigid lips.

The lips opened, the man gave his left shoulder the hysterical twist and drained the glass, but even with his head thrown back, his eyes bored into and scorched the brain of Cub Sterling, and held Matthew Higgins inert with horror.

It was Sally's, "Peaches! I smell peaches!" that brushed past their fear.

"Cyanide!"

As Cub barked the word, the tall man stiffened gauntly, his eyes still intent upon Sterling's; then his body, like a palm tree in a hurricane, cracked suddenly forward.

The medicine cabinet was within ten feet of the steps upon which Higgins, Cub and Sally stood, and the man fell so that his head just brushed the railing. His hands automatically spread through the railing and caught Sterling's knee.

The fall threw his hair forward and Matthew Higgins snapped:

"Who is he?"

Cub's eyes began disentangling themselves from the glassy vileness of the dead man's stare. Matthew Higgins reached down and savagely yanked at the stiffening hands around Cub's knees.

Sterling, his own hands gripping the railing for support, endeavored vainly to make his reeling mind bring his tortured eyes into focus.

Matthew Higgins threw the dead man's hand heavily back upon the floor; the body rolled half over.

Higgins rasped:

"Doctor who?"

Cub's brain snapped. His eyes focused.

"God! Baldy! It's Baldy!"

He lay upon the railing and carefully repeated in a dead monotone:

"Baldy Rath . . . bone . . . Baldy. . . ."

"Who's he?"

The sentence did not cut through and Higgins bellowed into Cub's ear:

"Doctor Rathbone . . . who's he?"

It reached. Cub stood straight and clipped:

"Baldy Rathbone. Not doctor. Chief pharmacist of the Elijah Wilson. But why in God's name! Baldy Rathbone!"

The incredulity returned. He looked again at the inert body with its eerie features.

Higgins nodded slowly. . . .

The long hair had flopped so that the wide part again led to the shiny spot. . . .

"The book!"

When the sentence finally reached Sally's lips, it whipped both Sterling and Higgins into action. They ran across the room and the sun took their gray and brown heads and played upon them. Through the cob-webbed windows it shone with prismatic beauty onto the now expressionless face of the dead man.

A terrible desire to get away from that hideous beauty gave Sally the will to mount the remaining steps and run to the table and to Cub.

Through the single open window, the late spring breeze played gently. It brought a hush to the horror-stricken air and a single fly entered, flew directly to the dead man's face and began walking upon his crooked lips, up his relaxed cheek and around his glassy eyes.

Matthew Higgins held, in his blunt hairy hand, a small stiff-backed notebook, such as the Elijah Wilson used for ward-addresses. The back was checkered and the pages ruled. It was open at a half-written page. The ink was still wet and the small, finely formed script stood out heavily.

Cub read over his shoulder:

"Cupola. . . . May 19th, 3:55 P. M. I have just failed to administer to the patient in Bed 11, Ward B, Medicine Clinic, a hypodermic of coniine. She opened her eyes suddenly and recognized me as . . . Cub Sterling! Nothing could be more fortunate.

Beforehand I presented to Bessie Ellis my usual token. I was followed by an orderly whom I suspect as a detective. I got away . . . but at last . . . at last . . . my brother may be arrested. . . . It has worked, perfectly!"

"My God! Lil!" Higgins said savagely as he dropped the book onto the plain deal table.

Nobody paid him any attention.

Cub Sterling said, " 'My brother?' "

And Sally Ferguson picked up the book and began reading aloud from the first page. Her voice was thin and pointed and she read:

"In 1883 there came to Heidelberg as a medical student a young American named Ethridge Sterling. He had studied at the Hotel Dieu and in New York. He lived at the Eagle Inn and attended lectures in surgery under Klotz.

"As a chambermaid at the Eagle Inn, there was a young Bavarian girl, Gretchen Seinrich. She was fair to gaze upon and full of country spirits."

Cub Sterling had sat down, his head buried in his cupped hands. Matthew Higgins rested against a corner of the table. He was suddenly old. Lil Parkins . . . for many years. . . .

They both listened, vacant of expression, and at the same time horrified with interest, to Sally's voice:

"From the spring of 1883 to the fall of 1884 young Sterling prevailed upon Gretchen Seinrich to live with him and she did so. I like to believe they were in love. I know she always was in love with him.

"In October 1884, Sterling was suddenly

called back to New York by the unexpected death of his father. He promised to write. He never did so. He promised to send his address. He did not do so.

"The last night he spent in Heidelberg he spent with her. While she was still asleep he arose and wrote the note containing all of the above promises, and before she woke he had packed and gone. . . .

"And I was conceived. . . .

"She returned to Bavaria and went to work as a seamstress. After my birth, my mother determined to come to America and find my father . . . and so she went to work at a more profitable profession . . . the oldest."

The utter and terrible stillness of Cub Sterling was more frightful than any words would have been.

"Go on!" Matthew Higgins was relentless and Sally continued.

"It took three years to earn enough money to come to America and then it took years of blind wandering to reach this hospital and . . . .

"When she reached it, her great love had grown, through endless pain and privation, to a great bitterness. She determined to reveal the Great Dr. Sterling and ruin him, and by mistake when she asked to see him, she was taken, instead, to his father-in-law, Dr. Jemison, and it was through the door of Dr. Jemison's office that she saw Ethridge Sterling standing with his arm around Dr. Jemison's daughter.

"She had a heart attack. Dr. Jemison pronounced her dead, and she was carted back through the dispensary door and handed over to a German Society for burial. The president of the society was Otto Weber. He burned her papers and I, then nine, was put into an orphan asylum.

"My father was already famous. He was Otto's best customer. But what we learn in the first eight years of our lives . . . if it is bitter . . . we never forget. . . .

"At the asylum we had candy at Christmas and mush for breakfast, and the Elijah Wilson operated upon us, free, when necessary. I remember quite vividly when I was operated upon. Double hernia, and endless pain, and a dispensary consultation. Dr. Sterling was designated to do the operation.

"Upon the day slated, his son was born and my case was turned over to an assistant resident. A man killed in the War. . . ."

"Fegus," Cub's voice was low.

"The doctor had never done the operation before. I was his first . . . the incisions were too deep.

"I lost my mother before I really knew her and my manhood before it began. . . .

"I lost both of them because my father was Dr. Ethridge Sterling, of the famous hands.

"At sixteen, when the boys in the orphanage discovered my inabilities, I determined to ruin my father . . . and began studying pharmacy with an idea of becoming connected, eventually, with his hospital.

"The orphanage farmed me out to a pharmacist. Otto Weber had become a political influence. I went to him and worked upon his sentiment. It was he, and the excellency of my work . . . and why not? I am the son of Dr. Sterling . . . that persuaded the Attorney-General to recommend me to Dr. Barton and Dr. MacArthur as assistant pharmacist.

"I passed my state boards brilliantly. I entered the pharmacy of the Elijah Wilson, the same year that Cub Sterling entered medical school.

"He spent ten years studying the science of medicine. I spent those ten years perfecting myself in the science of murder. At first I intended murdering the patients of my father, slowly, occasionally, over a period of years. Then I perceived if I waited until Wilkins died, became promoted as Chief Pharmacist and murdered my brother's patients, I would doubly ruin my father. ... .

"Then the gods smiled. . . ! Through the losing of my top hair, I, unconsciously, grew a nickname. For five years now, I have catered to that nickname. I shaved my center part to accentuate my bald spot. I pomaded my long front hair, which naturally is curly as my brother's, to slick behind my ears . . . to change my forehead line.

"There is not a famous doctor around this hospital who would not testify as to my baldness. . . .

"Around a hospital where so many people are constantly passing at stated intervals to stated places, the eyes of even a good observer become dulled into "seeing," when a person resembling a familiar doctor passes at an unexpected time, that doctor!

"It is upon that knowledge, a sudden assumption of my brother's queer angularity, and the combing of my recently washed hair to cover my bald spot, that I have built my resemblance . . . not upon the features. . . .

"Some day I shall be caught. When I am caught my father will be caught also."

"Is that all?" Higgins was still relentless. . . .

Cub Sterling's head jerked up from his folded arms and he said:

"God! It's enough!"

Sally Ferguson's voice cut into him:

"There is a diary of the murders, too."

Both men rose and came to her side. Their movement disturbed the fly and he began circling around the dead man's head.

Sally's voice drowned out his buzzing.

"Cupola, Friday, May 13th . . . 1:00 A.M. I have just committed my first murder upon the patient in Bed 11, Ward B. I know I have just completed it, because I filled, myself, the prescription to which I added Datura stramonium. The medicine was to be administered at midnight. The dose should, with the heavy bromide I included, have acted in an hour. It is unexpected and therefore not likely to cause an autopsy.

"The patient is one of my father's and also under the care of my brother.

"And she is now dead."

"Cupola, Sunday, May 15th . . . 1:00 A.M. The murder of the second patient in Bed 11, Ward B, is now completed. I tripled the perscription dose of Digitalis. It was to be administered at 12 M.

"She is a patient of my brother and observed by my father. Though autopsy is performed the condition of the organs will be such as not to suggest chemical analysis. Therefore I am protected.

"So far suspicion is not aroused, but patience is not a virtue in which I have been lacking. It takes time to make a reputation and time . . . to . . . my candle is almost gone. . . ."

"Cupola, Tuesday, May 17th . . . 1:15 A. M. I have just returned from Ward B where by the use of coniine administered with a hypodermic syringe, I have murdered the patient in Bed 11. My first traceable murder. Peters and Paton nearly caught me. If murdering ugly women is so much pleasure; a pretty woman. . . . Tonight I began an intriguing custom. I left upon the crib of Bessie Ellis a Ma-ma doll.

"Miss Kerr was on the ward at the time. She is stealing morphia again. So . . . even should she have recognized me, she will deny all knowledge. Most fortunate!

"The staff meeting yesterday, at which my brother escaped all censure, forces me into action. This autopsy will reveal murder and begin, I hope, the suspicion. My plan is working splendidly! But why not? Fifteen years' patient study

are behind it. I am tired and it is late. . . . Seeing Peters and Paton was luck. . . ."

"My eyes . . . I can't. . . ." Sally wailed.

Matthew Higgins took the book from her hands;
the fading light was eerie. Cub Sterling put his
arms around the girl and drew her into his lap.
She began to shiver and Higgins read:

"Cupola, Wednesday, May 18th . . . 1:30
A.M. The Gods are on my side. I have just
murdered Rose Standish. She was a pretty
woman, and my father had ordered a sleeping
potion . . . then he came by and asked me privately to make it bread pills. I did . . . plus
. . . an African sleeping drug. Ah! the murder
drugs are so fascinating and Heddis searched
for the obvious potions, only.

"Ah, luck! Ah, irony! Bear Sterling helping
his illegitimate son to ruin his legitimate one.

"Rose Standish was asleep by midnight. The
student nurse nearly caught me. It was exciting! She will testify against my brother.

"Yesterday I was called before the staff to
check drugs after Heddis settled upon coniine.
It is all so damnably easy. Of course no house
sold the supply. I made it from the hemlock I
gathered in the mountains of Pennsylvania
when I was east on vacation. I had thought so

long about what to use. Something which we did not keep in the pharmacy. I used to think something untraceable . . . and then when I met Heddis I saw he would discover. . . .

"Then coniine came to me. Out of a volume of Plato I found in a pullman seat in the Broad Street Station coniine came to me. Coniine, such a word! Coniine!

"The suspicion is growing. My brother and my father are panicky.

"I put another doll upon Bessie's crib. I passed no one in the corridor. Rose Standish was a pretty woman. . . ."

"Crazy. Dead crazy!"
Higgins' nerves were jumpy too.
"Anything else?" Cub's voice had become relentless, now.
"Yes."

"Cupola, Wednesday, May 18th, Noon. My father has pneumonia and will die without the knowledge of my brother's ruination unless I act quickly.

"There must be a daylight murder within the next twenty-four hours. If there is no patient in Bed 11, then upon the patient in a corresponding bed upon another floor.

"Before he dies, my brother must be under arrest. . . .

"It will take careful planning to execute a daylight murder . . . but years of careful planning prepare one. . . ."

"God! It makes me sick to read it! Lil Parkins, the best woman. . . ."

"A detective you put in the bed . . . ?"

Higgins nodded flatly, and turned the pages. At the back of the book was written, upon the stiff cover:

Murder Chart:

May 13th, 1:00 A. M.—goitre—E.S. & E.S. Jr.—
         Datura stramonium
May 15th, 1:00 A. M.—heart—E.S. & E.S. Jr.—
         overdose Digitalis
May 17th, 1:15 A. M.—operative E.S. obs. S. Jr.
         —Coniine
May 18th, 1:30 A. M.—nurse—E.S. Jr. obs. E.S.
         —Coniine
May 19th, 3:40 P. M.—heart—House & E.S. Jr.
         —failed to murder but
         ruined E.S. Jr.

The sunset breeze wound in the window and loosened the bands of Higgins' heated brain, and the hysterical tears of Sally Ferguson. She buried her head in Cub's shoulder and sobbed horribly.

Her sobs were long and rending and they forced Matthew Higgins into instant action. He struck a match, tore the pages from the front of the blank book and put them over the match.

The yellow-red flames ran up the crinkling paper as Cub Sterling's legs began untangling themselves and he threw Sally aside.

"Aw, what's the use?" Higgins' gray eyes shot into Cub. "He's dead and your father's dying. The body and the murder chart's all we need."

The contact with Cub had revived Sally's fight.

"How can we stop *The Call?*"

Higgins snapped around.

"Who owns it?"

Cub was half across the room toward Sally. He swerved.

"Barton told me half an hour ago that the Attorney-General had just bought it. . . . Now I see. . . ." His voice shattered.

Sally ran toward him. Higgins pushed a chair under his bending legs.

The fly rose from the dead man's face and slipped with the curling smoke out of the open window toward the distant river.

www.ingramcontent.com/pod-product-compliance
Lightning Source LLC
Chambersburg PA
CBHW030245030726
47493CB00023B/600